THE DENBIGH ASYLUM KILLINGS

A DI Ruth Hunter Crime Thriller Book #15

SIMON MCCLEAVE

THE DENBIGH ASYLUM KILLINGS

By Simon McCleave

A DI Ruth Hunter Crime Thriller
Book 15

About the Author

SIMON McCLEAVE

Simon is a million selling crime novelist. His first book, 'The Snowdonia Killings', was released in January 2020 and soon became an Amazon Bestseller, reaching No 1 in the Amazon UK Chart and selling over 350,000 copies. His twelve subsequent novels in the DI Ruth Hunter Crime Thriller Series have all been Amazon Best Sellers and many have hit the top of the UK Digital Chart. He has sold over 1.5 million books since 2020.

The Ruth Hunter Snowdonia books are currently in development as a television series to be filmed on location in North Wales in 2023.

Simon also has a very successful crime series set on Anglesey with Harper Collins (Avon). 'The Dark Tide', the first of the series, was the highest ever selling Waterstones' Welsh Book of the Month.

Simon McCleave was originally born in South London. When leaving University, he worked in television and film development. He was a Script Editor at the BBC, a producer at Channel 4 before working as a Story Analyst in Los Angeles. He worked on films such as 'The Full Monty' and television series such as the BBC Crime Drama 'Between The Lines'.

Simon then became a script writer for television and film. He wrote on series such as Silent Witness, Murder In Suburbia, Teachers, Attachments, The Bill, Eastenders and many more. His film, 'Out of the Game' for Channel 4 was critically acclaimed - 'An unflinching portrayal of male friendship.' (Time Out)

Simon lives in North Wales with his wife and two children.

Also by Simon McCleave

THE DI RUTH HUNTER SERIES

#1 *The Snowdonia Killings*
#2. *The Harlech Beach Killings*
#3. *The Dee Valley Killings*
#4. *The Devil's Cliff Killings*
#5. *The Berwyn River Killings*
#6. *The White Forest Killings*
#7. *The Solace Farm Killings*
#8. *The Menai Bridge Killings*
#9. *The Conway Bridge Killings*
#10. *The River Seine Killings*
#11. *The Lake Vyrnwy Killings*
#12 *The Chirk Castle Killings*
#13 *The Portmeirion Killings*
#14 *The Llandudno Pier Killings*

THE DC RUTH HUNTER MURDER CASE SERIES

#1. *Diary of a War Crime*
#2. *The Razor Gang Murder*
#3. *An Imitation of Darkness*
#4. *This is London, SE15*

THE ANGLESEY SERIES - DI LAURA HART
(Harper Collins / AVON Publishing)

#1. *The Dark Tide*

#2. In Too Deep

#3. Blood on the Shore

No part of this publication may be reproduced, stored, or transmitted in any form or by any means, electronic, mechanical, photocopying, recording, scanning, or otherwise without written permission from the publisher. It is illegal to copy this book, post it to a website, or distribute it by any other means without permission.

Names, characters, businesses, places, events, and incidents are either the products of the author's imagination or used in a purely fictitious manner. Any resemblance to actual persons, living or dead, or actual events is purely coincidental.

First published by Stamford Publishing Ltd in 2023

Copyright © Simon McCleave, 2023
All rights reserved

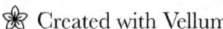 Created with Vellum

Your FREE book is waiting for you now!

Get your FREE copy of the prequel to
the DI Ruth Hunter Series NOW
http://www.simonmccleave.com/vip-email-club
and join my VIP Email Club

'To deny people their human rights is to challenge their very humanity.'
   Nelson Mandela

'Freedom means you are unobstructed in living your life as you choose. Anything less is a form of slavery.'
   Wayne Dyer

'Freedom is the open window through which pours the sunlight of the human spirit and human dignity.'
   Herbert Hoover

To Paresh, in fellowship x

Prologue

Taking a drag on his berry-flavoured vape, Carmel Chowdry let the vapour drift slowly out of his nostrils and watched as the wind dragged it away. He had tried various other flavours – mint, bubblegum and even coffee – but this was his favourite. Sitting quietly in the tatty, overgrown garden of a flat that he lived in in Denbigh, North Wales, he watched as a small bird landed on a rusty garden table nearby. It had a rust-coloured body, with white and black wings. Carmel thought it was a chaffinch. He remembered seeing one being attacked and killed by two crows when he was a child. Its screeches still haunted him.

Carmel was 21 years old and until three months ago lived in Borivali, a suburb at the north-west end of Mumbai. With a large Gujarati population, Borivali was relatively affluent compared to the slums of Dharavi in the south. Carmel and his 15-year-old brother had lived in a small two-bedroomed house with their mother, Nitira, who was a teacher at the local Catholic Francis De Assisi High School, located at the far end of the Mandpeshwar Road.

Their father had died from a heart attack when they were very young. Carmel could barely remember him but knew that he had worked on the railways.

Four months earlier, a Mr Kapoor had approached their mother at the local community centre. He claimed he was looking for bright young Indian students for an education programme abroad. Mr Kapoor could provide transport, a college education, and work for Carmel and Rishi in the UK. For 200,000 rupees, the brothers would fly to Britain, be provided with a place in catering college and gain well-paid employment in kitchens. Nitira jumped at the chance, knowing that her sons would have a much better life there than they could ever have in Mumbai. Even though she didn't have enough money, Mr Kapoor agreed to loan them the fees and her sons would pay back a small amount to him every month. The whole family had been incredibly excited by this opportunity for the boys.

Carmel and Rishi had flown into Manchester airport and then found themselves in a small town in North Wales called Denbigh. They soon realised that none of the things they had been promised were going to be provided. There was no college or catering course. Living with five other foreign nationals in a one-bedroomed flat, with little food, Carmel and his brother were quickly forced into working long hours in the kitchen of a local restaurant. They were then falsely accused of stealing, sacked, and then forced into other types of employment.

Even though Carmel had phoned his mother on several occasions to tell her that things weren't going quite to plan, he didn't disclose the true extent of his and Rishi's horrible and sometimes frightening existence. He didn't want her to worry or cause her undue stress.

As the wind picked up and rattled the leaves in the

trees, a downcast figure appeared at the back door of the flat. It was Rishi.

'Hey,' Carmel said, forcing a smile. Rishi might have been fifteen, but he was small and looked younger. Carmel had always felt very protective towards him ever since they were very young.

Rishi, who looked tired, put out his hand and Carmel handed him the vape.

'Where did you go last night?' Carmel asked, worrying that his brother looked so despondent.

'Nowhere,' Rishi snapped.

Carmel looked at him with a concerned frown. Rishi had been leaving the flat late at night and disappearing for hours on end. So far, he'd refused to tell anyone what he'd been doing.

'If you're in trouble or anything, you can tell me,' Carmel reassured him.

Rishi looked down at the ground. 'I don't want to talk about it.'

'Is it to do with what happened with that man outside the pub the other night?' Carmel asked.

Rishi didn't answer.

Carmel went over to him and put a comforting hand on his shoulder. 'You look scared, that's all.'

Rishi nodded but didn't look up. 'I am scared,' he whispered.

Carmel reached around the back of his own neck and unclipped the silver crucifix he was wearing. His uncle had given it to him on the day of his first Catholic Holy Communion. His mother and whole family were Catholics and attended the Our Lady of the Immaculate Conception Church in West Borivali. There had been Catholics in that area of Mumbai since the 1500s.

Carmel pressed the crucifix into the palm of his brother's hand. 'Take this.'

Rishi shook his head. 'I can't.'

'I want you to have it,' Carmel insisted. 'If you wear it, it will keep you safe. Remember, God is our protector and will protect us from all danger.'

Rishi nodded as he took the crucifix. 'Thank you,' he said. Carmel was pleased that the necklace seemed to have brightened his brother's spirits.

Rishi looked embarrassed but put his arms around his older brother for a moment. They hugged.

'Hey, it's going to be all right,' Carmel said gently. 'I promise you. Very soon, we will have our own home and jobs. And we can send for mother and she can come and live with us.'

'Really?' Rishi asked, his whole face brightening with that thought.

'Yes, really.'

Carmel glanced at his watch. He had arranged to meet someone to sort out a few things that were troubling him. Once that was done, it would be a great weight off his mind.

Carmel put his hand gently to Rishi's face and looked him in the eye. 'I've got to go, okay? But I'll be back later and we can sort all this out.'

Rishi nodded as Carmel turned and left.

Chapter 1

It had been nearly twenty-four hours since Amanda and her daughter Megan had been abducted by men posing as officers from Merseyside Police's Regional Organised Crime Unit.

Amanda looked out of the window from the back of the car where she was sitting once again. Megan lay with her head on Amanda's lap as she stroked her daughter's hair. It had been virtually impossible to explain to her why 'the nasty men' had taken them or where they were going. Amanda just had to try her best to allay Megan's fear and confusion while keeping calm herself. She couldn't let Megan see that inside she was a twisted ball of nerves that made her feel sick.

Having been forced into a car in North Wales late the night before, they had been driven across country. They had stopped at some kind of farmhouse where Amanda and Megan had been taken to a sparse bedroom, given food and drink and told to get some sleep. Amanda thought she might have managed about an hour. It had been a long torturous wait but, luckily, Megan had slept for a decent amount of time. Amanda assumed it was nervous exhaustion.

Now they were driving somewhere else. Amanda had tried to use the passage of the sun to calculate which direction they were going in. She thought they were going east which meant that they would eventually cross the border between Wales and England. And she knew that at some point they would pass a road sign that would allow her to work out where they were.

A man in his 40s with black hair, thick eyebrows and sharp features sat silently in the passenger seat. He had introduced himself as Detective Inspector Carl Doyle of Merseyside Police. He had even shown Amanda his police warrant card which looked identical to Nick's. She guessed that if you had the money and means, you could make a duplicate of anything.

As they turned right onto a long country road, Amanda tried to process all that had happened. It was the culmination of an ongoing feud between Nick and one of Liverpool's most dangerous and notorious gangsters, Curtis Blake, that went back decades. It had seen Nick falsely imprisoned for a murder in Llancastell that he didn't commit, and his subsequent escape from HMP Rhoswen. Nick had located and broken into Blake's safe house in Croxteth, Liverpool and managed to find the evidence that would clear his name.

Although Blake was now safely in custody, he had found a way of locating and kidnapping Amanda and Megan in revenge for Nick setting him up. Amanda had no idea what was going to happen next. She was clinging on to the hope that if Blake wanted to harm her or Megan, it would have happened already.

'Where are we going?' she asked calmly for the third time in about twenty minutes. So far, the two men in the front of the car had ignored all of her questions. 'You can't just ignore me,' she said, feeling herself getting angry and agitated, but she knew she needed to keep calm for Megan. And if they wanted to ignore her, then there was very little she could do about it.

A mobile phone rang from somewhere. Doyle answered it and spoke into it quietly.

Amanda strained to hear what he was saying. Mostly it was monosyllabic but then she caught him saying 'Yeah, that's right, Dublin.'

Dublin? Amanda thought to herself. Were they talking about her and Megan? Were they going to take them out of the country? Why? Her stomach tightened into a smaller knot as she took a breath. How the hell were they going to get out of this?

Doyle finished the call.

'Are you taking us to Dublin?' Amanda asked.

There was no response.

'What's Dublin, Mummy?' Megan asked as she stirred.

'It's a city, darling,' she replied.

'Where is it?'

'Ireland.'

'Is that where we're going then?'

Amanda stroked her hair gently. 'I don't know, darling.'

Chapter 2

It was dark as the three teenagers crept through the vast ruins of the Denbigh Asylum. An owl hooted in the distance, adding to the already eerie atmosphere. It had stopped raining, and the undergrowth was soggy beneath their feet.

The derelict asylum, also known as the North Wales Psychiatric Hospital or *Ysbyty Gogledd Seiciatrig Cymru*, was a colossal Grade II listed Victorian building that had been constructed to house psychiatric patients in the 1840s. At its height, it had over 1,500 patients. Built from local limestone, the buildings were Jacobean in architectural style. Covering over 20 acres, the hospital was comprised of three mammoth wings around a quadrangle, with a central clock tower that included a Gothic-styled chapel. Inside was an endless labyrinth of wards, corridors, treatment rooms and locked cells.

'Bro,' Alfie said as he adjusted his black baseball cap and gazed around at the wings which seemed to dwarf them with a sinister power. 'This is like a movie set. Or a computer game.'

Chloe rolled her eyes. Alfie, who was a very 'young' fifteen year old, had started to affect an American surfer accent, even though he was from Denbigh. It grated on her.

Conor, who was also in Chloe's class at school, was holding a small camera and moving slowly round to take in all the buildings. They were making a video for Chloe's YouTube channel. The asylum was supposed to be haunted. In fact, a TV programme had made a Halloween ghost investigation episode at the site. However, it had received fierce criticism in the press after entitling the show *Village of the Damned*, and carrying out paranormal experiments on presenters who had been wearing straitjackets in padded cells. There were many who thought the programme makers had mocked the mentally ill and that it had been in very poor taste.

As the moon peeked slowly from behind a thick cover of clouds, Chloe noticed the silence of the place. It had fallen over the asylum like a heavy blanket, muffling everything but the faint moan of the evening wind. Shadows fell in mighty blocks as the site sunk slowly into the inky darkness of night.

'Okay, guys,' Chloe called over quietly and gestured. 'Let's go inside and get set up.' She knew that if she didn't take charge, Conor and Alfie would wander around aimlessly and nothing would get done.

Glancing up, she observed that every glass window in the building had been smashed or cracked. She remembered hearing that ever since the hospital had closed in the 90s, local kids had broken in to smash things up, spray graffiti and even start fires.

From inside, there was a sudden hollow booming noise, like a heavy iron door being shut.

Chloe froze and held her breath. It sounded like

someone was moving around somewhere within the interior of the wing. Her skin shuddered into goose flesh.

'What the hell was that?' Alfie hissed with an agitated frown.

Jesus, this place is spooky, Chloe thought to herself – but she would not let the boys know she was scared.

Then another noise.

The short hairs on her neck prickled and stood up.

'I'm sure it's just the wind,' Chloe whispered, trying to reassure them and herself. Her heart was thudding in her chest.

Conor turned the camera to face them with an excited grin. 'Bro, we are definitely finding ghosts in this place.' He then gestured to a wide stone staircase that seemed to lead up to wooden double doors. 'Hey, that has to be the entrance. Come on.'

'Hey, go carefully bro,' Alfie warned hesitantly.

'Yeah, Conor. We don't know how safe the floors are inside,' Chloe warned him. 'Slow down.'

'It'll be fine,' Conor groaned. 'Come on, you pussies.'

'Jesus …' Chloe muttered under her breath as they followed.

The entire area was overgrown with weeds and wild grasses. On the far side, stones and bricks had been stacked into piles that were waist high. Old wooden cupboard doors lay haphazardly strewn in the undergrowth. A large patch of ground was burnt and black where someone had built a fire. Beer cans and bottles lay scattered all around.

'Woah, this place is crazy,' Conor said as they now had a much better view of the labyrinthine interior of the hospital through a vast hole in the brickwork. The inside was derelict and stretched away for as far as the eye could see.

Chloe looked at a thick oak tree. Its gnarled bark seemed to be shaped into a face, and low branches hung like grappling arms. She shuddered again. *Come on Chloe, pull yourself together.*

As they reached the stone steps, the wind groaned through the trees, and the fallen leaves rattled and skittered down the staircase as if trying to escape. The wind produced another faint, sorrowful moan from nearby.

For a moment, they all looked at each other. None of them wanted to admit they were scared – but the thought of going inside was unnerving.

'My brother and his mates were up here a few weeks ago,' Conor said. 'They said it was a right laugh.'

The metalwork and the splintered wood had all been painted a neutral green. Chloe remembered reading somewhere that the use of green could help ease anxiety and other mental health conditions. Maybe that was why it had been the colour scheme of choice.

Getting to the top of the steps, they went gingerly through the doorway and into a vast corridor. Walls were adorned with graffiti – *Matty was here, Jezzy C.* Sheets of corrugated iron had been used to block off some of the rooms.

It smelled of damp wood and plaster.

'Sick.' Conor gave a satisfied nod as he filmed. 'Hey guys, if I fall through the floor or something collapses on me, the video will get so many views.'

Chloe shook her head and rolled her eyes. 'Erm, you might also die, Conor,' she pointed out with dark irony.

Conor shrugged with bravado. 'Hey, it'd be worth it though, wouldn't it?'

Alfie caught Chloe's withering expression.

'Not really,' she muttered impatiently as she pulled out

a floor map that she had printed off. 'We need to find the morgue. That's the bit that's meant to be the most haunted.'

'You think there's still bodies in there?' Conor asked. 'That would be awesome.'

Spotting a red painted arrow and the words *SATAN THIS WAY*, Chloe pointed. 'It should be down here.'

Alfie looked at the words and stopped. The blood had drained from his face. 'What does that mean?' he whispered.

Conor shrugged. 'Just dickheads trying to scare people, bro.'

Chloe studied the floor plan that she'd found on the internet and soon saw the entrance on the right that she hoped led down into the basement of the asylum.

A large sign read – *DANGER – Structure Unsafe – KEEP OUT!* The entrance was cordoned off with yellow safety tape that looked like it had just been placed there. Another sign had a picture of falling rocks and read – DEMOLITION IN PROGRESS – KEEP OUT!

'We can't go down there.' Alfie pointed to the tape and the signs.

'Don't be a nonce,' Conor groaned. 'You can stay up here if you're too scared.'

'I'm not scared. It's just someone said that they kept people down there in cages like animals and tortured them,' Alfie whispered hesitantly as they looked at the stone steps that led down into the darkness.

'Cool,' Conor said. 'Maybe the cages will still be there.'

Then Chloe saw something that made her stop in her tracks.

There were wet footprints on the stone staircase. Someone was down there.

'Woah, dude,' Conor muttered as he filmed the footprints.

Alfie then looked worried and whispered, 'Shit.'

Chloe could feel her pulse quickening and her stomach tense. She took two cautious steps down. 'Hello?' she called. Her voice echoed and was then lost in the darkness. She tried to reassure herself that it was probably other teenagers looking around or messing about.

'Come on,' Conor said assertively with the camera held at shoulder height. 'Let's go down there. We can't go back now.'

Alfie raised an eyebrow. 'What if there's some psycho down there?'

'We're in Denbigh, dickhead,' Conor scoffed. He then reached into his pocket and pulled out a five-inch lock knife with a wooden handle. 'I've got this if anyone gives us any shit.'

'Jesus, Conor!' Chloe exclaimed. She knew that some of the nutters in her school carried *blades* and thought they were all *gangsta* or *roadmen*. A *roadman* was slang for a teenager who spent a lot of time on the streets in a gang and possibly got involved in drug dealing or violence.

'What you doing with that?' Alfie asked with a furrowed brow. Conor's knife had done little to calm Alfie's nerves. In fact, it seemed to have made him even more jumpy.

Chloe gave Alfie a reassuring look. 'We've come all this way to do this video. Let's just have a look, eh? Conor's right. Probably just some dickheads trying to scare us.'

They ducked under the yellow tape, and as they slowly descended the stone stairs the air became thick with damp and the smell of mould. The walls continued to be covered with flaky paint and graffiti.

The staircase turned right, and soon the light became

murky. Switching on her Maglite, Chloe used the beam of her torch to guide them all to the bottom of the steps.

'Hello?' Conor called in a mock spooky voice that echoed around the walls. 'Any psychos or paedos down here?'

Alfie gave a nervous laugh.

There was the constant, rhythmic noise of water dripping from somewhere nearby.

Suddenly, from out of nowhere, a dark shape came scurrying across the floor towards them.

What the hell is that?

Chloe jumped backwards.

It was a rat!

'Shit!' Chloe yelped as she jumped out of her skin.

The rat darted across their path and then disappeared down a hole. It was enormous and had to be eight or nine inches long.

'It's just a rat,' Conor laughed.

'I hate rats,' Chloe admitted as she shivered at the thought of it.

'So do I,' Alfie mumbled.

'Pussies,' Conor scoffed as they took careful steps along the basement corridor.

Stones and plaster crunched noisily under their feet.

A dark, cavernous room appeared to their left which Chloe illuminated with her torch. On the far brick wall, someone had painted a white Star of David. Within each section, there was a series of strange shapes and symbols.

The sight of it immediately spooked Chloe. She felt her whole body tense.

'What's that bro?' Conor asked.

'This must be where the paranormal stuff happens, dude,' Alfie said. 'And like rituals and stuff.'

Then the sound of something moving further down the corridor.

This time Chloe could see it was the shape of a person.

Oh fuck.

Before she could shine the torch in their direction, the figure had sprinted towards them.

Chloe's heart was in her mouth.

They're going to attack us!

'Shit!' Alfie hissed in fear.

Conor grabbed Chloe and pulled her back towards the wall as he pulled out his knife.

'Come on then,' Conor growled at the person approaching fast.

Bracing herself, Chloe clenched her fists. She wasn't going down without a fight! And now she was glad that Conor *was* carrying a knife.

In a shadowy blur, the figure, who was wearing black clothes and a black hoodie, hurtled past them, up the stairs and disappeared.

Trying to get her breath, Chloe looked at Conor and Alfie.

'Who the hell was that?' Conor asked, still standing with his knife clenched in his hand.

'No idea,' Alfie replied, his voice trembling.

Chloe narrowed her eyes as she peered down the dark corridor. 'Where did he come from?'

Conor and Chloe began to creep down the corridor towards where the figure had appeared.

'What if there's someone else down there?' Alfie asked nervously as he lagged behind them.

'Come on,' Conor hissed at Alfie as he raised the camera back to shoulder height.

Chloe felt broken glass crunch and crack under her feet. Even though she thought it was unlikely that anyone else was down there, she still took a nervous swallow as they pressed forward.

Another room, identical to the one where they had seen the spooky Star of David, loomed into view on their left.

'These must be the cells where they kept the psychos,' Conor said excitedly.

Chloe held her breath as she moved the torch to look inside.

It was still and silent.

Even the dripping seemed to have stopped.

At first, the room appeared to be empty.

Chloe waved her torch around, casting shadows across the walls and floor.

Then Chloe spotted a heaped shape on the floor over by the far wall, just under some bright red graffiti which read *@the Dead Zone.*

Taking a step inside, a large piece of plaster cracked noisily under her foot sending a loud, resounding CRACK around the cavernous room.

Alfie jumped. 'Jesus, Chloe!' he snapped.

She repositioned the torch beam, holding it up high.

What appeared for a moment to be a bag of old rags, was actually a figure lying down.

'Oh shit, is this one of those pranks?' Conor exclaimed too loudly and then pointed to the prostrate person on the ground. 'He's probably wearing a mask and someone's secretly filming. Then he jumps up and we run out of here screaming and they get like a gazillion views.'

Chloe wasn't sure how Conor was so certain about this theory. Maybe it was just bravado.

'Not everything is a social media stunt, Conor,' she sighed quietly.

'It could be a dead body,' Alfie suggested in a whisper.

'Don't be a dick, Alfie,' Conor groaned.

Taking very slow steps, Chloe and Conor moved closer and closer while Alfie hung back by the entrance.

And then it became apparent that it was a body.

'Oh God, Conor,' Chloe muttered, now terrified. 'We should call the police.'

'The Feds?' Conor sighed. 'No way. This is a set up.'

Chloe's blood ran cold as they got to about 10 yards away.

And then she saw his face.

She gasped.

The young man was Asian and looked like he might be Indian.

His eyes were wide open, and his mouth and nose were smeared with blood.

'Oh, fuck man!' Conor gulped.

The young man was definitely dead.

DETECTIVE INSPECTOR RUTH HUNTER OF THE NORTH Wales Police sat forward on her chair in the small inspector's office at the far end of Llancastell CID. Her stomach was churning, and she was finding it impossible to concentrate on anything. A television was tuned to the BBC News channel but had its volume muted. The news of Amanda and Megan's abduction 24 hours earlier was running on a loop. Every 15 minutes, photos of Amanda and Megan would pop up on the television screen with the latest news on a rolling banner underneath – *Police are continuing their search for missing mother and daughter, Amanda and Megan Evans, who were abducted yesterday from a house in Hanmer, North Wales. Police are appealing for anyone who has seen them or has any information on their whereabouts to come forward* …

Where the hell are they? Ruth wondered, taking a deep breath as she tried to compose herself.

She was being kept updated on developments as a common courtesy by officers from Merseyside Police. She was Senior Investigating Officer and ran Llancastell CID where Nick worked. She was also a close friend of his, and godmother to his daughter Megan. *Jesus, this is torture not knowing where they are or if they're safe.* What she really needed now was a cigarette, but she had promised that she would quit once and for all.

It took Ruth back to the terrible time in November 2013 when her partner Sarah Goddard had gone missing. That feeling of not knowing if someone was safe or what was happening to them. The overwhelming sense of powerlessness.

'Any news?' asked a voice. It was Detective Constable Georgie Wild.

'Nothing,' Ruth sighed.

Even though Georgie was young, she had a wise head on her. When she had first joined the CID team, Ruth had her down as ruthlessly ambitious and not a team player. She had also made a blatant move on Nick, even though she knew he was married. Nothing happened, but it hadn't exactly endeared Georgie to her. However, over the past six to nine months, Georgie had mellowed and looked to Ruth for more support and guidance. And under Georgie's hard exterior, Ruth had seen that she was a decent, caring young woman.

The whole of Llancastell CID was on tenterhooks waiting for news about Amanda and Megan. Nick had worked at Llancastell for many years and was a hugely popular member of CID. Ruth disliked trotting out the cliché that the CID team at Llancastell were like a big family. She'd heard it said at the police stations she'd worked at in South London, and often such a platitude couldn't have been further from the truth. But at Llancastell, it was genuine. They were a tight-knit unit. The fact that they'd lost two officers in the line of duty in recent years fostered their close bonds.

Ruth looked at Georgie. 'I've got DCI Parker from the ROCU keeping me in the loop. There was a tip-off that they'd been spotted in Liverpool but it came to nothing.'

The ROCU stood for the Regional Organised Crime Unit in Merseyside.

'It's my bloody fault,' Ruth hissed angrily. 'I thought Sarah's safe house would be secure.'

'You can't blame yourself, boss,' Georgie reassured her.

'Well, I do,' Ruth replied, aware that she sounded a little terse.

'Any idea how they found them?' Georgie asked.

Ruth shook her head. 'It must have come from someone in Merseyside Police.' Ruth knew the rumours that Blake had someone on the payroll in that force.

Georgie scratched her eyebrow nervously. 'Have you spoken to Nick yet?'

'No,' Ruth admitted. It was driving her mad that she couldn't have contact with Nick. The CPS and Probation Service were still working out if they were going to bring charges against him for his escape from HMP Rhoswen to clear his name. Even though there were mitigating circumstances – he had been framed for a murder that he didn't commit – it was still a criminal offence.

'Where are they keeping him?' Georgie asked.

'He's on remand on the VP wing in HMP Altcourse,' Ruth explained. Altcourse was a Category B prison in the Fazakerley area of Liverpool that also had a high percentage of prisoners who were on remand.

Georgie looked worried. 'Is he safe?'

Ruth shared her concerns. Blake and his gang were incredibly powerful in Liverpool, and even though Nick was being kept separate from the main prison population on the vulnerable prisoners wing, it still didn't mean he was completely safe. They were concerned that Blake would be able to get at Nick even on the VP wing.

'I don't know,' Ruth admitted, 'but Parker thinks they might transfer him over here to Rhoswen.'

'Well, that would be better,' Georgie said.

'I can't stop thinking about what Amanda and Megan must be going through,' Ruth admitted, feeling overwhelmed. 'They must be terrified.'

Georgie gave her a sympathetic look.

Detective Constable Jim Garrow appeared at her door and looked in. 'Boss, we've got a report of a body at Denbigh Asylum. First reports from uniform are that the death is suspicious.'

'Okay, thanks, Jim,' Ruth nodded. As hard as it was to concentrate, she needed to get her head back into DI mode. She had a CID department to run. *Come on Ruth, get your head back into DI mode.* 'Erm ... right ... take Dan down there with you and see what's going on. Keep me informed.' She knew that she sounded distracted.

'Yes, boss,' Garrow nodded as he turned to leave.

Ruth looked at Georgie. 'I can't do anything until I know that Amanda and Megan are safe.'

'No, of course,' Georgie said supportively. 'I don't think any of us can really concentrate at the moment.'

Ruth's phone rang. It was DCI Parker.

'Ruth?' he said.

'Hi there,' Ruth said, trying not to get her hopes up.

'We've got an eye-witness who's reported seeing something suspicious on Canada Dock,' Parker explained. 'I don't want to jump to too many conclusions yet, but his description matches Amanda and Megan.'

'Okay, thank you.' Ruth jumped up from her seat and grabbed her jacket. 'We're on our way.'

Georgie frowned. 'What was that?'

Ruth looked at Georgie and gestured. 'Come on. We're going to Liverpool.'

Chapter 3

Nick was keeping a low profile in the recreational area of HMP Altcourse. The VP wing mainly housed convicted sex offenders and rapists. Clearly, they would be targeted by other prisoners and so were kept separate. It also contained convicted police, prison or HM Customs & Excise officers, as well as any prisoner who was seen as a vulnerable witness in a criminal trial. The main prison population didn't care about the specifics. If you were on the VP wing – known as *the numbers* or *The Beast Wing* in prison slang – you were a *nonce* and deserved to die. Nick had been abused while entering the visiting area at HMP Rhoswen, with a young woman claiming he should be castrated and hanged for touching little kids. He'd also been spat at the last time he was in HMP Rhoswen before he escaped.

Rubbing his eyes, Nick's thoughts immediately turned to Amanda and Megan. Blake had ordered them to be kidnapped, and he had no idea where they were. His stomach was twisted with anxiety. Taking a deep breath, he tried to reassure himself that both the North Wales and Merseyside Police forces were out there looking for them.

Nick was also suffering from the flashbacks of being forced to drink two bottles of Jack Daniels. He had worked so hard at his sobriety in the past four years. There would be those who would argue that Nick clearly had done nothing wrong. Being made to drink alcohol doesn't count as a relapse in any addict's book. A relapse is when an alcoholic decides to pick up a drink. It's the mental decision to drink that defines a relapse – not actually having alcohol in your system. Nick remembered Huw, an old timer in AA with over 40 years' sobriety, recounting a story of going for dinner at his future daughter-in-law's home. She had cooked a beautiful lamb stew and dumplings. It was only when the conversation turned to Huw's ongoing sobriety and membership of AA that she broke down in tears. She had added nearly an entire bottle of red wine to the stew without thinking. Huw reassured her that all the alcohol would have disappeared in the cooking process. Even if there were remnants of alcohol, Huw also knew that he hadn't eaten the stew knowing that information – and therefore his ongoing sobriety hadn't been broken. However, Nick could still feel the remnants of a hangover and he was finding it hard to console himself that his recovery was still intact.

Nick had woken from a fitful sleep to find Duncan, his cell mate, doing press-ups on the cell floor. Nick would have been impressed by Duncan's ability to do one-handed press-ups, or press-ups where he could clap his hands, but he was so skinny that it didn't look that difficult.

It was 6.45am when Nick heard the keys unlocking the cells of prisoners known as 'the wing-workers' who went off to prepare breakfast. The breakfast in Altcourse was measly compared to Rhoswen. A scoop of cornflakes and some long-life milk.

'Evans!' barked a young male prison officer, breaking his train of thought.

'What's up, boss?' Nick replied, praying that there might be news about Amanda and Megan. *Boss* was the usual term of address for a screw. Especially if you wanted to toe the line and stay out of trouble.

'You're wanted downstairs,' the officer snapped in an unfriendly tone. That was the difference between the new, inexperienced screws and the older, veteran screws who had seen it all before and knew all the tricks, cons and scams. The new screws were keen to stamp their authority and show no weakness. The old screws didn't need to overcompensate. They were friendly and fairly reasonable but didn't take any shit.

'Is it my wife and daughter?' Nick asked as his pulse quickened. He was desperate for news. He followed the prison officer who was marching towards the stairs.

He didn't respond.

There was the sound of aggressive shouting of prisoners arguing nearby.

Nick followed the officer down the steel steps which clanged with the sound of their shoes. His head was spinning. What if something terrible had happened to them? Is that why they were taking him downstairs? His hands felt clammy with anxiety.

They reached the ground floor and walked through a series of locked doors until they reached the outside. As they strode along a wide tarmacked pathway, Nick glanced up at a window. Two inmates were giving him the throat-slitting thumb gesture. He didn't know if they knew he'd come down from the VP wing or were just fucking with him. At least they were behind glass. Nick realised that the best way to survive in prison was to always prepare for, and expect, the worst. As an old lag once told him, being in prison is like waiting at a bus stop at night in a very dangerous part of a city. You are just perpetually on your guard and anxious.

Eventually they went through another locked door and into the admin building and came into a long corridor of meeting rooms. This was where prisoners would meet probation officers, solicitors and police officers.

'In here, Evans,' the prison officer sneered, opening the door sharply.

Inside the room were two CID detectives that Nick didn't recognise. His heart was thumping heavily against his chest.

Please give me some good news. Tell me they're safe, said the pleading voice in his head. He could feel his whole body trembling.

'Sit down, Nick,' one of the detectives said. He was in his 30s and dressed in a smart navy suit and brown, shiny brogues.

Nick couldn't control his panic. 'Is it my wife and daughter?' he blurted out, feeling physically sick with worry.

'Yes,' the male detective stated with a nod. 'We've had a report of a woman and young girl being taken onto a boat at Canada Dock in Liverpool.'

Nick felt overwhelmed by a strange relief that they had been spotted, and then fear of what might come next.

'When?' Nick asked.

The detective looked at his watch. 'About half an hour ago. Officers are on their way. And I suggest you stay here until we have more news.'

'Is the boat still there?' Nick asked anxiously.

'As soon as we have anything concrete to tell you, we'll

be back,' he reassured him calmly. 'Until then, just sit tight.'

Nick looked at him. How was he meant to do that? Not knowing what was happening to Amanda and Megan was torture.

Chapter 4

The night air was full of drizzle as Detective Constable Jim Garrow and Detective Sergeant Dan French of the North Wales Police clambered through a mesh fence that led onto the derelict site of Denbigh Asylum. There were various signs warning people to KEEP OUT! and that TRESPASSERS WILL BE PROSECUTED!

The approach road to the hospital had been cordoned off and the night air was filled with the pulsing flash of blue lights and the crackle of police computer aided dispatch operators updating officers on the situation.

Pulling up his collar, French was trying to put a brave face on it. He'd been eating a *lonely man lasagne for one* and watching football on the telly when the call came through. It was technically his day off.

'He's been sent to Denbigh. That's what they used to say.' French stepped over weeds and a smashed piece of wood.

Garrow frowned. 'Sorry?'

'He's been sent to Denbigh,' French said. 'Or she. In fact, come to think of it, it seemed to be 'they've sent *her* up to Denbigh.'

Garrow gave him a quizzical look and shook his head. 'Sorry, you've completely lost me, Sarge.'

'When I was a kid,' French explained. 'If someone had …' He tried to think of the most tactful way of putting it. 'If someone had become mentally unwell …'

'You were going to say something like *gone loony* or *lost their marbles*, weren't you Sarge?' Garrow asked with a wry smile.

'Me? I don't think so.' French gave him a look of mock offence. 'I'm a changed man. I've had all the training.'

'Yeah, okay,' Garrow said dubiously. 'I heard you call a woman in the canteen *love* the other day. And when you pulled over a car last week, you greeted the occupants with *Afternoon ladies.*'

French was baffled. 'But both those things are me being friendly, aren't they?'

'Not really. Some would argue that both those are you being condescending to women. It's language designed to show that you, as a man, are superior to them.'

'Bollocks it is,' French snorted. 'Jesus.'

'That's okay, Sarge,' Garrow laughed. 'If you just toddle back to your cave …'

French looked at him with a raised eyebrow. 'Jim?'

'Sarge?'

'Fuck off.'

'Yes, Sarge.'

'Anyway, as I was saying before I was so rudely interrupted,' French continued. 'If someone had 'mental health' issues …'

'Very good.' Garrow gave an ironic smile.

'... they were sent up here to the Denbigh Hospital,' French explained.

As they moved from behind an outbuilding, the huge Victorian asylum loomed into view and towered above them.

Over by a doorway, SOCOs – scene of crime officers – who were dressed in white nitrile forensic suits, boots and masks, had set up huge halogen arc lights. A generator rumbled nearby to power them, and filled the air with diesel fumes.

French glanced up at the hospital's Gothic façade with its towering chimneys and central clock tower. He gave a shudder - it looked like an old, abandoned building from a horror film. A gloomy edifice made from dark stone and haunted by the ghosts of those who had lived there in centuries gone by.

'Certainly creepy looking,' Garrow admitted, looking up.

'Well, you know it's haunted,' French said nonchalantly.

Garrow rolled his eyes. 'Of course it is, Sarge.'

'No, seriously,' French insisted. 'There are ghost hunters and paranormal investigators roaming around here all the time. They reckon you can hear the screams of the patients at night.'

'Obviously,' Garrow scoffed dismissively.

'They had that TV programme,' French insisted. 'You know. *Britain's Most Haunted.*'

Garrow laughed. 'No, not really my thing.'

'You don't believe in ghosts then?' French asked.

'No, I don't,' Garrow said. 'It's totally illogical.'

'Thank you Dr Spock.'

'Sorry?'

'Never mind. Yet another cultural reference lost on you millennials,' French groaned.

French was pretty much on the fence when it came to the supernatural. However, there was an evening when he was about eighteen years old when he'd stumbled home from the pub. He'd woken with a raging thirst in the early hours and swore that a little girl was sitting on the carpet of his room, looking at him from over by the wardrobe. It had scared the life out of him and he'd spent the rest of the night sleeping under the duvet. His family had roared with laughter at the breakfast table the next morning, making all the obvious jokes – *Christ lad, how much did you have to drink? You been on the bloody wacky backy?* But the next few nights were sleepless until he could finally persuade himself that his imagination had been playing tricks on him.

A young male uniformed police officer with sharp features approached them. He was wearing a luminous yellow police waterproofed jacket with *Heddlu – Police* printed on it.

'Evening, constable.' French and Garrow flashed their warrant cards. 'DS French and DC Garrow, Llancastell CID.'

'Evening, sir,' the constable replied, addressing French.

'What have we got?' French asked.

'Teenagers were making some kind of video here.' The constable then gestured over to the abandoned building. 'They went down into the basement and found the victim there.'

Garrow took out his notepad and pen. 'What can you tell us about the victim?'

'He's an IC5 male,' the constable replied, 'and I would say he's in his late teens or early twenties.'

IC codes – or identity codes – were used by the UK police to describe the ethnicity of a victim or a suspect. IC5 meant that the victim originated from South Asia – India, Pakistan or Bangladesh.

French nodded. 'Any ID? Wallet, phone?'

'Nothing obvious I'm afraid, sir. I did a preliminary check but I couldn't find anything to identify him. I thought I should wait for you and the SOCOs to do a more thorough search.'

'And you think his death is suspicious?' Garrow asked.

'Yes, sir. The victim's face was smeared in blood. I also noticed some kind of wound to his abdomen. From the looks of it, he bled out where he was discovered in the basement. There's a lot of blood.'

'Right. Good work,' French nodded. The constable seemed keen to impress.

'There is something else, sir,' he added. 'The teenagers said that they saw someone run past them. This person had come from where they discovered the body.'

French frowned. 'Any description?'

He shook his head. 'No, sir. They said he came out of nowhere and was wearing a black hoodie. It's pretty dark down there so it would have been hard to see very much.'

Garrow gave him a quizzical look. 'You said they were shooting a video in there?'

He nodded. 'Yes.'

'Any idea if the camera was on when this person ran past or when they found the body?' Garrow enquired.

The constable took a moment. He was clearly annoyed at himself for not having asked. 'Actually, I didn't think to ask them.'

Garrow gave him a reassuring look. 'That's all right, we're going to need to interview them anyway.'

French gestured to the whole area. 'And we're going to need an inner and outer cordon here, constable.'

'I'll get that sorted right away,' he reassured him.

The young officer reminded him of when he'd first joined the force. Very serious, methodical and keen to impress senior ranks, especially those in CID. 'Has anyone set up a scene log yet?' French asked.

'Not as far as I know.'

'Can you do that for me? And make sure we don't get any press, general sightseers or busybodies down here trying to get a look. As soon as word gets out that we've got a possible murder in here, we'll get all sorts coming out of the woodwork.'

'Yes, sir.'

'Thanks constable.' French then looked at him. 'What's your name?'

'Liam Brooks.'

'Thank you PC Brooks. You've been very helpful,' French told him.

Brooks tried to hide his expression of pride as French and Garrow turned and headed towards the hospital, and the arc lights and SOCOs who were bringing out small bags and boxes of forensic evidence. The only noise was the rumbling of the diesel generator.

French took out his warrant card and approached a young female SOCO. 'Llancastell CID. Can you tell me who's the lead SOCO on site?'

'Professor Amis is down in the basement examining the victim, sir,' she explained from behind her mask as she handed them both a white forensic suit, rubber boots and a mask.

'Thank you.'

She then pointed to a wide stone staircase with iron railings. 'And the safest way inside is up those steps, sir.'

'Thanks,' French said as the drizzle in the air got heavier. He unzipped the suit, pulling it up as he plunged his arms through. He looked over at Garrow, who was fastening his suit, and grinned. 'This season, I'll be mainly wearing Issey Miyake.'

Garrow looked lost.

'The Fast Show?' French said by way of explaining that his little joke came from a 90s BBC comedy show.

'No, Sarge. You've lost me,' Garrow admitted.

'1990s comedy show?'

'Nope.'

'I don't know why I bother,' French laughed as they turned and made their way over to the stairs.

'I was born in 1996.'

French rolled his eyes. 'Jesus, that makes me feel very old.'

'No comment,' Garrow quipped, pulling out a torch as they climbed the stone steps up to a doorway. The steps were covered in dirt, moss and leaves. A wooden door lay to one side, smashed to pieces.

'Cheeky bugger,' French mumbled. He liked his and Garrow's growing connection and dark humour. They made a good team. Chalk and cheese, but that didn't matter. In fact, he thought that was why they were so effective.

Taking a cautious step inside the derelict building, French could see that the interior of the hospital was in ruins. Walls were stained and covered in graffiti. The floors were cluttered with old bits of wood and plaster, as well as cans, empty crisp packets and other rubbish. Ceilings had been damaged, and exposed wood hung down precariously from them.

A long line of aluminium stepping plates had been set up by the SOCOs along the corridor which was lit by several halogen forensic lights. Sharp shadows cut across the walls and ceilings.

'Looks like we go down here,' French said as he and Garrow moved from one aluminium stepping plate to the next.

For some reason, the SOCO had handed French a pair of white rubber forensic boots that were about three sizes too big. Every time he lifted his foot to move to the next stepping plate, he had to use his toes to prevent the boot from falling off.

'I'm glad we've got these plates,' French admitted, looking up to the exposed floorboards above his head. 'This place looks like a death trap.'

Garrow pointed to the plethora of graffiti emblazoned across the walls. 'Doesn't seem to stop kids coming down here.'

'Yeah, well, that's the problem with kids, isn't it?'

'What's that Sarge?'

'They think they're immortal.'

About a hundred yards down on the right, there was a doorway with a stone staircase leading down into the basement. It had clearly been taped off by builders. A sign showed a picture of falling rocks and read – DEMOLITION IN PROGRESS – KEEP OUT!

As they descended, French could smell the damp and mould in the air. The voices of the SOCOs talking below echoed upwards.

Getting to the bottom of the steps, French could see that they were now in the hospital's basement. The temperature seemed to have dropped suddenly, and he shivered. One of the arc lights began to move and shake, making the hooded shadows on the walls and on the ground jump momentarily.

Jesus, what was that? French thought, trying to hide the fact that he was feeling increasingly uneasy.

A figure appeared and looked towards them. 'Detective Sergeant French?'

French knew the voice. It was Chief Pathologist, Professor Tony Amis.

'Nice evening for it, Tony,' French quipped as they headed towards him. He never thought he'd be pleased to see the familiar face of Amis, but he was.

'Yes. It's just exquisite down here,' Amis laughed, joining in. 'Oh, and it's DC Garrow,' Amis said with a frown as he tried to remember. 'Now, is that correct?'

'Yes,' Garrow nodded with a bemused smile.

'Brilliant,' Amis chirped with satisfaction.

French didn't want to spend the whole evening in the dank, spooky basement of an old psychiatric hospital. 'What can you tell us, Tony?' he asked, gesturing to the room from where Amis had appeared.

'Come with me,' Amis replied, putting his mask back over his mouth and gesturing for them to follow. French noticed that he'd dispensed with the patchy ginger beard he'd been sporting in recent months and gone back to being clean shaved. It was definitely the way to go, French thought. Nothing worse than a man of a certain age with the patchy beard of an adolescent.

As they entered a large, empty brick room, French saw the victim lying on the ground over by the far wall. A SOCO was taking photographs, while another collected samples from the ground surrounding the body and placed them carefully into an evidence bag.

'So, we've got a young Asian male. My guess would be late teens,' Amis suggested as they approached. 'I think that cause of death was a stab wound to the abdomen but I can confirm that in the preliminary post mortem.'

'What about the blood around his nose and mouth?' Garrow asked.

'Your victim was in some kind of fight before he was killed,' Amis explained. 'I've checked his hands and I couldn't find any sign of cuts and bruising. It might be that he was restrained and beaten. It's too difficult to see down here.'

'Time of death?' French asked.

'Given the lividity and temperature,' Amis said with a frown, 'possibly a couple of hours. Maybe more. The damp and the temperature down here tend to skew things a little.'

French looked at his watch. 'So that gives a window of around 5pm to 9pm.'

'Roughly, yes,' Amis agreed.

French then narrowed his eyes with a slightly frustrated expression. 'And we've found nothing on him that might help with identification, have we?'

'I'm afraid not,' Amis said. 'Although, I might have something. It's purely guesswork on my part.'

French looked at him. 'I think we'll take anything at this stage, Tony.'

Amis crouched down, took the victim's right hand and turned it so the back of it was showing. 'You see these red marks and sores here on the knuckles and skin?'

Garrow nodded. 'Yes. What are they?'

'I have seen something like this before. Years ago,' Amis admitted. 'I think they are burns from hot fat and a grill, or something like that.'

French raised an eyebrow quizzically as he jumped ahead. 'You think he might have worked in a kitchen?'

'It's possible,' Amis shrugged. 'And given his ethnicity …'

'He might have been working in some kind of Indian or Asian restaurant,' French said, thinking out loud.

'As I said, it's a long shot,' Amis conceded. 'He might have got those marks from just cooking at home. Or he could have been working in a pub kitchen.'

French nodded and then looked at Garrow. 'At the moment, that's the only lead we've got.'

Chapter 5

The inside of the boat was small and cramped with a very low ceiling. It was only 40ft long. Amanda and Megan sat on a white padded bench seat beside a small Formica-topped table. While the other gang member busied himself in the cockpit to the front of the boat, Doyle had paced around in the darkness outside on the deck in constant and animated conversation while on his mobile phone.

They had arrived at Canada Dock in Liverpool about thirty minutes earlier and been frogmarched from the car to the boat. Amanda had caught the word 'Dublin' again in conversation and assumed that they were going to be taken from Liverpool to Dublin by boat.

'Where are we going, Mummy?' Megan asked as she moved herself closer to Amanda and snuggled into her.

'It's a secret, darling,' Amanda said under her breath. It was the third time that Megan had asked, and Amanda suspected that her vague answers weren't going to appease her for much longer.

Megan looked at her and frowned. 'I don't like secrets. And you and Daddy told me it was bad to keep secrets.'

'It is,' Amanda replied, 'but sometimes there can be a good secret if it's a nice thing that's happening.'

Megan looked confused. 'So do you know where we're going?'

'Yes,' Amanda said calmly.

'Then why won't you tell me?' Megan was looking upset.

At that moment, Doyle shouted loudly from outside.

It startled both Amanda and Megan, who flinched. She then pushed her head into Amanda. 'I'm scared, Mummy,' she whispered.

'It's okay,' Amanda whispered back, putting her arm around her protectively. 'We're going to be fine.'

'Why can't I see Daddy?'

'We can see Daddy very soon.'

'Promise?'

'Yes. I promise,' Amanda said. 'We'll soon be home with Daddy and everything will be back to normal.'

Suddenly the air outside exploded with gunfire.

CRACK! CRACK! CRACK! CRACK!

Amanda and Megan jumped out of their skin.

Doyle was shouting anxiously to his accomplice as they ran across the deck, their shoes thudding noisily on the hull.

CRACK! CRACK! CRACK!

Megan gave a squeal and buried her head in Amanda's chest. She covered Megan's ears with her hands.

'It's okay, it's okay,' Amanda tried to reassure her daughter, but she was trembling with fear.

The two men burst in to where Amanda and Megan were sitting.

'What the hell is going on?' Amanda demanded. Her

fear had been replaced with anger that Megan was so scared.

'Shut up!' Doyle snapped at her as he took a black gym bag and threw it down onto a nearby table. He then pulled out half a dozen grey blocks that looked like moulding clay. Then she saw wires protruding from each block.

Amanda's stomach lurched. *Oh God. They're explosives.*

Doyle then moved around the inside of the boat, placing the blocks of explosives at regular intervals against the hull.

Amanda's heart hammered inside her chest as she took a nervous swallow. She had no idea what or why Doyle was doing what he was doing.

Doyle then looked at Amanda and narrowed his eyes. 'Sit very still and keep quiet, and you and your daughter stay alive,' he hissed.

He then marched over to a switch, clicked it off and the whole boat was plunged into darkness.

Chapter 6

By the time Ruth and Georgie had made their way across the English/Welsh border to Liverpool's Canada Dock in Kirkdale, it had stopped raining. To their left, low clouds full of black rain, pregnant and ready to burst, were moving north.

Ruth took a turning for the A565 – Liverpool Freeport and passenger ferries to Belfast. The Canada Dock, which they could now see in the distance, was around four miles long and had been opened in the late 1850s. The Port of Liverpool itself enclosed an eight-mile stretch of the waterfront that ran from Brunswick Dock in Liverpool, Seaforth to the east, and Birkenhead Dock to the west. Canada Dock was so-called as it received timber from Canada in the 19th century.

As Ruth and Georgie turned, the quayside came into view. The dark sky was ablaze with flashing blue lights which throbbed menacingly. A long line of emergency vehicles – police cars, ambulances, an armed response unit and a fire engine – were all parked along the waterfront.

Uniformed figures stood in small huddles, talking in low voices.

Ruth's stomach lurched at the enormity of the scene. She knew a major incident was unfolding but it was terrifying to think that Amanda and Megan could be at the centre of it. Were they being held somewhere in a boat on the docks? She couldn't imagine how Megan would be coping. She was so young. Her whole life had been turned upside down in the past few weeks. Would such a traumatic incident have any lasting effect on her as she grew up? It didn't bear thinking about.

There was a thundering noise from above as a black and yellow police Eurocopter EC135, with its spotlight cutting through the black sky, went overhead. It circled over the wharf as it tried to get a fix on something down in the water. Ruth couldn't see, but she could only assume it was the boat where Merseyside Police believed Amanda and Megan were being held. The fierce wind from the helicopter blades produced great circular ripples on the water's surface.

'Jesus!' Georgie muttered under her breath as she surveyed the scene. Two enormous steel cranes loomed menacingly in the distance, like great sculptures scarring the skyline.

Ruth shook her head. Normally in a potential hostage situation like this, the police would tread very carefully, especially as there was a child involved. A covert team of officers would try to assess where the hostages were and how much danger they were in. A trained negotiator would be on the scene as quickly as possible. Eventually police marksmen might be called for. But everything would be done to cause the least amount of panic or anxiety to the hostage-takers.

With the lights, helicopters and teams of armed officers, Merseyside Police seemed to be dealing with the situation with all the subtlety of a sledgehammer. It was making Ruth feel very uneasy.

'Is there something we don't know?' Georgie asked – she was obviously thinking the same thing.

Ruth reached for the door handle and opened the car door. 'There must be. It's hardly a covert operation, is it?'

As they got out of the car, the helicopter circled again and then rose up into the night sky and disappeared into the darkness.

Ruth took a deep breath. She felt her face being battered by the icy wind that swept in from over the Mersey. It seemed to pull her skin back. Despite the faintest crackle of police radios, there was a sudden eerie quietness to the scene. As they walked, their feet crunched on the stones and broken bits of concrete under their soles.

A young female uniformed police officer, who was standing by the police cordon dressed in a luminous jacket, gave them a quizzical look as they approached.

'DI Hunter and DC Wild, North Wales Police,' Ruth explained as she flashed her warrant card. 'We're looking for a DCI Parker.'

'Yes, ma'am,' the officer replied politely as she scribbled their names down on the scene log. 'Shall I tell him you're here?'

'Yes, please,' Ruth replied warmly.

The officer walked away a few feet, clicked her radio and spoke into it before returning. 'DCI Parker will be here in a minute, ma'am.'

Ruth gave her an affable nod. 'Thank you.' Then she surveyed the scene again, still feeling confused.

A few seconds later a mixed-race man with a goatee, dressed in a black raincoat, approached. Ruth could see that underneath the raincoat he was wearing a Kevlar bulletproof vest and was carrying a Glock 9 handgun.

'DI Hunter?' he asked. He had a soft Liverpudlian accent.

'Yes,' Ruth replied anxiously. The sight of his vest and gun only added to her apprehension. 'DCI Parker?'

'Yes …'

Ruth narrowed her eyes enquiringly. 'Can you tell us what's happening?'

Parker gestured across the length of the concrete docks. 'A witness saw a car pull up just over an hour ago. A woman and a young girl were forced out of the car, taken over to that dock and then onto a boat that's moored at the far end. They matched the descriptions of Amanda and Megan. The witness also had the foresight to take a photo of the car and its licence plate. The car is registered to a known associate of Curtis Blake.'

Ruth nodded. There was clearly no doubt now that it was Amanda and Megan on the boat. She frowned as she looked around. 'What's with all the shock and awe tactics?'

'I sent a small unit of AROs down that pier about forty minutes ago,' Parker explained as he pointed at the small jetty that went out into the water from the concrete dock. Ruth could now see a small pleasure cruiser which had been moored at the end of that jetty. 'Before they got halfway down, they came under fire from the boat. One of my DS's got shot in the leg. She's going to be okay but I'm not risking any more of my officers.'

'Have you got a negotiator?' Ruth asked as they strolled down the quayside.

'Yeah,' Parker replied. 'We can't seem to make any contact. I don't know if it's deliberate or if the boat's radio just isn't working or even switched on properly. We tried a loud hailer but got nothing.'

'So, now what?' Ruth asked as she peered over at the boat. For a moment, she was overwhelmed by her worry for Amanda and Megan sitting there, frightened to death.

'We've let them know that we're here and mean business,' Parker explained. 'We have to wait it out until they make some kind of move. They can't sit in there forever.'

'What if they make a run for it?' Georgie asked, furrowing her brow. 'It's not like you can blow the boat out of the water.'

'No,' Parker agreed, but then pointed further down the dock. 'We've got police pursuit launches down there. We have to follow them wherever they go.' He then gestured to a dark blue van. 'I'd like you guys to put vests on in case we have any more gunfire.'

Ruth looked at Parker. 'Thank you for keeping me in the loop.'

'Of course,' Parker reassured her. 'If it was my goddaughter, I'd want to be here too.'

Parker's radio crackled. He took his Tetra radio and walked a few yards away as he began to murmur.

Ruth and Georgie approached the van. From a side door, two armed response officers – AROs – in full combat equipment got out. Within the police, AROs were referred to as 'shots', and they were clad in black helmets, Perspex goggles, balaclavas, Kevlar bulletproof vests and Heckler & Koch G36C assault rifles.

Their appearance spooked Ruth for a second as she reached in, took out a heavy vest and pulled it on. It had been a while since she had worn one and she had forgotten how much they weighed down on her shoulders. Maybe it was a sign she was getting old?

Ruth glanced over at Georgie. Given the fact that she was in the early stages of pregnancy, it suddenly dawned on her that taking her into a dangerous situation like this was completely irresponsible.

'I think you should wait in the car, don't you?' Ruth suggested with a nod towards Georgie's tummy to let her know why she was making such a suggestion.

Georgie shook her head adamantly as she pulled the straps of the vest tight. 'No way. I'm coming with you,' she insisted.

'Georgie,' Ruth said with a frown. She knew how stubborn she could be.

'I'm going to be fine,' she reassured her sternly. 'You can't wrap me in cotton wool for the next nine months, boss.'

Parker looked over at Ruth and said under his breath, 'Anyone asks, you're here in an advisory capacity.'

'No problem,' Ruth replied quietly. 'And thank you again.'

Technically, there was no reason for Ruth and Georgie to be there. They were officers from North Wales Police and this was way out of their jurisdiction. And it had no ties to any of their ongoing investigations. However, Ruth had explained the extenuating circumstances and her overwhelming desire to be around. Parker seemed like a good guy and had kept Ruth in the loop all the way along.

'You okay to come with me now?' DCI Parker asked, gesturing for them to follow.

'Of course,' Ruth replied.

As they continued along the dockside, Ruth spotted half a dozen AROs fan out as they moved into position, crouching low against a stone wall. They had Glock 19 pistols and G60 stun grenades attached to their belts.

There was a sudden glint of light from over by the boat.

What was that?

They all stopped for a moment. It looked like someone was moving around the boat and a light had been switched on inside the cockpit.

Georgie glanced at her. 'Did you see that?'

'Yes …' Ruth said, now frozen to the spot. She squinted to see if she could make out who was out on the deck but it was too dark.

Then the sound of the boat's engine burst into life.

Shit.

Ruth's heart now pounded against her chest as she exchanged an uneasy look with Georgie and then Parker.

This is not good.

Parker clicked his Tetra radio on as he took a few nervous steps towards the edge of the quayside and squinted at the boat again. 'Gold Command, Gold Command to all units.' He sounded concerned. 'Target vessel has started its engine. I need pursuit craft up and ready to go, over.'

'Gold Command. Alpha Five Zero receiving,' replied a crackly voice. 'Pursuit craft are ready to follow target vessel and awaiting further instructions, over.'

Parker clicked his radio. 'Alpha Five Zero, received. Proceed with caution …'

CRACK! CRACK! CRACK! CRACK!

Suddenly there was machine gunfire from the boat in their general direction.

Everyone dived for cover.

'Get down!' Parker yelled. 'Everyone get down!'

Even though they were over seventy yards from where the boat was moored, a couple of bullets hit the ground beside their feet, throwing dirt into the air.

Ruth flinched and jumped backwards before Parker grabbed her and pulled her to the ground.

Jesus Christ!

The burst of automatic gunfire was deafening.
Another flash from the gun's muzzle on the boat.
CRACK! CRACK! CRACK!
Glancing frantically around, Ruth looked for Georgie.
She was lying face down, about twenty yards away.
'Georgie?' Ruth yelled.
Georgie wasn't moving.

Chapter 7

The three teenagers who had found the body at Denbigh Asylum were now sitting on a small stone wall close to an ambulance where the paramedics had checked them over. Covered by emergency foil blankets, they were drinking hot sugary tea as they were all suffering from shock. They were pale and shivery.

Taking off his oversized white rubber forensic boots, French looked at Garrow and pointed to the teenagers. 'I guess we'd better go and see what these guys have to say.'

'They look pretty shaken, Sarge,' Garrow said in a cautious tone as he folded his white nitrile forensic suit and handed it to a SOCO.

'Yeah, we'll tread very carefully,' French replied. 'But if they saw someone fleeing the scene, I'd like to find out what they remember while it's fresh in their memory.'

'Of course,' Garrow said with a nod as they approached them.

'Hi guys,' French said lightly as he took out his warrant card. 'We're detectives from Llancastell CID. You must have had a bit of a shock tonight?'

They nodded but didn't reply.

Garrow pulled out his notepad and pen. 'Can I just check your names?' he asked gently.

'I'm Chloe,' a girl with a purple beanie hat and an eyebrow piercing replied as she cupped her tea with both hands which were visibly shaking. The make-up around her eyes was smeared from where she had been crying.

Garrow gave her a reassuring nod. 'Can I get your surname, Chloe?'

'Hill,' she whispered. 'Do you know when we can go home?'

'Once we've got your details and had a quick chat,' French reassured her. 'Shouldn't be more than ten minutes.'

'We can get a patrol car to take you all home,' Garrow suggested.

'My mum is driving over, but thanks,' Chloe explained.

'No problem.' Garrow then turned and looked at a blond boy who was about the same age.

'Alfie May,' the boy said, his voice quivering. He looked terrified.

'Thanks, Alfie,' Garrow said calmly.

'Conor James,' the dark-haired boy who was chewing gum said. He was trying to pretend that he wasn't quite as shocked as the other two. Typical teenage bravado, French thought to himself.

'Thank you, Conor,' Garrow said. 'And you're all friends are you?'

They nodded.

'Yeah, we go to school together,' Conor explained.

Garrow looked over. 'And what school would that be?'

'St Joseph's in Denbigh,' he replied.

French narrowed his eyes. 'Can you guys tell me what you were doing in the basement of this place this evening?'

There was an awkward silence as they looked at each other. French assumed that they were scared and didn't want to get told off.

'It's okay,' French assured them. 'You're not going to get into trouble. We're only interested in hearing what you saw tonight, that's all.'

Chloe frowned. 'But we were trespassing, weren't we?'

'Well technically, yes.' French gave her a wry smile. 'But that's not why we want to talk to you. I just want you to tell us what you were doing here.'

Conor had a slightly surly expression. 'We were just making a video anyway.'

'A video?' Garrow asked as he stopped writing for a moment.

Chloe nodded. 'We've got our own YouTube channel. And we go to places that we think might be haunted or have some kind of paranormal stuff going on and we make videos.'

'Right.' French nodded encouragingly. 'So, you came here and went down to the basement hoping you might see or hear some ghosts.'

'Yeah,' Conor replied defensively as though French had somehow mocked them – which he purposefully hadn't. 'This place is meant to be haunted. They made a TV show here about it.'

French gave Garrow an amused look as if to say *I told you so*.

'Yes, I think I saw that,' French admitted. 'Can you tell us what happened when you went down into the basement?'

'Conor was filming. Then we saw wet footprints on the steps going down,' Chloe explained as she pulled some congealed mascara from an eyelash.

'The steps going down to the basement?' Garrow asked to clarify.

'Yes,' Chloe said with a nod. 'We thought someone must be down there. You know, because of the footprints.'

'But you went down there anyway?' French asked with a frown. He wondered why seeing the footprints hadn't freaked them out.

'We thought it was just some kids messing about,' Conor admitted in a withering tone as if he and his two friends weren't kids and were there to do something serious and meaningful.

'And what did you see when you went down there?' French enquired.

'It was very dark,' Chloe said. 'The first room we came to had this weird cross painted on the wall with all these symbols.'

'Yeah, it was probably done by devil worshippers or something,' Conor chipped in.

'And then when we came out of there …' Chloe continued, '… this person came running down the corridor towards us. Then they ran past, went up the stairs and disappeared.'

'Can you describe this person?' French asked, thinking that there was a strong chance that this was their killer.

Conor shook his head and replied hastily, 'No. It was too dark and they were wearing a hoodie.'

French watched Conor for a moment. Maybe it was his imagination, but Conor's reply didn't ring true. Was there something Conor wasn't telling them?

Garrow looked at them. 'Did this person say anything?'

'No,' Conor said insistently.

'I think I saw something,' Alfie mumbled.

French gave him an encouraging nod. 'Right. Can you tell us what you saw?'

'I saw some of him for a second,' Alfie admitted nervously.

'So, was it a man?' Garrow asked.

Alfie thought for a second but then looked uncertain. 'I don't know. Maybe.'

Great, that's helpful.

'I thought they looked small,' Chloe piped up. 'I mean like they were young.'

'A teenager?' Garrow said.

'Yes,' Chloe nodded uncertainly.

'Is there anything else you can remember?' French enquired.

The three of them shook their heads but didn't reply.

'And then you found the victim in the next room along?' Garrow asked quietly. 'Is that right?'

'Yes,' Chloe said under her breath, and looked like she was about to cry at the thought of it.

French looked at them. 'Had you ever seen the person in that room before?'

They all shook their heads.

'And did any of you touch the victim or his clothing?' French asked, as this could contaminate the body with DNA or fibres.

Chloe widened her eyes as if this was a horrible suggestion. 'No, of course not,' she whispered.

'Who has got the camera now?' French asked.

Conor half raised his hand that was holding the small video camera.

'Were you filming the whole time you were down in the basement?' Garrow asked.

Conor nodded. 'Yeah.'

'Have you had a look at what you filmed yet?' French asked.

Conor shook his head. 'No.'

'I'm going to need to take that as it's evidence, but you will get it back later,' French explained as he reached out his hand for the camera. He hoped that whatever was on there would provide a big clue as to the mystery person who had fled the scene.

Chapter 8

The paramedics had pulled Georgie urgently over to a nearby ambulance. For a few seconds, Ruth held her breath. She searched the paramedics' faces for an indication of how badly Georgie was injured. Ruth knew it was her fault for not insisting that Georgie go and wait in the car.

Please, let her be okay.

'Has she been shot?' Ruth asked frantically.

'No,' the paramedic replied.

Then Ruth saw Georgie opening her eyes and trying to get her breath.

'Is she okay?' Ruth asked.

'Fine. She's fine,' the paramedic reassured her as they checked her pulse and other vitals. 'I think she just winded herself when she dived to the floor.'

Thank God, Ruth thought as she let out an audible sigh of relief.

Ruth then looked at the paramedic with an additional concern. 'She's pregnant.'

The paramedic looked worried. 'Right ... we'll take her to the Royal Liverpool and get her checked over.'

'Thank you,' Ruth replied as Georgie was helped up to her feet and into the back of the ambulance. They passed her an oxygen mask to help with her breathing.

'I'm fine, really,' Georgie insisted as she put up her hand. She looked at Ruth and gave a forced smile. 'Maybe I should have waited in the bloody car,' she quipped.

'Don't make jokes,' Ruth groaned, rolling her eyes. 'You scared me to death.'

Georgie frowned. 'I don't think I need to go to hospital. I'm just winded.'

Ruth pointed a finger. 'You're going and that's an order.'

'Yes, boss.'

'Better safe than sorry,' Ruth said. 'I'll keep in touch.'

As the paramedics closed the doors, Ruth's thoughts immediately turned to Amanda and Megan. Jogging back towards the dockside, she saw Parker approaching.

'How is she?' he asked, gesturing over to the ambulance.

'I think she's going to be fine,' Ruth replied. 'It's just that she's pregnant so they don't want to take any chances.' Ruth's heart was pounding. She couldn't see exactly what was going on, but the boat had left where it was moored. 'Where's the boat gone?' she asked as her anxiety went through the roof.

Parker pointed left. 'It's heading down river but we have a vessel following it.'

Ruth turned to look across the Mersey and could see the two boats heading away. 'What are you going to do?' she asked. Her breathing was shallow, and she felt sick in the pit of her stomach.

'While Amanda and Megan are on board,' he said, 'we have to keep our distance.'

'Any communication with the kidnappers on board?' Ruth asked as she swallowed nervously.

'Nothing yet,' Parker admitted with a dark look.

Suddenly, the air filled with the distant sound of gunfire. It came from the direction of the two boats.

Then the gunfire stopped for a few seconds.

'What's going on?' Ruth asked under her breath as she broke into a run towards the direction of the boats.

'I wish I knew,' Parker replied with a growing sense of concern as he followed her.

Ruth narrowed her eyes and peered over. From inside the police vessel, the outline of four AFOs in full black protective equipment appeared on deck. They lined up on the left-hand side of the police launch.

Bloody hell! This is not good, she thought as she realised she was verging on a panic attack.

'Gold Command,' a voice crackled on Parker's Tetra radio. 'This is Alpha Five Zero, over.'

'Go ahead, Alpha Five Zero,' Parker said, looking concerned.

'We're taking gunfire,' the voice said. 'Request permission to take evasive action and board target vessel, over.'

The request made Ruth's blood go cold. *Board the target vessel?* The thought of armed police officers storming the boat where armed gangsters were holding Amanda and Megan captive made her feel sick with fear.

Ruth looked at Parker horrified. 'You can't.'

Parker blinked nervously and looked at her. 'I don't think we have a choice. If they continue to fire on my officers, they will have to back off. And if that happens, we could lose visual contact with the target vessel.'

Ruth didn't know how to respond. She wasn't in

command but she knew how dangerous boarding the boat would be for the officers and for Amanda and Megan.

The air filled again with gunfire that was clearly coming from the kidnappers.

'Gold Command to Alpha Five Zero,' Parker said. 'Order is to board target vessel immediately. Repeat, order is to board target vessel immediately. Proceed with caution, over.'

Ruth held her breath and prayed. *Let them be safe.*

Suddenly, there was a huge orange explosion that lit up the sky.

What the hell was that?

Both boats disappeared in a thick wall of smoke that obscured that part of the river.

For a second, there was a terrible silence.

'Oh my God!' Ruth gasped as she froze. She had no idea what was going on as she roamed up and down the quayside trying to see what had happened to the boat carrying Amanda and Megan.

Had the kidnappers rigged the boat with explosives which they had detonated as the AROs had boarded? It didn't bear thinking about.

Please be all right, she prayed to whatever higher power was up there.

The waiting was excruciating.

Silence.

The smoke hung like a thick blanket on the surface of the river.

Come on …

Her heart was thumping like a drum in her chest.

Everything seemed unnaturally still for what seemed like an eternity.

Then a dark shape appeared and came out of the smoke towards them across the water.

Taking a terrified step forwards, Ruth squinted.
What is that?
Then she could see the shape of the police vessel now powering through the water back towards the dock.

'Are they okay?' Ruth gasped, hardly daring to breathe. Then she grabbed at Parker's arm who was now by her side. 'Are they okay?' she snapped.

'Gold command from Alpha Five Zero,' came the voice on the radio. 'We have two female hostages safely on board. There are two fatalities on board target vessel. No officers down, over.'

'Thank God,' Ruth gasped as her eyes filled with tears.

Parker looked at her and nodded. 'Thank God indeed.'

Ruth closed her eyes as the emotion of the past hour swept through her whole being. Now she needed to get a message to Nick that his wife and daughter were safe.

Chapter 9

Nick had spent the past 90 minutes sitting in the meeting room in Altcourse prison worried sick. He'd given up pacing the room and now sat staring at the carpet wondering quite how his life had become thrown into such disarray in the past two weeks. He ran his hands over his short hair. Then he felt his jawline which was now thick with stubble. He was no longer on the run so it was time to regrow his beard.

Part of his 12-step programme as a recovering alcoholic was to believe in a higher power. There were some who favoured a traditional Christian God. Of course, there were Jewish, Muslim and Buddhist alcoholics who had their own version of God. However, the world was a very secular place in 2021 so AA was eager to point out that a higher power could be anything. The main point of any faith or belief was to remember that you weren't the centre of the universe and that there was something more powerful than you. It was about lessening the ego and arrogance of an alcoholic, which was often an integral part of their makeup. Selfishness, self-absorption and self-loathing were all traits.

Nick was happy to believe that there was a power out in the universe that was more powerful than he was. It didn't take much to convince him. He lived in a universe that was 13 billion years old and was over 90 billion light years in diameter. He assumed it would be incredibly arrogant to think that because his small brain couldn't comprehend the idea of a benign, external force, it just didn't exist. He supposed that there was a fair amount within an infinite universe in terms of time and space that was beyond his understanding. As his sponsor Dundee Bill once told him, just remember you are but a grain of sand on a vast beach. You're no more important than that. Nick remembered thinking that it was actually a relief to feel his insignificance and irrelevance in the grand scheme of things. It allowed him to live his life with a much healthier sense of perspective and gratitude.

At that moment, he had yet another word with whatever benign force was out there to deliver his wife and daughter back to him safely. He would do anything for that to happen. And he couldn't even allow himself to think that anything awful might have happened to them.

The door opened, breaking his train of thought and startling him.

Jesus!

It was the detective he'd spoken with earlier.

Nick's pulse went through the roof as he jumped to his feet.

The detective gave him a reassuring nod. 'It's okay, Nick. They're safe.'

'Are they?' Nick asked, hardly daring to believe what he'd said. 'They're okay?' he asked again just to check he hadn't misheard.

'Yes. Amanda and Megan were rescued about twenty minutes ago,' he explained. 'And they're both okay.'

'Thank you,' Nick said as he let out an audible breath and tears filled his eyes. 'Sorry,' he gasped as he let out another long, audible sigh of relief.

'It's fine … They are being checked by the paramedics who are at the scene,' the detective said. 'I spoke to a DI Hunter. She's with them at the moment.'

'Good.' Nick nodded as he wiped the tears from his face. He couldn't think of anyone else he'd want looking after them at that precise moment. 'Can I get to see them?'

The detective pulled a face. 'I don't think that's going to happen any time soon. DI Hunter said that your wife and daughter are being taken to an undisclosed hotel and placed under 24-hour armed guard.'

'Of course,' Nick nodded. Even though he was desperate to see them, he knew they were safer with Ruth and being guarded permanently, especially after what had happened with the members of Blake's gang impersonating police officers.

'We're going to transfer you out of here tonight back to HMP Rhoswen. You'll stay there on bail on the VP wing until the CPS and Probation Service can get you into court. Maybe that's something that can be arranged from there, but I'm making no promises.'

Nick nodded and looked at him. 'Thanks. I really mean it.'

'You don't need to thank me, Nick,' the officer said. 'I've read your file. And if I'd been in your shoes, I would have done everything in my power to clear my name and save my family too.'

Chapter 10

Ruth came out of the lift at the country hotel on the border of Wales and England. It had been three hours since Amanda and Megan had been rescued. They had both been checked and given the okay by the paramedics. Then they were taken by armed officers to a hotel where they would be under armed guard until police were certain they were safe. Ruth had flagged up her concerns that someone in Merseyside Police had tipped off Blake that Amanda and Megan had been in the safe house in Hanmer. She didn't want the same thing to happen again. Parker reassured her that Amanda and Megan's whereabouts was now on a need-to-know basis and that the Independent Office for Police Conduct – IOPC – would run a full inquiry into how Amanda and Megan had been abducted.

Carrying a bag of snacks that she'd bought from a nearby 24-hour supermarket, Ruth saw the two uniformed AROs sitting on chairs in the hotel corridor. Their Heckler & Koch MP5 sub-machine guns were by their sides. It felt disturbing to have that kind of firepower in such a quiet, mundane setting. But she knew it was for the best.

'Evening, ma'am,' said one of the AROs as Ruth flashed her warrant card again. Even though the AROs knew who she was and why she was there, they weren't taking any chances.

Ruth knocked on the door and waited for Amanda to answer.

'It's Ruth,' she said under her breath.

The door opened, and Amanda ushered her inside the hotel room. She immediately spotted Megan fast asleep in bed.

'She's asleep,' Ruth whispered. It broke her heart to see her goddaughter lying in bed with her tiny hand resting on the sheets. She looked so innocent and peaceful. And she'd been through so much.

'Yeah,' Amanda replied as she and Ruth went to a sofa on the other side of the room and sat down. 'I was worried that she wouldn't be able to sleep but …'

'She's probably exhausted.'

Amanda's eyes filled with tears.

Ruth reached out her hand and put it on her shoulder. 'Hey, it's okay. She's safe. You're both safe now,' she whispered.

Amanda nodded as she wiped the tears from her face. 'It just feels like we've been in this horrible nightmare that we can't seem to get out of.'

'Yeah, I know,' Ruth reassured her. 'It's going to take a while for you both to take in what happened to you. But I promise you that you are safe. And we can put support in place for Megan if she's struggling with what's happened.'

Amanda acted as if she was still in a bit of a trance and she pointed to the shopping bag as if to distract herself. 'What did you get?'

Ruth looked in the bag. 'Pringles, cheese, Haribo, chocolate, biscuits, crisps, nuts.'

'That's brilliant.' Amanda forced a smile. 'What would we do without you?'

Ruth pointed to the phone. 'And make sure you order room service as well.'

'I never get room service,' Amanda admitted. 'Too expensive.'

'You're not paying.'

'Of course ...' Amanda looked at her. 'I really need to talk to Nick.'

'I'm working on it,' Ruth explained. 'They're transferring him from Altcourse to Rhoswen tonight. As soon as you can talk to him there, I'll let you know.'

'Thank you,' Amanda said, and then shrugged. 'I just want to hear his voice.'

'Of course you do,' Ruth comforted her. 'Let me work on getting you a phone call first thing tomorrow from Rhoswen.'

Amanda nodded and then frowned. 'He's safer in Rhoswen than Altcourse, isn't he?'

'Yes, much.' Ruth nodded.

'How are we going to get our lives back while Blake can get to us even when he's in prison?' Amanda asked with a pained expression. 'He's not going to be satisfied until we're all dead, you do know that?'

Ruth didn't know what to say for a moment. She suspected that what Amanda feared was true, but now wasn't the time to face hard facts.

'I'm not sure, to be honest,' Ruth said. 'It all depends what happens now he's back inside. The longer Blake's away, the less control and power he has.'

Amanda gave Ruth a dark look. 'Yeah, well, I would happily stick a knife in him and watch him die right now.'

Ruth didn't blame Amanda for her anger. Blake had made their lives hell for the past few weeks, and there didn't seem to be a way out.

'Yeah, well, it wouldn't be the worst thing if he was no longer on the planet,' Ruth admitted. 'I agree with you on that.'

It had just gone 2am. The air inside the prison transporter was thick with body odour and the smell of stale cigarette smoke. Nick's hands were cuffed in front of him. Along with five other prisoners, he'd been waiting for nearly half an hour for the journey from HMP Altcourse in Liverpool to North Wales and HMP Rhoswen. The transporter was only half full, and the prisoners were well spaced out along both sides. There had been the odd joke, but they had sat mostly in silence.

The doors clattered open and two AROs, in full operational equipment, hopped in and sat down. They were carrying Glock 9s in their holsters, as well as Heckler & Koch machine guns.

What the hell are they doing on here? Nick wondered as he scanned the other prisoners. The only reason that Nick could think of was that there was a prisoner on the transporter whom they believed was possibly going to be involved in an escape that would require the use of firearms. Looking at the others, he could see that they were thinking the same thing and trying to suss each other out. Who was the *Mr Big* who posed such danger that armed police officers were needed? No one looked like they fitted the bill.

There was more movement from the back of the transporter, and an officer brought another prisoner up the steel steps.

'Sit down there and don't fucking move a muscle,' the officer growled.

'Eh, calm down there lad,' the prisoner joked in a thick Scouse accent. 'The last time I moved a muscle, your wife didn't complain.'

There were some sniggers from the other prisoners.

But Nick wasn't laughing.

He recognised the voice instantly, and it had sent a shiver down his spine.

As the officer moved out of the way, Nick saw the face of the man he hated more than any other in the world.

Curtis Blake.

Are you fucking joking? he thought as he took a deep breath.

Blake was giving his usual cocky grin as he looked around the transporter. Then his eyes locked onto Nick's.

'Fucking hell, lad,' Blake snorted with a sneer. 'If I'd known I'd have to share this ride with you, I'd have asked to go later.'

'Yeah, well, I'm not thrilled at the idea,' Nick muttered.

The other prisoners looked a little confused.

'Don't worry, lads,' Blake explained with a smirk. 'Me and Detective Sergeant Nick Evans go way back. Don't we Nicholas?'

Nick could feel the mixture of utter fury and fear sweep through his whole body. He was also aware that the other prisoners were glaring at him – he was just glad they were all handcuffed. However, it meant that his identity was now known to all of them once they were inside Rhoswen. As long as none of them were heading to the VP wing, that shouldn't be an issue.

'Oh sorry, Nick,' Blake joked. 'Didn't mean to let on

that you're a bizzie like.'

Nick fixed him with an icy stare. 'I wouldn't worry about it, Curtis. I'm getting out in a couple of days.'

Blake raised an eyebrow. 'That's not what I heard.'

Nick knew that Blake was trying to fuck with him and get inside his head. He wasn't prepared to give him the satisfaction of rising to it.

'Yeah, I'm getting out so I can see my wife and daughter,' Nick said with a glimmer of *fuck you* in his face.

'Good for you,' Blake said, but something had got to him. Maybe Blake didn't know that Amanda and Megan had been rescued. If he didn't, Blake certainly wasn't going to admit it. They were essentially playing a dangerous game of poker.

'Yeah, I thought I'd get on with the rest of my life,' Nick said with a sarcastic smile. 'You up to much for the next thirty years, Curtis?'

'You make me laugh, Nicholas. You think you're going to fuck me over and just crack on in the world?' Blake growled with a cold, deadly stare. 'Not a chance. You just keep looking over your shoulder. And keep an eye on your wife and daughter. Because it won't be this week. And it won't be this month. And it might not even be this year, but someone is going to be coming for you all. And it's going to be painful for all of you … So, while I'm still breathing, you and your family are as much in prison as I am.'

That was it. Blake had said it. *While I'm still breathing.*

In that moment, Nick knew that until Blake was dead, he wouldn't be able to get on with the rest of his life.

'Food for thought then, Curtis,' Nick said with a smile that was intended to unsettle Blake. 'Food for thought.'

Blake laughed and shook his head with contempt. 'Yeah, whatever bizzie.'

Chapter 11

It was 7am the next morning when French and Garrow drew up outside the Simla Indian Restaurant and takeaway in Denbigh. The brickwork had been painted white but now looked a little tired and patchy. The word *Simla* was spelt out in large black letters that were slightly slanted as if they were in italics. Underneath, in smaller letters – *Authentic Tandoori and Balti Dishes Served.*

Simla was the only Indian restaurant and takeaway in the area, but it was still a complete long shot. However, French and Garrow had to revisit the crime scene at Denbigh Asylum anyway, so French concluded it was worth a try – despite the early hour.

The forensics team at Llancastell nick had already used photographs of the victim and computer technology to produce an accurate image of his face. All they knew was that he was South Asian, possibly Indian, and in his late teens or maybe early 20s. The burn marks that Amis had spotted on the back of his hands might indicate that the victim had worked in a kitchen.

Getting out of the car, French and Garrow walked

along the pavement towards the Simla. The paving stones were uneven and strewn with weeds. The thunderous, deep bark of a dog echoed around the street.

If anyone was hoping for a lie in, that ship has sailed, French thought dryly to himself.

Gazing up at the first floor, French could see that there was a flat above. He wondered if the occupants had anything to do with the restaurant.

'Boss,' Garrow said as he cupped his hands and looked inside. 'Someone's in there hoovering.'

Garrow gave an authoritative knock and gave French a look. They were in luck.

A few seconds later, an Asian man in his early 20s peered through the glass of the door at them and frowned.

French flashed his warrant card. The man's eyes widened as he nodded and opened the door apologetically.

'Hello. Can I help you?' he asked politely with a slight Indian accent.

'DS French and DC Garrow from Llancastell CID,' French explained. 'Can we come in for a second?'

'Yes, of course. Please,' the man said as he opened the door wide and gestured.

They went inside.

Another man continued hoovering on the far side of the restaurant. He looked over at them quizzically, but continued.

'Don't worry, it's just a few routine questions, that's all,' Garrow reassured him as he took out his notepad and pen. 'Could I get your name, sir?'

'Rohan,' he replied. Garrow gave him a look and before he could ask, the man had said, 'Rohan Chopra.'

'Thank you, Rohan,' Garrow said with a kind expression.

'Do you work at this restaurant, Rohan?' French asked

as he looked around. It looked like a hundred others he'd been to.

'Yes, sir,' Chopra replied, but he seemed jittery.

French then took his phone, tapped on the forensic image of their victim's face and showed it to Chopra. 'Do you recognise this man?'

Rohan frowned, leaned forward, and peered at the phone for a few seconds. Then he shook his head. 'I'm sorry. No.'

'You're sure?' French asked. For some reason, he wasn't convinced by Chopra's manner.

'Yes.' Chopra nodded, blinked, and then his mobile phone began to ring. He looked at it. 'I need to take this. I'm sorry that I couldn't help you.'

Chopra turned with the phone to his ear and wandered away, talking to someone in a language that French didn't understand – Hindi? Was that right?

Garrow went towards the door. 'Worth a try, Sarge.'

French hesitated. He still wasn't convinced by Chopra's reaction to the photofit and he usually trusted his *copper's instinct*.

'Bear with me,' French said as he gestured to the other man who was hoovering. Chopra had now disappeared out the back of the restaurant and wasn't anywhere to be seen.

'Everything all right, Sarge?' Garrow asked with a frown.

Grabbing his warrant card, French went over to the man who was hoovering and showed it to him. The man turned off the hoover, looking nervous.

'Hi,' French said in a friendly tone. 'We're police officers. We were just talking to your colleague, Rohan.'

'Yes, sir,' the man replied politely.

'I wonder if you could look at something for me?' French said.

'Of course, sir,' the man said.

French took out his phone and showed the man the forensic photofit of their victim. 'Do you recognise this man?'

'Yes. It looks like Carmel,' he stated immediately, sounding surprised.

French looked at Garrow. There had been no hesitation in the man's response.

'Carmel?' Garrow asked, implying he wanted the surname.

'Erm, yes, sorry. Carmel Chowdry,' the man replied.

'And you are?' French asked.

'Aakash,' he replied. 'Aakash Patel.'

'Is Carmel a friend of yours?' French asked, pointing to the image.

'No, no,' Aakash replied, shaking his head. 'Not really. He worked in the kitchens here about two months ago.'

Garrow looked at him. 'And how long did he work here for?'

'Only a couple of weeks,' Aakash explained.

French frowned. 'Why was that?'

'He and his brother had a row with the owner,' he said. 'He sacked them both.'

French looked at Garrow. The fact that Carmel had a brother was news to them. 'Do you know where they went to work after that?'

'Sorry, no.'

'Can you tell me his brother's name?' Garrow said.

'Rishi.'

'So, Rishi Chowdry?' Garrow asked to clarify.

'Yes, sir. That is correct,' Aakash replied with a serious nod. 'Are they in trouble?'

'I'm afraid that Carmel is dead,' French said gently. 'And we suspect that he's been murdered.'

'Oh, that is terrible news,' he said under his breath, shaking his head.

Garrow stopped writing and looked over at Aakash again. 'Do you know if Rishi was older or younger than Carmel?'

'Younger,' Aakash replied immediately. 'Rishi told us he was seventeen, but I thought he was younger.'

'Do you know where they were living?' French asked.

'No, sorry. But the owner, Mr Kabir, should have the details.'

'And where would we find Mr Kabir?' Garrow said.

Aakash pointed to the ceiling. 'He has offices above the restaurant. But I know he's not around today.'

'Do you know where we might find him?' French asked. They needed to find out as much as they could about Carmel Chowdry. In particular, they needed to inform his next of kin, probably his parents, of his death as soon as possible. They also needed to find out where he had lived and if, and where, he had been working.

Aakash shook his head. 'I am sorry. No.'

Garrow looked at him. 'And the last time you saw Carmel Chowdry was the last day that he worked here?'

'No,' Aakash replied and then pointed down the high street. 'I actually saw him about a week ago with his brother down there.'

'Did you talk to them?'

'Yes, a little.'

'Did they tell you anything that might help us? Where they were living or working, something like that?'

Aakash took a few seconds to respond. He had clearly thought of something. 'Actually, there is something.' He then pointed to his own face. 'Carmel had blood on his mouth. He said someone sitting outside the pub had punched him in the face.'

French narrowed his eyes. 'Did Carmel tell you why?'

Aakash nodded, looking a little distressed. 'This man was shouting racist things at him and Rishi. And Carmel told this man to fuck off, so he punched him.'

Garrow nodded. 'Can you give us the name of the pub?'

'The Royal Oak,' he replied. 'It's only a few minutes down there.'

At that moment, Chopra came back into the restaurant. Aakash glanced over at him and looked very anxious.

'Anyway, that is all I know, sir,' Aakash said, but French got the distinct impression he didn't want Chopra to see him talking to them. 'You see, I have to get on now.' Aakash started up the hoover again and moved away.

French glanced over at Chopra and gave him a nod as they headed for the door. However, he got the feeling that there was more to the Simla restaurant than first met the eye.

Chapter 12

Taking a slightly nervous sip of his coffee, French looked out at the assembled CID team at Llancastell nick. Ruth had let him know that until she had made sure everything was okay with Amanda, Megan and Nick, he was going to be the acting SIO – Senior Investigating Officer – for the investigation. It was the first time she'd ever asked him. Technically, he was still an *acting sergeant*, as opposed to Nick, who had been a DS for several years now and always stood in for Ruth.

Okay mate, you've got this, he said to himself as he walked over to the scene boards that had recently been erected in IR1. He could feel the tension in his stomach as he took a shallow breath. Georgie looked over and gave him a supportive smile. Even though she'd been instructed to take the day off, Georgie had arrived in CID bright and early as though nothing had happened. French knew that Georgie was a tough cookie, but it took a strong character to be shot at and taken to hospital, only to arrive at work the following day full of the joys of spring.

'Morning everyone,' French said, trying not to show

them that he was feeling uncomfortable. 'Until DI Hunter is back at the station, she has asked me to step in as acting SIO on this.' He waited for a barbed joke or a snigger, but there was nothing. The team was fully focused on what he was saying. *Phew.* 'Right,' French said with growing confidence. He pointed to a forensic image on the board. 'This is our victim, Carmel Chowdry. Forensics' initial assessment is that he was attacked, stabbed and left in the basement of Denbigh Asylum sometime last night. At a rough estimate, we're looking at a time of death between 5pm and 9pm. We know he worked at the Simla restaurant with his brother Rishi about two months ago. I know we're struggling to find out much more about him. Anyone got anything?'

Garrow signalled from his desk that he had something. 'Sarge. I've spent the morning checking the victim's name against the Inland Revenue, HMRC, electoral register. I've checked him against the PNC and HOLMES too.'

'Anything?' French asked.

'A huge blank,' Garrow said. 'I took a guess that our victim may not have lived in this country until very recently. I ran his name past immigration.' Garrow looked down at his notes. 'Carmel and Rishi Chowdry arrived just over three months ago from Mumbai on one-month student visas, which have now expired.'

'Student visas?' Georgie asked. 'Where were they meant to be studying?'

'I can't seem to find that out,' Garrow explained. 'Carmel was twenty-one. And Rishi is only fifteen.'

'And we don't know where the brother Rishi is?' Georgie asked to clarify.

'No,' French replied. 'We just know that they were both working at the Simla.'

'What about the owner?' Georgie asked. 'Doesn't he have at least a phone number or an address for them?'

French looked over at her. 'The owner, Mr Kabir, can't be contacted at the moment.'

Georgie narrowed her eyes. 'They were on student visas from India? But Rishi is only fifteen. That doesn't add up.'

'Sarge.' Garrow pointed to his computer screen. 'The Home Office has just been in touch. They're arranging for Nitira Chowdry, the boys' mother, to fly in from Mumbai to identify the body.'

'Right, okay. I will deal with that when she arrives,' French said. 'We have the eye-witness testimonies of the three teenagers that found Carmel. What about the video footage they shot?'

'Digital forensics are taking a look,' Garrow explained. 'Their initial analysis was that it's very dark, grainy and not a huge amount of use to us.'

'Really?' French sounded disappointed. He had hoped that the teenagers had caught the person who had fled the murder scene on their camera.

'They are going to see if they can clean it up and take another look, but that's going to take time,' Garrow added.

'I'm trying to see if either Carmel or Rishi had a mobile phone, but I'm not getting very far,' Georgie admitted.

'We know that Carmel was attacked outside The Royal Oak pub in Denbigh in what appears to be a racially motivated attack,' French said. 'Jim and I will go there and see if there's any CCTV and speak to the bar staff to see if they know anything about it.' French looked at the board again. 'I'm also very concerned about the safety of Rishi Chowdry. He's fifteen years old, in a foreign country, and his brother has been murdered.' French looked out at the team. 'We need to find out where he is as soon as possible. And I think we definitely need to take another look at whatever was going on at the Simla restaurant.'

Garrow put down the phone and looked over. 'Sarge, there's a DI Stewart from the Modern Slavery Human Trafficking Unit downstairs. He wants to talk to someone from CID.'

French glanced over at Georgie. 'You okay to see what he wants while Jim and I head over to Denbigh?'

'Of course, Sarge,' Georgie replied.

Chapter 13

Amanda sat in the hotel room trawling through news on her phone. She had been banned from contacting anyone or even using social media, for obvious reasons. However, it was making her feel incredibly isolated. Checking her watch, she saw it was 9.28am. Ruth had called her earlier to say that Nick had a phone call booked in and would call her at 9.30am. She felt a twinge in her stomach. There was part relief and even excitement of being able to talk to him. But also fear at how everything was going to pan out.

'Look Mummy!' Megan said proudly from where she was curled up on the bed. She had been drawing quietly for the past twenty minutes. Megan held up a drawing she had been working on. It included a house with a man, woman and child standing outside surrounded by flowers. She assumed it was Megan, Nick, and her. There was a small dog beside them.

'Is that us?' Amanda asked, feeling a little overwhelmed.

'Yes, of course,' Megan said with a frown, as if that was a stupid question.

'And who's that?' Amanda asked, pointing to the dog.

'That's our dog, Jack,' Megan replied.

Amanda raised an eyebrow. 'We don't have a dog, Megs.'

She shrugged. 'I know. But I like dogs.'

'Would you like a dog?' Amanda asked.

Megan nodded as her face lit up. 'Yes … Can we?'

Amanda smiled and nodded. 'I don't see why not.'

'Really? When Daddy gets home, can we go and get a puppy?' she asked with growing excitement. Amanda was glad that Megan was happy and distracted.

'Actually, I think Daddy is going to ring any minute now,' Amanda said, pointing to her phone. 'Do you want to come over here?'

Right on cue, her phone rang, and she immediately answered it and put it on speaker.

'Hi there,' Amanda said in an upbeat voice. 'I've put you on loud speaker so Megs can talk to you.' She didn't want Nick to launch into anything dark or serious while Megan could hear.

'Oh right. Hi,' Nick said brightly. 'How are you guys? You both okay?'

'We're getting a dog, Daddy,' Megan blurted out straight away.

'Are we?' Nick asked.

'Mummy said,' Megan replied.

'That's a great idea. What are we going to call it?'

'It's a 'him' and his name is going to be Jack.'

'Jack? That's a brilliant name for a dog. Ruth said you're in a hotel? Is everything okay?'

'We got room service, and I got a pizza,' Megan said.

'Sounds good to me. How was the pizza?'

'It was all right.'

'I haven't got long, sweetheart,' Nick said. 'So, I'm going to talk to Mummy now if that's okay? I love you.'

'Love you Daddy,' Megan chirped and then she skipped happily to the bed. Amanda was so relieved as, understandably, Megan had been quiet and withdrawn since their dramatic rescue the night before.

Turning off the speaker function, Amanda put her phone to her ear. 'Hi it's me. We're not on speaker anymore.'

'Right. How are you?' Nick asked, sounding concerned.

'Yeah, we're okay, all things considered,' she admitted.

'You must have been terrified?'

'Yeah, it wasn't an experience I'd want to repeat,' Amanda said, trying to keep her tone relatively buoyant.

'God, I'm so sorry.'

'It's not your fault, is it?' Amanda said under her breath.

There were a couple of seconds of silence.

'Blake's here in Rhoswen,' Nick said darkly.

Amanda's stomach lurched. 'How have they let that happen?'

'Rhoswen is the main remand prison in the area now,' Nick explained. 'And I don't suppose my safety was of paramount importance when they moved him.'

'Jesus, Nick,' Amanda gasped.

'It might be a blessing in disguise,' Nick said in a hushed voice.

'How?' Amanda asked as her imagination ran away with her.

'It's not something I can discuss on the phone,' Nick explained.

'Bloody hell, Nick, the last time you had a good idea,

you escaped from prison,' Amanda said as her pulse quickened.

'Trust me, we're getting our lives back,' Nick promised her. 'And frankly, I'm beyond caring how that happens.'

'Hold on, Nick,' Amanda whispered. 'You're beginning to scare me.'

'You've got to trust me,' Nick said urgently.

Then silence.

'I love you so much,' Nick said.

'I love you too,' Amanda replied. 'Please be careful.'

'I will. Listen, my time is up now. Just hang on in there. I'll see if I can speak to you tomorrow, okay?'

'Okay.' Amanda knew that her voice was trembling with emotion. 'Just please don't do anything stupid.'

'I won't,' Nick said. 'Bye now. I love you both.'

The line went dead and Amanda sat back in her chair and let out a breath.

Chapter 14

The Royal Oak pub in Denbigh sat on the main road. With its grey and white façade, it looked like it had been modernised recently – although French was glad to see it retained its traditional pub sign outside.

Garrow and French pulled into the pub car park, got out, and headed for the rear entrance. The spring sunshine gleamed down on them. The air was filled with the noise of a middle-aged man mowing the pub garden, and the smell of freshly cut grass was instantly redolent. As they walked inside, it was immediately replaced by the odour of beer and food. French made a mental note that it was too early in the day to be hit with the smell of alcohol.

The pub had just opened and was virtually empty. French and Garrow went to the bar, showed their IDs and explained why they were there. The young barman nodded with a suitably serious expression and went off to get the landlord.

'You know what kind of pub you're in when the menu is written on a blackboard,' French said dryly, pointing.

'And why would anyone want a tomato and caper compote with their food?'

'Sounds nice to me. Better than frozen burgers that have been microwaved.'

'Oh God, here we go.' French rolled his eyes. 'When I was younger, I thought vegans were a race of aliens from Star Trek.'

'I'm not a vegan, Sarge,' Garrow protested. 'I'm a vegetarian.'

'I fancy this new carnivore diet,' French said. 'You can only eat meat and dairy products. Hardly any veg.'

Garrow smirked. 'I thought that was your diet already?'

'Very funny,' French replied with a smile.

'Morning,' said a voice. 'I understand you're police officers?'

A rotund man in his 50s, smartly dressed in a salmon-coloured shirt and dark blue jeans, approached. He had the ruddy face of a drinker.

'We're from Llancastell CID,' French explained. 'Are you the landlord?'

'Geoff Symes,' he said with a nod and shook their hands firmly, which wasn't how most people greeted them – but each to their own.

'We understand there was an incident outside this pub about a week ago?' Garrow said.

'Was there?' Geoff looked a little confused.

French showed Geoff his phone and the computer image of Carmel Chowdry. 'It involved this man and someone sitting outside.'

'Oh yes. That's right. It was last Tuesday night,' Geoff nodded slowly, but he seemed to be hiding something from them. 'Just a bit of a scuffle, that's all. Just handbags really.'

'Can you tell us what happened?' French asked.

'Not really, as I didn't see it myself,' Geoff admitted. 'I was in the kitchen. But I know Gareth had to go to A&E.'

That doesn't sound like 'just a bit of a scuffle' or 'handbags'.

'Gareth?' Garrow asked.

'Gareth Steel,' Geoff said. 'He's a regular here. Good bloke. Bit of an eccentric but I like him.'

French and Garrow shared a look. 'Were the local police called?'

'I don't think so,' Geoff replied cautiously. 'He said that a couple of kids attacked him outside but he didn't want the police involved.'

'Did he say why?' Garrow asked.

'No,' Geoff said with a shrug. 'I suppose he didn't think it was serious enough.'

French could sense that Geoff was very uncomfortable talking about it. Were he and Gareth Steel friends? French wondered that if there really had been a racial element to the fight between Gareth Steel and Carmel, Steel wouldn't want the police involved. Maybe Steel decided he would get his revenge for the attack a few days later?

Garrow looked at him. 'Do you have CCTV of the outside of your pub?'

'Erm … Yeah,' Geoff said with a slight hesitation. French wondered if there was a reason why Geoff didn't want them to see the footage.

'We're going to need to take a look,' French explained.

'Right,' Geoff nodded, but just stood there rooted to the spot.

Why is he stalling? French wondered.

'We're going to need to look now,' French said.

'Erm, oh right, okay.' Geoff gestured to a door. He looked flustered. 'It's in here.' He opened the door, which they could see led into an office that was cluttered with some stock, papers and files.

French and Garrow followed him inside. The room was windowless. There were two desks, a couple of computers and office chairs. Work rotas were pinned up on a board, and shelves were tightly stacked with folders.

Sitting down at the computer, Gareth grabbed the mouse, moved it around, and then clicked on an MPEG file.

There was an awkward silence as they waited.

A CCTV image of the outside of the pub appeared on the monitor. Gareth moved the footage forward until the timecode read 22.10pm. A man was sitting at a table on the pavement outside the pub. French assumed it was Gareth Steel. He was smoking and nursing a pint.

Two figures wearing hoodies walked past and Steel clearly said something to them because they stopped in their tracks and looked back at him.

As one of the figures turned, French could see that it was their victim, Carmel Chowdry. The person next to him was a teenage boy. It had to be Rishi Chowdry, his fifteen-year-old brother.

Steel stood up and walked forward with his chest puffed out. There was clearly some kind of argument going on. There was a lot of finger pointing, aggressive gesticulating and shouting.

Then from out of nowhere, Steel punched Carmel in the face.

The two brothers immediately exploded into violence, dragging Steel to the floor, kicking and stamping on him before running away.

Even though it had been provoked, it was a brutal attack.

French and Garrow exchanged a look – they needed to find Gareth Steel, get his version of events and find out where he was at the time of Carmel Chowdry's murder.

'Do you know where I can find Gareth Steel?' French asked.

'Yes.' Geoff nodded.

French looked at him. 'We're going to need an address.'

Chapter 15

Georgie sat quietly at the long oval table in the main meeting room on the ground floor of Llancastell nick. At the far end, the badge of the North Wales Police was attached to the wall. Beside that, a photo of James Appleby, the current Police and Crime Commissioner for North Wales.

Taking a deep breath, Georgie felt another twinge deep inside her stomach. The scan she'd had at the University Hospital in Llancastell had revealed that everything was okay with the pregnancy, although it was too early to see very much yet. She had phoned Pam and Bill during the evening to tell them about what had happened at Canada Dock in Liverpool, but to reassure them she and the baby were okay. There were still moments when she completely forgot that she was carrying a baby. And then the enormity of it hit her with all the doubt, fear, but also excitement that her pregnancy generated when she remembered.

Her thoughts were interrupted by a knock at the door. A man then opened it, poked his head in, and gave her a quizzical smile.

'I'm looking for a Detective Constable Georgina Wild?' he said.

Woah. He is seriously good looking, she thought instantly.

'Hi. Yes, that's me,' Georgie replied with a half-smile, aware that her breathing had changed due to the man's presence. 'It's Georgie.'

'DI Ben Stewart,' he said as he came over and shook her hand firmly. He was in his late 30s, piercing blue eyes, dark blond hair and very handsome - like a young Robert Redford. 'I'm from the Modern Slavery Human Trafficking Unit. We're part of the NCA out of Manchester, but I'm based in North Wales,' he explained as he sat down.

The NCA stood for the National Crime Agency. It was the UK's primary law enforcement unit against organised crime and human, weapon, and drug trafficking.

'Right.' Georgie couldn't take her eyes off him.

'And we're working in tandem with the Gangmasters and Labour Abuse Authority in North Wales.' Ben looked over at her.

'Okay.' Georgie shifted in her seat. 'So, how can we help?'

'We've been tracking a gang working along the whole North Wales coastline,' he replied. 'We believe they are trafficking young people and children from India and then forcing them into slavery. We got intel you were investigating the murder of a young Indian male, is that right?'

'Yes. It happened last night. His body was discovered in the basement of a derelict psychiatric hospital in Denbigh. We believe he was stabbed,' Georgie said as she grabbed a folder and then took out the forensic photofit. 'The victim's name is Carmel Chowdry. He was twenty-one. He entered the UK three months ago with his fifteen-year-old brother, Rishi. They were travelling on student visas. We've contacted their mother, and she's flying in to identify her son's body.'

'Yeah, that does sound very familiar,' Ben nodded with a serious expression as he studied the photofit for a few seconds. 'The gang are promising families in India that their sons and daughters will be at a catering college while working in restaurant kitchens.' He then pulled out a photo from the folder he was holding. It showed a tiny room packed with mattresses and sleeping bags. 'Instead, they're being kept five or six to a room like this. Not being fed properly. And they're being used as cheap labour in care homes and car washes. Others are kept for weeks on end on fishing boats.' He gave her a dark look. 'We're also finding some teenage girls and boys are being forced into prostitution.'

'That's why we're concerned about the whereabouts of Rishi Chowdry,' Georgie explained.

'You haven't found an address?' Ben asked.

'Not yet. We know that they worked briefly in an Indian restaurant in Denbigh called Simla but they were sacked about six weeks ago,' Georgie said. 'Two officers are over in Denbigh now, trying to find out as much as they can.'

Ben reached over, took a folder, and then pulled out a photograph of a bearded Indian man in his 50s. 'This is the man our investigation is focussing on. Pavan Singh. He first came to our attention in 2015 after the earthquake in Nepal. It left thousands of children as orphans. Singh and his gang sold the children as domestic slaves to rich families in the West. Since then, he's expanded his operation south into Punjab, as well as some of the major cities like Delhi and Mumbai.'

Georgie nodded. 'Carmel and Rishi Chowdry flew in from Mumbai.'

Ben looked at her. 'I'm fairly certain your victim was part of Singh's operation. Looks like we might need to team up on this.'

Oh good, Georgie thought.

Chapter 16

Nick was now back in a cell on the VP wing of HMP Rhoswen. The worrying thing was that being there was starting to feel both normal and even comfortable. Nick had checked and there was an AA meeting later that he could go to. It was a place where he felt safe and where he could try to get his head together. It was especially important that he worked hard at his recovery after Blake had forced alcohol down his throat. So far, Nick hadn't felt any overwhelming cravings to drink more booze – and for that, he thanked whoever or whatever was up there looking out for him.

Laying back on his bed, he took a moment to also thank whatever higher power was up there for getting Amanda and Megan back safely. He just needed to make a plan to keep them all safe permanently and get their lives back on track. It had been so nice to hear their voices earlier. However, he was concerned that he had alarmed Amanda rather than reassured her.

His encounter with Blake in the prison transporter had shaken him a little. Even though it wasn't a surprise, Blake had made it very clear that Nick and his family would never be safe while he was still alive. Effectively, that gave Nick two options going forward. Move himself and his family away from North Wales and go into hiding while never being absolutely certain that they were safe. Or eliminate Blake once and for all. Nick couldn't believe that he'd been driven to the point where he needed to seriously consider killing someone to get his life back. But that was the truth. It went against everything he believed in, both as a police officer and a recovering alcoholic with a 12-step programme.

The door to his cell opened and his cell mate, Danny, a very skinny 30-year-old Geordie, came in out of breath. Even though Danny had been ravaged by heroin addiction, Nick hadn't been able to persuade him to come along to the AA meeting with him later. Danny had been out to an organised park run that the prison held twice a week. It was a 5-kilometre run around the site of the prison. Danny's philosophy was that he was going to get himself fit by going to the gym and running. Then he was going to stay away from drugs and booze when he left prison and rebuild his life.

'Jesus,' Danny panted. He was still out of breath as he sat down on his bed.

'How did it go?' Nick asked.

Danny smiled. 'Third place.' He had a strong Geordie accent. 'All those muscle dickheads out on the yard three times a day. They can't run to save their lives. They're all top heavy. Big chests, big arms, legs like bloody twiglets. I was like a fucking whippet out there, man.'

Nick smiled. 'Sounds like you enjoyed it?'

'Aye ... and they're all going, eh how come that skinny Geordie twat's goin' flying past us, like,' Danny said. 'I told them. Years of bloody practise, man.'

Nick frowned. 'How do you mean?'

'Running away from Five O,' Danny snorted. 'I mean, there weren't any garden fences or walls out there, but I've been running like that all me life.'

Nick laughed. 'Yeah, I see what you mean.'

Five O was slang for the police.

'Got to play 5-a-side later too,' Danny said. 'You fancy a game?'

'No thanks,' Nick replied. 'Rugby's my game. Or it was when I was younger.'

Nick spotted Danny looking over a copy of The Big Book that he'd managed to get hold of. It was the essential text owned by every alcoholic, as well as drug addicts.

'Don't know why you bother with all that AA shite, man,' Danny said with a frown. 'It's all God and that, isn't it?'

'Not at all.' Nick shook his head. 'Most people I know in AA aren't religious at all. My sponsor is an atheist, and he's forty-five years sober.'

Danny pulled a face. 'Yeah, but it's full of weirdos, isn't it?'

The irony of Danny's comment while they were sitting in a cell in prison wasn't lost on Nick. He didn't know why Danny was on the wing, and he didn't care. Nick didn't intend to be sharing a cell with Danny long enough for it to matter.

'It's just people like you and me.' Nick knew he had no chance of persuading Danny that going to AA or NA was going to help him in any way. 'I have a drink to make me feel better. To turn my head off. But I can't stop at one drink. And once I've started, I just can't stop until I pass out.'

Danny rubbed his jaw. 'Yeah, that's me. One smoke and I'm back on the smack and I can't stop.'

'I'm going to that meeting in about an hour, if you fancy it?' Nick said.

'Thanks.' Danny shook his head. 'I might go another time, like.'

With an urge to stretch his legs for a few minutes, Nick got up from his bed and wandered slowly out onto the walkway. There were the usual shouts and booming laughter that reverberated around.

Nick went over to the steel railings that looked down on the ground floor of the prison. Most prisoners on the VP wing kept away from the railings as it only antagonised the prisoners below, who would shout up obscenities and threaten to kill them.

Glancing down into the rec area, Nick saw two men playing pool.

The prisoner on the far side was wearing sports kit with shorts, a luminous bib and black astroturf boots. He must have been playing 5-a-side.

The other man potted the black and then punched the air in celebration.

It was Curtis Blake.

Nick stared down at him, almost daring him to look up at him. He remembered from intel that Blake always ran his own 5-a-side team in prison, made up of his cronies from Croxteth.

Fuck him, Nick thought.

Blake peered up, caught his eye and then went over to the prisoner he was playing pool with and whispered something.

They both laughed and turned to look up at Nick.

Nick gave Blake a grin and a wink before turning to go.

He knew in that very moment that he was going to have to kill Blake if he and his family were ever going to be truly safe. He just needed to work out how.

Chapter 17

French and Garrow pulled up outside the address they'd been given for Gareth Steel. It was a small bungalow that looked like it had seen better days. The front garden was strewn with weeds and there was a rusty bicycle leaning against a mouldy wall.

They walked up the garden path and knocked on the door.

After a few seconds, the front door opened slowly. A man in his early 50s peered out at them. He was shaven-headed, with sharp features and a swollen left eye. He was wearing a white vest and camouflage cargo shorts.

'Yeah?' he asked as he squinted at them suspiciously.

'Gareth Steel?' French asked as he showed him his warrant card.

Steel nodded. 'Yeah. What do you want?'

'Mind if we come in for a minute?' French asked. 'Just a couple of questions we'd like to ask you.'

'You got a warrant?' Steel sneered.

'No,' French admitted. Most people were too scared to challenge police officers on their doorstep and ask to see a warrant. Especially when they'd explained they were only there to ask a couple of questions. It implied that Steel had had prior dealings with the police. It also might suggest that he had something to hide.

French frowned. 'You're not under arrest.' He then gestured to Steel's swollen eye. 'We'd like to talk to you about an incident last Tuesday night outside The Royal Oak pub.'

'Yeah, well, I don't want to talk about that,' Steel replied.

French took a moment and then fixed him with a look. 'Right, if you want me to go and get a warrant, then I can do that. But that would mean me coming back here with half a dozen uniformed officers who are then going to trample all over your house … or we could just come in for a minute?'

They stared at each other for a few seconds.

'Jesus,' Steel growled, opening the front door begrudgingly.

They followed him inside. The house was untidy and cluttered. It smelled of fried food and stale cigarette smoke.

Steel wandered into the living room and then plonked himself down in an armchair. The floor was littered with empty beer cans and old takeaway cartons. The ashtray that sat on the arm of his chair was overflowing with cigarette butts.

It was a depressing sight, although French had seen worse.

Up on the wall was a huge Welsh flag. Lower down was a poster for a local Reform UK politician who was standing in a coming local election. Steel clearly wasn't hiding his politics.

'We understand that you were involved in an altercation outside The Royal Oak pub last Tuesday night?' Garrow fished out his notebook and pen.

Steel nodded as he took out a cigarette and popped it into his mouth. 'Yeah, that's how I got this, isn't it?' he mumbled, pointing to his swollen eye.

French took out his phone and showed Steel the photofit of Carmel. 'Was this one of the men who attacked you?'

Steel shrugged. 'I dunno. They all look the same to me.'

Jesus, here we go, French thought. He moved the phone closer to Steel. 'If you could have another look …'

Steel peered at the image and nodded. 'Yeah, I suppose so.'

French narrowed his eyes. 'You suppose so?'

'Yes. For fuck's sake, yes. That's the little fucker that attacked me. Him and some other fella.'

'Can you tell us what the altercation was about?' Garrow asked.

'No idea,' Steel said. 'I was having a beer and a smoke outside. And these two bastards attacked me.'

French glanced at Garrow. They knew that was bullshit.

'You didn't say anything to them?' French asked in a tone of disbelief.

'No,' Steel replied, shaking his head as he lit his cigarette.

'Had you ever seen the two men who attacked you before?' Garrow enquired.

'I don't think so,' Steel said. 'Like I say, I can't tell one from the other, if you know what I mean?'

Garrow frowned. 'No, I don't know what you mean.'

Steel bristled and then looked at French. 'Why are you asking me about this? I never reported it.'

'Can you tell us why you didn't report it?' French said.

Steel blew a plume of blueish smoke into the air. 'It's just the way I was brought up.'

'You mean you were brought up to settle stuff like this yourself?' French asked.

Steel nodded. 'Yeah, I suppose so. You don't go running to your lot if someone gives you a slap.' He tapped some ash into the ashtray. 'You still haven't told me what this is all about.'

Garrow looked over. 'Can you tell us the last time you saw the men who attacked you?'

Steel frowned for a few seconds. 'I haven't seen them since that night.'

'You're sure about that?'

'Yeah,' Steel said, starting to sound uneasy.

'Can you tell us where you were last night?' Garrow enquired.

'I was here.'

'On your own?'

'Yeah.'

'Can anyone verify that you were here?'

'No,' Steel stated, now sounding agitated. 'What's this all about?'

French pointed at his phone. 'This man's name is Carmel Chowdry, and he was found murdered last night.'

The blood drained from Steel's face. 'Fuck that. I didn't have nothing to do with that. No way.'

French fixed him with a stare. 'You're sure about that?'

'Yeah. You're not gonna pin that on me. And I want my solicitor before I say anything else,' Steel snapped. 'Either you arrest me or I want you to leave. I know my rights.'

Chapter 18

Amis had been examining Carmel Chowdry's body for over an hour when Ruth and Georgie arrived at the Llancastell University Hospital mortuary. Ruth had checked and rechecked the security arrangements for Amanda and Megan. They were going to be under armed guard at the hotel for the next few nights before being moved to a safe house, which would also be guarded by armed officers. Parker had promised her that there would be no more compromises or mistakes in their protection, and she felt secure in the knowledge that the security around them was incredibly tight now. What she couldn't gauge was what Amanda and Megan would be doing in the long term. Ruth supposed that would depend upon whether Nick received a custodial sentence. She knew she needed to talk to Nick during the day, now he was back at Rhoswen.

'You okay, boss?' Georgie asked.

Ruth blinked, bringing herself back into the present. 'Yes. Sorry. Miles away.'

As they went inside, Ruth immediately felt the chill of the room and the eerie hum of the refrigerators.

'I forgot to ask,' Ruth said. 'How was DI Stewart from the Modern Slavery Human Trafficking Unit?'

'Ben,' Georgie replied with a smirk.

'Ben?' Ruth said with a raised eyebrow. She then looked at Georgie for a beat, picking up on her expression. 'Oh God, you fancied him, didn't you?'

'No.'

'Liar.'

'No, not really.'

'Don't lie,' Ruth said. 'What's he like?'

'Well, you know when people say *He's no Brad Pitt* ... Well, he actually is,' Georgie explained with a knowing expression.

'Oh, I see what you did there,' Ruth laughed. 'You do know that being pregnant makes you horny?'

'I'm not *horny*,' Georgie whispered with a defensive expression. 'He was just very attractive.'

Before they could continue, Amis turned on an electric saw, which then squealed as it hit the body's breastbone. Not only did it grate on Ruth's teeth, but it made her stomach churn.

Jesus! That's horrible.

Ruth pulled a face as they made their way over to the metal gurney. 'Yeah, well that's killed my mood a bit,' she said over the noise.

Turning off the saw, Amis noticed Ruth and Georgie. He pulled down his green surgical mask.

'Ah, the cavalry has arrived,' Amis quipped with a winning smile.

'What can you tell us, Tony?' Ruth asked.

'Cause of death is what I suspected,' Amis said. 'Stab wound to the abdomen. It cut the apical pericardium, diaphragm and liver. Damage to the abdominal aorta causing a major retroperitoneal haemorrhage.'

Ruth rolled her eyes. 'You've just said a load of words that I don't understand, Tony. What does that mean for those of us who aren't medically trained?'

'Oh yes, sorry,' Amis guffawed. 'In laymen's, or laywomen's terms in your case, your victim was stabbed, haemorrhaged and bled to death.'

'Thank you,' Ruth said with a forced smile.

Ruth looked at Carmel's youthful face. Having now caught up on the details of the investigation, she thought it was such a tragedy that he and his brother had tried to escape the poverty of their lives in Mumbai by coming to the UK, only for him to be murdered. There must have been such hope that they were going to make a better life for themselves and their family. Ruth knew they needed to find whoever had killed Carmel and get justice for his family.

And wherever Rishi Chowdry was, they needed to find him and return him safely to his mother. Ruth couldn't allow her to lose two sons.

Chapter 19

Ruth and Georgie were in Interview Room 3, sitting opposite Nitira Chowdry, Carmel and Rishi's mother, whom the Home Office had flown in from Mumbai. She was in her 40s, with soft features, and wore an orange patterned sari. Fiddling with the hem, Ruth could see how nervous she was. Her gold bracelets jangled as she raised her hand to move a strand of dark hair from her face.

An hour earlier, Nitira had been taken over to the University Hospital morgue in Llancastell to identify her son's body.

Ruth gave her an empathetic look. 'I'm so sorry for your loss, Mrs Chowdry.'

'Nitira, please,' she replied quietly. She then stared into space, lost in her grief. Then she looked at them. 'Please, I need you to find Rishi,' she pleaded with them.

'We're doing everything we can to find him,' Ruth tried to reassure her.

'I just need to know he's safe,' she said, her voice trembling with emotion. 'Carmel was supposed to be looking after him. What if something happened to Rishi too?'

Ruth looked at her. 'As far as we know, no harm has come to Rishi. Maybe he's hiding from whoever attacked Carmel, which is why it's been so difficult to locate him.'

Nitira nodded, as if Ruth's words had calmed her slightly. 'Yes. That does make sense.'

'Would you be up to answering a few questions?' Ruth asked gently. 'It might help us catch whoever attacked Carmel and help us bring back Rishi safely.'

Nitira blinked as though she hadn't heard Ruth's question, but then gave an almost imperceptible nod. 'Yes. Of course.'

Georgie clicked her pen as she opened her notebook. 'Nitira, could you tell us why Carmel and Rishi flew to the UK?'

Nitira composed herself and then looked over at them. 'A man came to our village. We live maybe ten miles outside Mumbai. He told some of us that he could arrange for our children to go to college in Britain and learn to be cooks. He could arrange the student visas, the accommodation and the flights. He told us that maybe if our children settled there, we could one day go and live with them in the UK.'

'And he asked for money to arrange all this?' Ruth asked.

'Yes.' Nitira nodded sadly. 'It would cost 200,000 rupees. I think that is about £2,000. We told him that we didn't have that kind of money. But he told us not to worry. That he would lend us the money and then our children could pay him back each month. He said they would be earning good wages, so it wouldn't be a problem. He made it sound so easy.' She took a breath as she started to cry. 'I just wanted my sons to have a better life. There is nothing for them where we are from.'

Ruth took a tissue and handed it to her. 'Here you go.'

Nitira sniffed. 'I'm sorry ... Thank you.'

'Please don't apologise,' Georgie said reassuringly.

After a few seconds, Nitira composed herself and looked back over at them. 'Please,' she whispered, indicating that she was happy to continue.

Ruth gave her a kind smile. 'And this was three months ago?'

'Yes.'

'Did you speak to Carmel and Rishi once they'd arrived here?' Georgie asked.

'Yes. At first, we spoke a lot,' Nitira explained. 'But then less. They told me there was some delay in them going to college. They said they had to work very long hours cleaning and washing up in a restaurant kitchen. It wasn't what we were told it was going to be like.'

Georgie gave her an understanding nod and then pulled a photograph from a nearby folder that contained intel that Ben had brought with him from the Modern Slavery Human Trafficking Unit.

'Could you look at this man and tell me if you've seen him before?' she asked.

Nitira moved the photograph closer, peered at it, and then looked at Georgie. 'Yes, this is the man who came to our town. Mr Kapoor.'

Georgie shot a meaningful look at Ruth and then said, 'We believe that his real name is Pavan Singh and he's being investigated by the British police.'

Chapter 20

The CID team had assembled for an impromptu briefing on the investigation so that everyone could get up to speed. Ruth walked over to the scene boards and pointed. 'Pavan Singh. This is the man who we believe runs the trafficking gang from India, arranging for children, teenagers and young people to come to the UK. He promises them college and decent jobs. Instead, they are sold and exploited. Car washes, kitchens, care homes and even prostitution.' Ruth looked out at the team and then gestured to Ben. 'We're now working with DI Stewart from the Modern Slavery Human Trafficking Unit. If Pavan Singh is in the UK, we need to know where he is. Check passport control and see if they can run a check on him.' Taking a sip of water, Ruth perched herself on a desk. 'What about Rishi? Are we any closer to finding him?'

Garrow looked over. 'I'm running a check on the mobile phone number that his mother gave us. And we're going to talk to Kabir Malik, who owns the restaurant where the two brothers worked two months ago.'

Ruth nodded. 'If Malik is the owner, then maybe he's

part of the trafficking ring. Let's run him through NPC and do some background checks.'

Ben looked over. 'If Singh is promising families in India that their children will get valuable experience working in kitchens, maybe the Simla restaurant is part of that scam. Otherwise, how would two boys from Mumbai find their way into working there?'

Ruth agreed. 'Okay. Dan and Jim, if you need to pull Malik in for questioning, then do that. But our priority has to be to find Rishi.'

'I've checked the main hospitals and shelters in the area but no one's seen him,' French said.

Garrow pointed to his computer. 'I'm trying to see if either of the brothers had any kind of social media presence, but at the moment I'm drawing a blank.'

Ruth frowned. 'As far as we know, Rishi doesn't have any money and no relatives. So where is he staying and who's looking after him? He's fifteen and his brother has been murdered. My assumption is that he's terrified. Maybe he knows who killed Carmel and he's now hiding away out of fear.' Ruth looked at the team. 'So, we need to get to Rishi before the person who killed his brother does.'

Chapter 21

French and Garrow were driving through the centre of Snowdonia National Park as they cut through North Wales, heading from Llancastell to Denbigh to interview Kabir Malik at an office above the Simla Indian Restaurant.

Above them, the clouds were breaking up to reveal pale streaks of sky. The hazy semi-circle of the sun cast light across the mountain peaks opposite. French thought what a magnificent sight it was and one that he usually took for granted. The tops of the mountains looked like raw, jagged teeth.

To their right, the summit of Snowdon, which was partially covered by cloud and a dusting of snow.

Garrow looked over. 'What do you think about the plans to call Snowdon and Snowdonia by their proper names?'

'What? Yr Wyddfa and Eryri?' French said, slightly showing off his knowledge of Welsh and what he considered to be his flawless Welsh accent. 'I'm all for it. Snowdon and Snowdonia are bloody English names.'

Garrow laughed. 'Remember I'm bloody English.'

French grinned. 'That's why I said it.'

'Don't you think it might be confusing for tourists?' Garrow asked.

'I think it's bloody disrespectful not to use the Welsh language for Welsh landmarks,' French said, realising that he sounded annoyed.

Garrow smiled and held up his hands. 'I'm just asking a question, boyo,' he joked.

'Yeah, well, I was reading how in India in the 90s they changed the city names from the English Raj names back to the Indian names,' French explained. 'Bombay is now Mumbai. We're just doing the same in Wales.'

'Everest is still called Everest, and that's in Nepal,' Garrow reasoned.

'Yeah, well, they want to change that too,' French stated, feeling himself getting carried away. 'Apparently, it was an Indian bloke that first measured the mountain. Sikdar, I think his name was. It had nothing to do with some English toff called Sir George Everest, who worked for the British. In fact, George Everest never even saw the mountain, let alone set foot on it.'

Garrow gave French a wry smile. 'Right.'

French shrugged. 'What?'

'I just didn't know you felt so passionately about the oppressive nature of British colonialism, Sarge.'

'Don't take the piss, Jim,' French said. 'Just because I went to the local comprehensive doesn't mean that I don't have any opinions.'

Garrow nodded. 'Hey, even as an Englishman, I agree with everything you said. For what it's worth.'

'You would.'

'Why?'

'Because you're an over-educated Guardian-reading leftie,' French said as his face broke into a smile.

'Thanks, Sarge,' Garrow chortled. 'I love being reduced to a stereotype.'

Ten minutes later, they pulled into Denbigh and parked up outside the Simla restaurant.

Getting out, they walked down the pavement and then rang the bell that French assumed was for the offices or flat above the restaurant.

A few seconds later, the door opened and an Indian man in his 40s, slim, well dressed with a goatee beard, peered out at them.

'Kabir Malik?' French asked, as they both showed their warrant cards.

'Yes?' Malik replied with an assurance that let them know he wasn't remotely fazed by their visit.

'DS French and DC Garrow,' French explained. 'Llancastell CID. Is it okay if we come in for a few minutes? We've got some routine questions we'd like to ask you.'

'Of course, of course,' Malik said, immediately opening the door. French could smell his aftershave, which was bordering on overwhelming. 'Come upstairs.'

French and Garrow followed Malik up some stairs to a landing. A door was open. Inside, there was an office with a large table and computers. A young woman in her 20s, smartly dressed, was tapping away at a keyboard. Opposite her, a young man was on the phone.

'Shall we go in here?' Malik suggested, pointing to what looked like a smart meeting room with an oval table and stylish padded chairs.

French exchanged a look with Garrow. It certainly wasn't what French had been expecting to see above an Indian restaurant in Denbigh. And whatever Malik was in to, he clearly had lucrative businesses other than the restaurant.

'Can I get you any tea, coffee, water?' Malik asked politely.

French held up his hand. 'We're fine. Thanks.'

Pulling out a chair, Malik sat down. French noticed he wore stylish cufflinks on his cobalt blue shirt and his hands looked manicured.

'Of course, I was expecting a visit,' Malik admitted. 'I know you spoke to Rohan the other day. And I've seen the local news. It's terrible what happened the other night.'

'You remember Carmel Chowdry?' Garrow asked.

'Yes,' Malik replied with a serious nod. 'I try to remember everyone who works for me.'

French looked at him. 'What about his brother, Rishi?'

'Yes. I believe they came to work here together.'

'Were you aware that Rishi was only fifteen years old?' French asked in a stern tone.

'No. Of course not.' Malik frowned for a second and then shook his head. 'I'm sure that can't be correct.'

'I'm afraid it is,' French said sternly.

'To be honest, Rohan does the day to day running of the restaurant and the hiring of staff,' Malik explained calmly, 'but we don't employ anyone under the age of sixteen. And usually we don't employ anyone under eighteen. It's against the UK employment laws for a start.'

'Could you tell us how Carmel and Rishi came to be working in your restaurant?' Garrow asked.

'As I said, Rohan deals with the staff for the restaurant.' Malik scratched his nose as if the question had made him feel uncomfortable. 'But I'm sure that he said that they were Indian nationals who were in the UK on student visas. And they were looking for part-time work while they were at college.'

'Do you know which college they were studying at?' French asked.

'I'm afraid not, no.'

'How long did Carmel and Rishi work for you?' Garrow said.

Malik pulled a face. 'I think it was just a few weeks.'

French raised an eyebrow. 'Can you tell us why that was?'

Malik thought for a few seconds. He clearly wasn't comfortable explaining what had happened.

'We do need you to answer the question,' French explained. 'This is a murder enquiry, so we need to get a full picture of what Carmel had been doing in the lead-up to his death.'

'Unfortunately, Rohan said that Carmel and Rishi had been stealing from us.'

Garrow narrowed his eyes. 'Stealing?'

'Food, alcohol and then some money,' Malik explained.

'Right,' French said. 'Did you report this to the police?'

'No, no,' Malik replied, as though this was an absurd idea. 'I didn't want to get them into trouble. I just couldn't trust them to work in my restaurant anymore.'

French gave him a stern look. 'We are currently working with the Modern Slavery Human Trafficking Unit. I assume that you have the relevant paperwork for everyone that works for you.'

'Naturally,' Malik said with a nonchalant shrug, as though it didn't need saying.

'Have you ever heard the name Pavan Singh?' French enquired.

'No, I'm afraid not.' Malik shook his head. 'Is there any reason why I should?'

'Just a routine question,' French reassured him. 'I'm

assuming that you kept records of Carmel and Rishi's local address and phone numbers?'

'Possibly. They will be here somewhere,' Malik replied in a blasé manner.

'Could you check for us please?' Garrow asked, indicating that they needed that information as a matter of urgency.

'Of course.' Malik got up from where he was sitting and went into the office next door.

Garrow looked at French. 'What do you think?' he asked under his breath.

'I'm not sure,' French admitted. There was nothing in Malik's manner or response to their questions that suggested he was hiding anything from them. Maybe he was just a very good liar.

'Actually, you're in luck,' Malik said, pulling out a document. 'I have phone numbers and an address here in Denbigh.'

Malik came over and handed the piece of paper to French.

Chapter 22

'Hi, my name's Kenny and I'm an alcoholic,' said a young man sitting in a wheelchair at the AA meeting in HMP Rhoswen.

'Hi Kenny,' replied the other prisoners.

Nick remembered Kenny from the AA meeting the last time he was in Rhoswen, just before he escaped. Kenny was 25 years old and cross-addicted to alcohol, heroin and crack cocaine. His heroin abuse had been so severe that he'd had his left leg amputated.

'Yeah, it's been a good week, really,' Kenny admitted. 'I'm getting the hang of my prosthetic leg. I did about an hour on it this morning.'

'Yeah, lad, that is good,' remarked another prisoner encouragingly. 'Won't be long before you're whizzing round the fuckin' park run, eh?'

The other prisoners laughed.

'Yeah,' Kenny said with a self-effacing smile. 'As I've shared before, I've made my mind up this time to stay clean and sober. Normally I'd be sitting in my pad, smoking spice, completely out of it. Or getting some pills or hooch. But since I've been coming to these meetings, I can see that I can stay sober and clean. I always thought AA was just a load of rubbish, but it really has helped me. In fact, I look forward to coming. And talking about stuff helps. So, when I get out of here, I'm going to a rehab in Colwyn Bay to come off the methadone. Then I'm going to find out where the local AA and NA meetings are, because I don't want to end up in here again. This is my third recall for dealing and I'm sick of being in this place.'

There were some murmurs and nods of agreement.

Kenny looked at Phil, a man in his 60s, who lived locally and came in to run the meetings.

'Thanks, Kenny.' Phil glanced at his watch. 'That's it for today, lads. But I think it's been a great meeting and I'll see you next week.'

The prisoners got up and went over to shake Phil's hand and thank him for running the meeting and bringing biscuits.

The AA meetings took place in a recreation room in a wing that also housed the prison's chapel and prayer room, as well as the chaplaincy offices.

The prison's Substance Misuse Service Officer, Mike - in his 40s, intelligent and stick thin - arrived with a set of keys. He was wearing a tracksuit, trainers and had a whistle hanging around his neck.

'Right, lads,' Mike said with a friendly smile. 'I need you out of here pronto so I can lock up and go and ref the bloody 5-a-side.'

'Rather you than me,' a prisoner joked. Prison 5-a-side could get very competitive and there were often fights.

Nick stood up, went and shook Phil's hand and thanked him. He hadn't shared at the meeting. There was no way he could go into the details of what had happened.

In fact, he was just happy to be sitting in an AA meeting where he felt safe.

As the prisoners filed out into the corridor, Nick looked down at Kenny.

'Good share, Kenny,' Nick said. 'I've got a few contacts in AA in Colwyn Bay if you want? I can see if someone can meet you over there and take you to a meeting?'

'Yeah, that would be great,' Kenny replied gratefully.

Nick glanced down the corridor. He spotted four prisoners coming out of the chapel further down.

'What are they up to?' Nick asked.

'It's that Catholic Bible study group, isn't it?' Kenny stated, rolling his eyes disapprovingly.

'Right.' Nick nodded and spotted a group of eight prisoners coming out of a meeting room. He immediately recognised one of them as Tony Connell. Nick knew Connell was an addict because he'd previously seen him queuing up for methadone downstairs. Nick also remembered him from way back. He was a member of the notorious Bootle Crew Gang in Liverpool. And the Bootle Crew Gang had an ongoing feud with Curtis Blake and the Croxteth Boyz dating back a decade. A 15-year-old member of the Bootle Crew called Reece Harding had been shot dead in a drive-by in 2011. Everyone knew it was the Croxteth Boyz and that Blake had been driving the car, but the police came up against a wall of silence. Instead, the Bootle Crew bided their time and shot Blake's best friend, Marcus Kane, coming out of The Crown pub six months later. Kane survived but had brain damage from the gunshot wound to his head.

Connell was talking to another prisoner who Nick recognised as Jayden Roberts, who was also part of the Bootle Crew.

'And that's the NA meeting,' Kenny informed Nick, gesturing to them. 'Bloody junkies, eh?' he joked.

'Yeah,' Nick laughed and then looked at him. 'So, there's the AA, NA and Bible studies over here at the same time?'

'Yeah,' Kenny nodded. 'And there's some Muslim thingy in the prayer room after us.'

Nick watched Mike as he locked the door to the recreation room. He then walked over to a door on the other side of the corridor that Nick remembered led to stairs that went down to the astroturf pitches. Using his security card, Mike opened the door, went through, and then disappeared.

Nick took all this information in as he started to hatch a plan.

Chapter 23

French and Garrow arrived at the door of a ground-floor flat in a side road in the centre of Denbigh. It was the address that Malik had written for Carmel and Rishi Chowdry.

As they approached, they saw that the frosted glass panel in the door had been smashed.

'That's weird,' French said under his breath as he inspected the broken glass. As soon as he got closer, there was an unpleasant smell from inside the flat. 'Jesus, what the hell is that?'

Garrow took out his blue forensic gloves, reached for the door handle and opened it. Pushing the door open slowly, they went in.

Garrow pulled a face at the smell. 'I see what you mean.'

The flat was tiny and virtually unfurnished. Floorboards were bare, and the paint was flaking from the walls. A bulb hung from the ceiling of the hallway and the floor was littered with flyers and unopened post. The air was thick with the smell of body odour, rotting food and something like sour milk.

The first room to their left was some kind of kitchen. While French went in, Garrow continued to look through the flat.

Over by the sink, there was an old rusty kettle unplugged, and a toaster covered in crumbs. French, who had now put on his forensic gloves, went over to the small fridge. Opening it, he saw it was empty except for a bottle of milk that had congealed.

'I can't believe anyone is living in here,' he muttered under his breath.

'Sarge,' Garrow called.

'What is it?' French asked as he left the kitchen and marched down the hallway.

Garrow pointed to a bedroom. The smell of body odour was overwhelming.

Glancing inside, French could see that the floor was covered in two stained mattresses. There were about half a dozen old ripped sleeping bags and some filthy clothes piled up in the corner. It was something he'd only seen before in police photos, but it definitely looked like the flat had once been occupied by several people who had slept crammed together in a bedroom.

'If I was looking for signs of illegal immigrants being used for forced or slave labour, this is what I would guess it would look like,' Garrow said darkly.

'And it looks like they've been moved on somewhere else,' French said.

Garrow moved one of the sleeping bags to one side. Underneath, there was a large bloodstain.

Garrow and French exchanged a look.

'We'd better get SOCO down here now,' French said.

The pool of blood wasn't big enough to suggest anyone had been stabbed or bled out in that room. But it was significant enough to warrant further investigation.

Especially as this was Carmel and Rishi Chowdry's last known address.

Chapter 24

Ruth strolled through IR1. Most of the CID team were out checking leads, addresses or witnesses. She remembered the days when she first joined the Met in the early 90s when it was a matter of trawling through the London telephone directory or the Yellow Pages. Witness reports were typed up on typewriters, often by designated typists, and carbon copies were made and filed away by hand. She recalled the looks of excitement when the first few word processors had been set up. Everyone had to learn to use the Word Perfect 5.1 programme. Most of the older coppers dismissed it all as 'bollocks' and continued to handwrite everything. Sometimes it astounded her how much the world of policing had changed in 30 years.

'Boss.' Georgie approached, breaking her train of thought. 'We've got some forensics back on Carmel Chowdry. 'They found significant traces of isopropyl alcohol under his nails, in his hair and on his clothes.'

'What is it?' Ruth asked.

'It breaks down dirt, oil, and grime,' Georgie explained. '*And* it's often found in car shampoo.'

'Okay ... Maybe he was working at a car wash,' Ruth suggested. 'Can you find me every car wash in the area, especially anyone offering hand washing and valeting? And then have a look on the PNC and see if we've got any intel on car washes in North Wales.'

'Yes, boss,' Georgie replied.

'Where's DI Stewart?' Ruth asked. 'We could do with his expertise on this.'

'He's gone to meet his CHIS,' Georgie explained.

CHIS stood for Covert Human Intelligence Source, which essentially meant an informant.

'Right you are,' Ruth said.

Garrow looked over. 'Boss?'

'Jim?' Ruth replied as she turned.

Garrow then pointed to his computer screen. 'I've done some digging on Gareth Steel and it makes for pretty unpleasant reading.'

Ruth frowned. 'Why?'

'First of all, Gareth Steel isn't even his real name. He was born Gareth Pratt in 1968. He changed his name by deed poll to Gareth Steel in 1995.'

'I'm not surprised. Can't be easy going around with the surname Pratt.' She then looked at Garrow. 'That doesn't make him a murderer though, does it?'

'Oh, it gets better,' Garrow explained. 'Steel was a member of the North Wales British Movement, which was a Neo-Nazi group. In 2008, he served 18 months of a three-year sentence for unfurling a Nazi swastika flag and performing Nazi salutes outside the gates of Auschwitz in Poland. He posted the photos and videos on the British Movement website. Since then, he's been photographed at various rallies with Hitler banners.'

'Jesus,' Ruth groaned, shaking her head.

'Oh, and he's in a band called *The Good Ole Rednecks*

who perform in Klu Klux Klan hoods and hang 'golliwogs' on stage.'

'Bloody hell,' Ruth said, pulling a face. 'So, I'm guessing for a man like that, being beaten up by two Asian boys is utterly humiliating.'

'It's definitely a motive. Maybe he tracked Carmel down?' Garrow suggested.

'And his alibi is weak.' Ruth nodded. 'Let's get the CCTV in Denbigh on Friday night sent over. Talk to the DVLA and see if he has a car and then run that plate past traffic. We might even get a hit on the ANPR.'

'Yes, boss.'

ANPR stood for Automatic Number Plate Recognition. It was fitted to certain traffic cameras. When a vehicle passed, its registration number was read and instantly checked against a database of vehicles of interest. Sometimes that could be done retrospectively.

Ruth then gestured for Georgie to follow her towards the DI's office, asking under her breath as they went, 'How are you feeling?'

'Yeah, still a bit sick in the mornings,' Georgie whispered as they entered the office and sat down. 'I just hope it doesn't develop into full-blown hyperemesis.'

Hyperemesis was severe nausea and vomiting in pregnant women that was sometimes so serious that it required hospital treatment.

Ruth frowned. 'I don't think we even had the term *hyperemesis* when I was pregnant with Ella. It was just called morning sickness.'

'A bottle of folic acid arrived in the post yesterday from Pam,' Georgie explained with a wry smile. 'I didn't have the heart to tell her that I was already taking it, so I rang to thank her anyway.'

'Bless her.' Ruth smiled. 'Remember, anything you

need? And no more diving around docks in bulletproof jackets, please.'

As Georgie laughed, Ben entered IR1 and headed their way.

'Here he comes,' Ruth said in a knowing tone.

Ben looked at Georgie as he got to the door and smiled. 'Georgie, have you got a minute?'

'Yeah, no problem.'

'I've got a couple of things I'd like to run past you,' Ben explained.

'Mind if I sit in?' Ruth asked.

'Of course. No problem.' Ben sat down, took out his laptop and opened it. A moment later, the image of a young Indian man appeared on the screen. 'As you know, our investigation is focussed on Pavan Singh. However, we've come across this young man, Rohan Chopra.'

Ruth frowned as the name instantly rang a bell. 'I think two of my officers spoke to him a couple of days ago.'

'Yes.' Ben nodded. 'Chopra works at the Simla restaurant in Denbigh. But we believe that he is also working for Singh recruiting Indian nationals to work at several hand car washes in the area.'

Georgie raised an eyebrow. 'Our victim had car cleaner under his fingernails.'

'Right, that is interesting,' Ben replied. 'The only problem we have is that the car washes keep moving as soon as there is any sign of them being watched.'

'We could get Chopra in for questioning,' Georgie suggested.

'I suspect that he won't give us anything,' Ben said. 'Plus, it would tip off Singh and whoever else is involved that we're investigating them. They could shut up shop, move their workers on somewhere else and start again.'

Ruth nodded. It was a well-reasoned argument. 'Are

you suggesting running a surveillance operation to start with?'

Ben nodded, clearly glad that Ruth had predicted what he was going to suggest. 'Exactly. But if you guys are looking at Chopra and the restaurant, it seems prudent for us to team up?'

'Sounds good to me,' Ruth said. 'We know he works at the Simla, so my guess is to wait for him to finish and see where he goes after work.'

Ben nodded. 'Sounds good.'

Ruth gave Georgie a knowing look. 'Georgie would be more than happy to team up on surveillance tonight.'

Chapter 25

It had taken nearly half an hour to find two prison officers to escort the prisoners from AA and NA back from the chaplaincy, across the yard and walkways and back to the main body of the prison.

Keeping his eye on Connell, Nick knew that he had to talk to him now before he got separated and taken up to the VP wing.

Picking up speed, Nick manoeuvred himself so that he walked next to Connell who was talking and laughing with Roberts.

'Tony?' Nick asked.

Connell turned and frowned. 'Who the fuck are you?' he asked aggressively.

'I remember you from Bootle,' Nick said.

'Yeah, well I don't remember you lad, so fuck off,' Connell snapped and then turned away.

Roberts laughed.

This isn't going well.

Nick racked his brains for snippets of intel that he could remember.

'I used to serve you in the Sports and Social,' Nick said. 'I knew your brother, Kev.'

Connell looked back at him and studied his face for a second. 'Yeah, lad, I remember you. You didn't have a beard, though.'

Great. He must have me mixed up with someone else.

'That's right,' Nick said, playing along. 'Must be hard to see that scumbag from Croxteth swanning around here.'

Connell's face darkened as he frowned. 'Blake?'

Nick nodded. 'Thinks he owns the bloody place.'

Connell gestured to Roberts and hissed angrily, 'Yeah, well if he wasn't surrounded by his cling-ons all the time, Jay and I would slice his face off and send him out of here in a box, know what I mean?'

'What if I told you I could get you, Jay and Blake in a room on your own? No cameras,' Nick said.

Connell exchanged a look of disbelief with Roberts. 'I'd say you were a fucking magician.'

'But you'd be interested?' Nick asked.

'Interested?' Connell snorted. 'I'd be made up, mate. But it ain't gonna happen.'

The group of prisoners arrived at the main block and stopped beside a large door.

'I'll be in touch,' Nick promised as they walked inside.

'Eh, what's your name, pal?' Connell asked, clearly intrigued by what Nick had said to him.

'Andy,' he replied.

Chapter 26

Georgie and Ben had been sitting outside the Simla Indian restaurant for about twenty minutes. They guessed that Rohan Chopra would be leaving the premises between 11.30pm and midnight.

As Ben looked out from the passenger seat of the car, the moon overhead stole slowly behind a swollen grey cloud and the sky darkened. Denbigh High Street was deserted and there wasn't a soul to be seen. A nearby church bell struck to signal that it was 11.45pm.

Ben checked the lens on the surveillance camera for the third time. So far, they had talked *shop*, but nothing more than that.

'I guess your husband has got pretty used to you staying out late on obs,' Ben said nonchalantly as he twisted the telephoto lens.

Georgie wasn't an idiot. She knew that Ben was a detective and at some point he would have checked out her wedding finger. She did it herself all the time. Not because she was interested in someone, but because it was useful to know if someone was married. It was an instinctive thing that all detectives did, so she wondered why he'd said it.

Georgie gave a wry smile. 'I don't have a husband.'

He looked at her with a quizzical smirk. 'What?'

'You know I'm not married,' Georgie replied, looking directly at him. He might be handsome, but she wasn't going to let him play her.

'How would I know that?' he asked innocently.

'Come on. You're an experienced detective. It's something you check on everyone you come into contact with. It goes with the job,' Georgie said.

Ben took a few seconds, but she had him on the ropes. 'Okay. But I was just making conversation.'

'Really?' Georgie smiled at him. 'You ask me what my husband thinks of me being out late? I tell you I don't have a husband. You then shrug and say something like 'Well your boyfriend then.' At which point I tell you whether I have a boyfriend or if I'm single.'

Ben's face lit up with a smile. He held up his hands. 'You're good,' he laughed.

'Yeah, well, this isn't my first rodeo,' Georgie grinned.

'So?' Ben asked.

'So what?' Georgie asked, playing along.

'What does your boyfriend think of you sitting in cars with strange men late at night?' Ben joked.

'Yeah, well, I suspected you were strange. That's true,' Georgie said playfully. 'Any man who keeps playing with his telephoto lens like that is definitely overcompensating for something.'

Ben's eyes widened in mock horror. 'Jesus …'

'Don't tell me. You've had no complaints so far,' Georgie laughed.

'Well, I don't like to brag,' he replied with a wry smile. 'You still haven't answered my question.'

Georgie raised an eyebrow. 'Oh, which question is that?'

'Do you have a boyfriend?' he asked with a confident smile.

'And how is that relevant to this joint surveillance operation?' Georgie asked.

Ben scratched his face. 'I don't know how long we're going to be stuck in this car together. I'm just trying to make conversation.'

'You said that already.'

'Well, I'm just trying to get to know you better.'

'Right.' Georgie looked at him with a disbelieving smirk. There was something incredibly sexy about the way their teasing conversation had gone back and forth. 'You do know that I'm not going to sleep with you, don't you?'

'Wow!' Ben gasped with a laugh. 'That's not what this is. I have no intention of trying to sleep with you.'

'Why, do you have a girlfriend?' Georgie asked.

'No, I don't but …'

'But you just don't find me attractive? Is that it?'

'No, I didn't say that.' Ben shook his head. Then he looked at her with an amused expression. 'This is not how I saw this surveillance operation going tonight.'

'Oh, how did you see it going?'

Ben sighed. 'No comment.'

Georgie laughed and then saw movement out of the corner of her eye. 'Looks like we're on.' She gestured to a figure leaving the Simla. It was Chopra.

Grabbing his surveillance camera, Ben took a series of photographs as Chopra walked across the road and got into a BMW.

Georgie looked puzzled. 'That's an 18 plate BMW,' she frowned. 'It's a nice car for a 23 year old who works in an Indian restaurant, isn't it?'

'Yeah, that doesn't add up.'

Turning the ignition, Georgie readied herself to follow Chopra to wherever he was going.

The BMW indicated, pulled out from where it was parked and zoomed away at speed.

'Great,' Georgie growled. 'We've got a bloody boy racer on our hands.'

Ben glanced over at the speedometer and saw that Georgie was having to drive at 60 mph to keep up. 'Twat,' he sighed.

Taking a left-hand turn, the BMW then slowed rapidly, red brake lights glowing brightly, beside a few shops set back from the road. Georgie wondered what he was doing, given that all the shops were closed.

A figure wearing a hoodie ran out of the darkness and stopped by the car. They opened the back door of the BMW and jumped inside.

Georgie pulled over to the other side of the road, trying to maintain a decent distance between them. After a few seconds, the BMW pulled away again.

'That looked like a woman or girl to me,' Ben observed.

Georgie thought about the figure's diminutive stature and height. 'That was my instinct.'

Ben smiled. 'Great minds, eh?'

For the next few minutes, they followed the BMW out of Denbigh, heading northwest towards Abergele and the North Wales coastline.

'Where the hell are they going?' Georgie asked under her breath.

'Is it me?' Ben said, 'Or did you think it was strange that whoever got into that car sat in the back … It might be nothing.'

'No, I think you're right,' Georgie agreed. 'It definitely

suggests that they're not friends and that they don't know each other very well.'

The BMW indicated left, pulled off the road and entered the car park of a Travelodge hotel. Trying to keep her distance, Georgie was worried that there were so few cars on the road that Chopra would spot them.

Pulling into the car park, Georgie made sure that she took a completely different route so that they were no longer behind Chopra's BMW.

However, instead of parking, the BMW drove up to the hotel's entrance and stopped. The back door opened, the figure got out and trudged inside. The BMW then pulled around and parked in a space nearby.

Ben had been taking photographs the whole time. He looked over at Georgie. 'What do you think?'

'If I had to guess,' Georgie said, 'I would say that Rohan Chopra has just delivered a sex worker to someone inside that hotel and he's waiting for her to finish, and then he'll drive her home.'

'Yep. That was my guess too,' Ben said. 'See? Great minds, eh?'

'You talk to Chopra,' Georgie suggested. 'I'll go in and see who that was in the car and what they're doing.'

'Well, be careful,' Ben said.

Georgie rolled her eyes.

Ben shrugged. 'What?'

'You wouldn't say that if I was a male police officer,' she said.

'Wouldn't I?' Ben frowned.

'No. But it's okay. Even though I'm a woman, I can handle myself,' she said sarcastically.

Getting out of the car, they headed for the BMW where Chopra was sitting, waiting.

Ben looked at her. 'I can see you can handle yourself. That's what I like about you.'

Georgie didn't reply.

Ben knocked on the car window and Chopra buzzed it down.

'Can you get out of the vehicle please sir?' Ben asked, showing him his warrant card.

Georgie turned and marched towards the hotel, wondering what to make of the time she had spent with DI Ben Stewart. Her instinct was that he was a bit of a *player*, but she couldn't help but be attracted to him. However, she wasn't about to be another notch on his bedpost. Of course, there was the small matter of being pregnant to throw into the mix, so it might be best for her to leave any carnal thoughts well alone.

Striding through the automatic sliding doors, Georgie spotted a young woman sitting at the reception desk.

She looked up as Georgie approached and gave her a friendly smile. 'How can I help?'

'A woman came in here about five minutes ago. She was wearing a hoodie,' Georgie explained. 'I need to know which room she went to.'

The receptionist frowned, but before she could say anything else, Georgie had fished out her warrant card. 'I'm a police officer from Llancastell CID. It's very important that you tell me where she went.'

The blood had drained from the young woman's face. Maybe she or the hotel were in on whatever was going on.

'Yes, of course,' she said, clicking the computer. 'Room 343. It's on the third floor. But …'

'Thank you,' Georgie interrupted, and headed for the lift. This wasn't the first time she'd worked a case where sex workers had been using a hotel to ply their trade. On the surface, she didn't have a problem with two consenting adults agreeing to have sex for money. However, she knew that, in reality, sex workers were often desperate addicts who were being abused, exploited and threatened by those they worked for. And that definitely wasn't okay.

As she got to the third floor, she headed left down the corridor and quickly arrived at Room 343.

She knocked on the door and took a step back.

After a few seconds, the door opened by about an inch and a middle-aged man peered out at her.

'Llancastell CID,' Georgie said. 'Is it okay if I come in for a second, sir?'

The man looked horrified – and guilty as sin. 'I … I'm … Not really … I …'

Georgie didn't wait for him to stammer out his answer as she gave the door a decent shove, knocking him backwards.

She could see he was standing dressed in just his shirt and boxer shorts.

From out of nowhere, the person in the hoodie ran into Georgie, knocking her backwards across the hotel corridor. Georgie grabbed the wall to stop herself from falling over.

Trying to regain her footing, she spotted the person running full pelt down the corridor back towards the lifts.

'Stop, Police!' Georgie shouted as she ran after her.

Getting into her stride, Georgie gained pace as she crashed through the double doors that led out to the third floor lobby and the lifts.

She glanced around. They had literally vanished.

What the fuck?

Then she spotted that the fire exit door was open by about an inch.

Grabbing the door, she flung it open and immediately heard footsteps further down the stairs. Whoever it was, they were heading down to the ground floor. Georgie knew she couldn't let them escape.

Hammering down the stairs, she could feel the muscles in her legs burning as she tired. She clasped the handrail as she jumped down the steps two or three at a time.

So much for taking things easy, she thought ironically.

As she got to the first floor, she paused and could hear that the footsteps had stopped.

Where the hell has she gone now?

Seizing the fire exit door, she threw it open and found herself out on the first floor lobby.

The person was heading towards the lifts, but they were both on different floors.

Got you!

They were trapped.

'Right,' Georgie gasped, trying to get her breath. 'Stay there. You're not in trouble …'

The person turned to look at her.

Georgie was shocked to see that it was a teenage Indian boy wearing the hoodie. Even though he looked terrified, he pulled out a knife and held it aggressively.

Woah, that's not good.

Taking out her warrant card, Georgie showed it to him. 'I'm a police officer,' she panted. 'I just want to talk to you, that's all. So, I'm going to need you to put down the knife, okay?'

Then the penny dropped.

'Are you Rishi?' she asked.

She saw a spark of recognition in the boy's eyes. He gave a slight nod.

'Rishi,' Georgie said in a gentle tone. 'I really need you to put down that knife for me. Okay?' She looked at him. 'Can you do that for me?'

Rishi shook his head anxiously.

'Your mum, Nitira,' Georgie said. 'She's here. She's in North Wales.'

'What?' Rishi's eyes widened in disbelief. 'Why? Why is she here?' Then he realised as he looked at Georgie. 'Carmel? Where is Carmel?'

Georgie looked at him with an empathetic expression. 'I'm so sorry, Rishi.'

For a second, Rishi shook his head in disbelief. He dropped the knife to the floor. 'No, no. Carmel is okay, isn't he? Tell me he is okay?'

Georgie took a step towards Rishi, whose eyes had now filled with tears. 'I'm really sorry.'

Rishi slid to the floor, with his back to the wall. He then reached into his pocket.

Georgie crouched down. 'I'm going to need you to come with me now, Rishi. Is that okay?'

Rishi didn't seem to be listening. He opened his palm and inside was a crucifix on a chain. He looked up at Georgie and gestured to the crucifix. 'He gave me this the day he disappeared.'

'Carmel did?' Georgie asked to clarify.

'Yes,' Rishi nodded as he wiped a tear from his face. 'He said that if I had it, it would keep me safe. But now he's dead, so it's my fault. He should have been wearing this.'

'It's not your fault.' Georgie gave him a sympathetic look. 'I promise you.' She reached out her hand. 'I really think it would be a good idea if you come with me now, Rishi. Okay?'

Rishi nodded, held out his hand, and Georgie pulled him up to his feet.

Chapter 27

Ruth pressed the button on the coffee machine in the Llancastell nick canteen.

'You look miles away, boss,' said a voice.

It was Georgie.

'Oh, right.' Ruth blinked as she gave a self-effacing smile. 'Yeah, I was ... We've let Nitira Chowdry know that Rishi is safe. Once we've interviewed him, they can be reunited.'

'Thank God.' Georgie nodded. 'She's been through enough already.'

'How was DI Stewart last night?' Ruth asked with more than a hint of a knowing smile.

'Oh, you know,' Georgie replied as she reached for a cup and put it under the coffee machine. 'Very full of himself. I get the feeling that he's a bit of a player.'

'Yeah, well keep him at arm's length then,' Ruth said warily. 'That's the last thing you need at the moment.'

'You don't need to worry about that, boss,' Georgie said, pulling a face. 'I have no intention of going anywhere near a man for a very long time.'

'Glad to hear it,' Ruth said.

'Spoken like a true lesbian,' Georgie joked.

'Come on,' Ruth laughed as she glanced down at her watch. 'I've got a briefing in five minutes and I'm running late.'

The canteen was about half full. Tables were populated by mainly uniformed officers eating bacon butties and swigging from mugs of tea.

Getting to the double doors, Ruth sidestepped two burly male uniformed officers as she and Georgie went through and headed for the back staircase that led up to the first floor, the CID offices and IR1.

'Rohan Chopra's brief arrived about an hour ago to look through our initial report,' Ruth said with a knowing look.

Georgie frowned. 'He's got a brief?'

It was definitely unusual for a man in his early 20s, like Chopra, to have a solicitor on board that quickly. Most suspects like Chopra relied on the duty solicitor in the early stages after an arrest. They might then seek counsel if they were charged and were going to trial.

'Yeah,' Ruth nodded as they got to the top of the stairs. 'Definite red flag in my book.'

The fact that Chopra already had a solicitor in place was suspicious. Ruth's instinct was that it was a sign that Chopra was working for more seasoned criminals who had access to that kind of legal help with one phone call.

'I think Chopra is part of a much wider network,' Georgie agreed as they headed for the doors of IR1.

'Well, we'll see what he has to say for himself after briefing,' Ruth said.

'Unless he goes *no comment*.'

Pushing open the doors to IR1, Ruth could see that

most of the CID team were sitting at their desks, chatting or tapping at computers.

'Right, morning everyone.' Ruth strode over towards the scene boards. 'Let's get cracking, shall we?'

She spotted Ben sitting on the far side of IR1. He gave her a nod to say hello.

'Georgie, do you want to kick us off with the events of last night?' Ruth asked.

Georgie, who hadn't yet sat down, turned and headed over to where Ruth was standing.

Georgie pointed to a photo on the scene boards. 'DI Stewart and I followed this man, Rohan Chopra. He left the Simla restaurant around 11.30pm, and drove to this location in Denbigh.' She pointed to a map. 'Here he picked up this boy, Rishi Chowdry, the 15-year-old brother of our victim Carmel. He then drove Rishi out to this hotel, dropped him off and parked to wait. I entered the hotel and found that Rishi had gone to the room of a Phillip Owens, a 50-year-old salesman. Owens admitted he had used a website to book Rishi as a male prostitute, although he claimed he had no idea of Rishi's age. DI Stewart and I then arrested Rohan Chopra for sexual exploitation, although once we've interviewed him and Rishi, and spoken to the CPS, those charges might encompass modern slavery too.'

French looked over. 'Do we think that Chopra had forced Carmel into prostitution?'

'Possibly,' Ruth replied. 'We also have forensics that show that Carmel might have been working at a hand car wash but we haven't located that yet. Run Chopra's number plate through traffic and ANPR and see if we get a hit.' She then looked over to Garrow. 'Jim, let's recheck if Carmel had any social media.' She then looked out at the team. 'Carmel's mother is sitting downstairs. Let's do our best work today so she can have some justice for her son. Thank you, everyone.'

Chapter 28

By the time Georgie and Ben arrived to interview Rohan Chopra, his tough-looking solicitor, Frank Clinton, with black slicked-back hair and weasel-like features, had arrived. Chopra was now dressed in a regulation grey tracksuit, as his clothes had been taken for forensics. He had also been swabbed for his DNA. He sat with a smirk on his face as his eyes roamed around the room, which immediately irritated Georgie.

Taking a sip of water, she took a deep breath. She was feeling a little nauseous, and it was making her irritable.

'You okay?' Ben whispered as he leaned into her. She got a waft of his aftershave.

Usually that would be nice, but it's actually making me feel worse.

She nodded. 'Yeah, I'm fine.'

What was she going to say? *Actually, I'm feeling a little queasy as I'm pregnant.*

Georgie composed herself, then reached across the table to start the recording machine. A long electronic beep sounded as Georgie opened her files and gave Ben a quick look of acknowledgement.

'Interview conducted with Rohan Chopra, 10.45am, Interview Room 3, Llancastell Police Station. Present are Detective Inspector Ben Stewart, the suspect's solicitor Frank Clinton, and myself, Detective Constable Georgina Wild.' She then glanced over. 'Rohan, do you understand you are still under caution?'

'Yeah,' he mumbled with a nonchalant shrug.

Georgie opened a file and pulled out one of the photos that Ben had taken outside the Simla restaurant the night before. 'For the purposes of the tape, I'm showing the suspect item reference 383F.' Georgie turned the photograph to show Rohan. 'Can you tell us what you can see in this photograph please, Rohan?'

He didn't respond for a few seconds. Then he leaned into Clinton and they talked in hushed voices.

'No comment,' Rohan said, looking directly at her.

Oh great, we're doing that are we? Georgie thought as she shared a frustrated look with Ben.

'Okay. The photograph shows you leaving the Simla restaurant in Denbigh last night at 11.30pm and getting into this BMW.' Georgie pointed to the image. 'I assume that you own this vehicle?'

'No comment.'

'Can you tell us where you were going last night please, Rohan?'

'No comment.'

'Myself and DI Stewart followed you to Victoria Road,' Georgie said, 'where you picked up a passenger. Could you tell us who you picked up at this location, Rohan?'

He gave an audible huff. 'No comment.'

Ben leaned forward and fixed him with a stare before

pointing to another photograph. 'We believe that you picked up this 15-year-old boy, Rishi Chowdry, at the location. Is there anything you'd like to tell us about that?'

Rohan now had his hands thrust deep into his grey tracksuit trousers and was looking intently at the floor. 'No comment.'

'You then took Rishi Chowdry to the Marine Hotel,' Ben continued. 'For the purposes of the tape, I am now showing the suspect item reference 286H.' Ben pulled out another surveillance photograph and turned it to show Rohan. 'Can you tell us what you can see in this photo, Rohan?'

'No comment.'

'The photograph shows you stopped outside the Marine Hotel and Rishi Chowdry getting out of your car to go inside,' Ben said coldly. 'Can you tell us why you took Rishi Chowdry to the Marine Hotel?'

Chopra scratched his ear nervously. It was the first time that he'd shown that sitting in the interview room being questioned was getting to him. 'No comment.'

Georgie shifted her chair forward. 'Rohan, you then parked at the Marine Hotel and waited. Can you tell us why you were waiting for Rishi in the car park?'

'No comment.'

Georgie looked over at Rohan, but he continued to stare at the floor. 'We have a statement from a Mr Phillip Owens. He has described how he had used a website to book Rishi to come to his hotel room. Is there anything you can tell us about that?'

'No comment.'

'Are you aware that earning a living from someone else's prostitution is a criminal offence?' Ben asked calmly.

Rohan blinked nervously.

'And that forcing a minor to have sex also contravenes

the Sexual Offences Act of 2003,' Georgie stated, and then waited for a few seconds. 'You could be facing fourteen years in prison, Rohan. And you can imagine how popular men who prostitute boys are in a prison.'

There were a few seconds of tense silence.

By now, Chopra's foot was jerking slightly. The pressure was clearly getting to him.

Ben leaned forward and stated quietly, 'Rohan, we know that you weren't doing this on your own. We know that there are other men who are organising the travel of young Indian men and boys into this country, who are then exploited for sex or modern slavery ... Can you tell us who you are working for?'

Chopra took a visible breath. 'No comment,' he mumbled.

Ben pulled out a photo from a folder. 'For the purposes of the tape, I am showing the suspect item reference 382D. Rohan, can you tell me if you recognise the man in this photograph?'

Chopra continued to look at the floor. He shook his head, but he was starting to shake.

'Come on, Rohan,' Ben encouraged in a friendly tone. 'Just take a look.'

Chopra didn't respond.

'For the purposes of the tape, item reference 382D is a photograph of Pavan Singh,' Ben explained. 'Does the name Pavan Singh mean anything to you, Rohan?'

Chopra shook his head again, but refused to look up. Something about the name seemed to have spooked him.

'Come on, Rohan,' Georgie said gently. 'Why are you protecting men like Pavan Singh? If you help us, we can make sure that is taken into account when you go to trial.'

Chopra put his head in his hands. He looked broken as he glanced over at Clinton.

'I think my client needs a break, don't you?' Clinton enquired in a steely voice.

Ben looked at Georgie.

She gave Clinton a withering look. 'He can have fifteen minutes. Then I want him back in here.'

Chapter 29

Ruth and French were sitting in Interview Room 1 with Rishi and Molly Davids, a 40-year-old 'appropriate adult' provided by the Youth Justice Service.

Ruth looked over at Rishi and stated gently, 'Just to let you know we are recording this interview, Rishi, in case we need to use any of what you tell us in court. Do you understand that?'

Rishi nodded slowly, but he looked very nervous. 'Yes.'

Ruth took a few seconds and gave Rishi a reassuring look. 'Rishi, could you tell us when you last saw your brother, Carmel?'

Rishi blinked and took a breath. He was clearly upset. 'It was two days ago.'

'That was Friday?'

'Yes.'

'What happened?'

'They picked him up to go to work, but he didn't come back.'

Ruth gave him an understanding nod. 'Who picked Carmel up for work?'

Rishi was hiding something.

French scratched his chin and frowned. 'Was it Rohan Chopra that collected Carmel for work?'

Rishi nodded slowly but didn't say anything.

'Did anyone tell you why Carmel didn't come back?' French asked.

'They said that he had run away,' Rishi replied in a virtual whisper as he shook his head.

'Can you tell us when you and your brother Carmel arrived here from India?' Ruth asked.

Rishi thought for a few seconds. 'I think it was maybe three months ago, but I cannot tell which date it was.'

'Okay, thank you,' Ruth said. 'Did you travel on your own?'

Rishi shook his head. 'No. There was a man on the plane with us.'

'Was it just you, Carmel, and the man on that plane?' French said.

'No,' Rishi replied. 'There were two girls who came with us. They were from Jaipur.'

'And you were promised a place at a catering college and a job in a restaurant so that you could learn to cook,' French said. 'Is that correct?'

'Yes,' Rishi said quietly. 'That is what the man told my mother.'

French pulled a photograph of Pavan Singh out of a folder. 'Was this the man that told your mother this?'

Rishi nodded, but again he didn't say anything. The sight of the photograph had scared him.

'And did this man travel on the plane with you?'

'Yes.'

'But you and your brother never went to a catering college while you were here?' Ruth asked.

'No,' Rishi replied.

'But you worked in a restaurant,' Ruth stated, 'called the Simla. Is that correct?'

'Yes. Me and Carmel worked there,' Rishi explained.

French rubbed his jaw and then enquired, 'Can you tell us how you got the job?'

'We were given a name and an address.'

'You were given the address of the Simla restaurant when you arrived here?' Ruth asked to clarify.

Rishi fiddled nervously with his hands. 'Yes.'

French glanced over. 'What was the name you were given?'

There were a few seconds of silence. Rishi was clearly frightened to give them a name.

'Rishi?' Ruth asked gently. 'It's okay. You're safe now.'

'Rohan Chopra,' Rishi muttered as he looked at the floor.

'But you didn't work there for very long, is that right?' French said.

'Yes,' Rishi replied, sounding indignant. 'They made up a story that we had stolen from them and then told us we could not work there anymore.'

Ruth looked at him. 'Did you and Carmel steal from there?'

'No, no.' Rishi seemed horrified by her suggestion. 'We would never steal. But there were others who told us this happens to everyone.'

Ruth shared a look with French. She didn't know what Rishi meant, and neither did French.

'Can you explain what you mean by that, Rishi?' Ruth asked softly.

'These men. They say you can work in the restaurant,' Rishi struggled to explain. 'Then they say that you steal, but they will not call the police. But they said I must work going to hotels and Carmel must work in the car wash for

The Boss. Carmel got very angry, but they said if we didn't, The Boss would hurt our family back in India.'

'The Boss?' Ruth asked. 'Do you know who they meant?'

Rishi shook his head. 'No.'

'Did they mean Pavan Singh, the man who was on the plane with you?'

'No. They said it was another man,' Rishi explained, sounding like he was on the verge of tears. 'But they said he was very dangerous.'

'So, they threatened you?' French asked to clarify.

'Yes, threatened,' Rishi nodded.

'And they made you go to hotels to meet men, is that right?' Ruth asked.

Rishi nodded slowly, but she could see that the shame of it was making him upset.

'Rishi, I know this is difficult,' Ruth stated gently. 'But we need to know if you were forced to go to these hotels?'

Rishi brushed a tear from his eye and nodded again. 'Yes,' he whispered, but his voice broke with emotion.

Ruth's heart went out to him. 'It's okay, Rishi.'

Rishi wiped away more tears. 'Can I see my mother?'

'Yes, of course,' Ruth reassured him. 'There are just a couple more questions that I need to ask you. Is that okay?'

'Yes,' Rishi mumbled.

French pointed to the notepad in front of him on which he had been taking notes. 'Rishi, can you tell us where you and Carmel were staying?'

He looked confused and frowned. 'It was ... erm ... a little flat.'

French pulled out a photo of the ground-floor flat that he and Garrow had been to in the centre of Denbigh. 'Is this the place where you and Carmel were staying?'

'Yes,' Rishi nodded as he peered at the image.

'But not anymore?' Ruth enquired.

'No. They said we must go somewhere else now,' Rishi explained.

Ruth looked over at him with a quizzical expression. 'When you say 'we', how many of there were you?'

Rishi thought for a few seconds. 'There were six. Three boys, three girls.'

'Are they all from India?' French asked.

'No. Two girls are from India. There is a girl from Syria too,' Rishi explained. 'And a boy from Afghanistan.'

'How old do you think they are?' Ruth asked.

Rishi shrugged. 'Maybe fifteen or sixteen.'

French glanced up from where he was making notes. 'Do you know their names?'

'Yes,' Rishi nodded. 'The girls are Sita and Amulya.'

'Do you know what they do when they work?' Ruth asked.

Rishi nodded, but looked guarded.

'Does Rohan make Sita and Amulya visit men at hotels too?' Ruth asked in a quiet voice.

Rishi nodded but didn't reply.

'What about the others?' French asked. 'Do you know what they do?'

'They are a bit older,' Rishi explained. 'They work at the car wash.'

'Do you know where that car wash is?'

'No.'

'When we visited the flat you were staying at,' French said, 'we found some blood on one of the mattresses. Do you know anything about that?'

Rishi looked upset again as he nodded. 'It was Carmel.'

'Carmel?' Ruth said. 'You mean it was Carmel's blood?'

'Yes …'

'Can you tell us what happened?'

Rishi thought for a second. 'Carmel got very angry. He told Rohan that they couldn't keep us like that. And they couldn't make us do those things. He said it was against the law and he would go to the police. Or he would find a journalist who would be interested in what was happening.'

'What did Rohan say to that?' French asked.

'He punched Carmel in the face and kicked him,' Rishi explained in a whisper. 'Rohan told Carmel that if he went to the police, or anyone, that would be a very serious problem.'

Ruth and French exchanged a look.

Chapter 30

Sitting on his bed in his cell, Nick was using a tiny burner phone to talk to Amanda. Danny had 'rented' him the phone and was charging £25 for a 5-minute call. It was 8pm, so way past 'bang up', the time when the cell doors were locked for the night.

'I have a hearing with the CPS and Probation,' Nick said to Amanda.

'Okay,' she replied, sounding concerned. He didn't blame her. Nick was going to find out in that meeting whether he was going to be charged with the offence of escaping from prison. Or if the CPS had decided not to press charges, as there were mitigating circumstances.

'And I've got some good news …' Nick said.

'Thank God,' Amanda sighed.

'I spoke to my Police Federation rep,' Nick explained. 'James Appleby has made a direct approach to the judiciary and the Welsh Home Secretary on my behalf to ask for leniency.'

'James Appleby?'

'Sorry. He's the Police and Crime Commissioner for

North Wales,' Nick said with a positive tone. 'Basically, he's the boss of North Wales Police.'

'Great,' Amanda said brightly. 'That is good news, isn't it?'

'It has to be,' Nick replied. 'But I just don't want to get my hopes up quite yet.'

'No. And we do have another major problem at the moment, too,' Amanda said darkly. She was referring to Blake. Nick hadn't even told her about Blake's direct threats to him, Amanda and Megan in the prison transporter. She was scared enough already.

'Yeah, well, I'm dealing with that,' Nick said, trying to reassure her.

'That's a phrase that convinces me you're about to do something stupid,' Amanda sighed.

'Trust me,' Nick said, trying to project an air of confidence. 'I'm going to sort it out.'

Danny glanced over with a look. Nick checked his watch and realised he'd been on the phone for seven minutes already.

'Listen, I've got to go,' Nick said quietly. 'But I will ring you again tomorrow.'

'I love you,' Amanda whispered.

'I love you too,' Nick said. 'Hang on in there.'

'We're in a hotel with room service,' Amanda joked. 'You're the one in prison.'

'Hopefully not for too much longer.'

'Yeah,' Amanda said. 'Love you.'

'Love you.' Nick ended the call and handed the phone back to Danny. 'Cheers mate.'

'No problem,' Danny said with a smile. He was engrossed in reading a printed sheet of A4 paper.

Nick sat back and let out an audible breath. The phone calls to Amanda always left him emotionally drained.

'Everything okay with the missus and the bairn?' Danny asked.

'Yeah, they're fine,' Nick said. He hadn't gone into any detail about what was really going on. Like most things in prison, personal information was on a need-to-know basis. 'What's that?' Nick asked, gesturing to the sheet of paper that Danny was studying.

'Just the booking up sheet for the astroturf pitches,' Danny said with a shrug.

'Mind if I have a look?' Nick asked, his interest now piqued.

Danny handed it to him. 'You can have a look now. Why, do you fancy a game?'

'Maybe.' Nick took the sheet. He had no interest in playing as he ran his finger down the hourly slots available and bookings for the next seven days.

Then he saw exactly what he was looking for.

A booking for the following day – *3pm – Pitch 1 – C Blake 'Croxteth Albion'*.

Bingo!

Chapter 31

Wandering over to the scene boards, Ruth sipped her coffee and looked closely at the photograph of Carmel Chowdry which his mother Nitira had given them. She wondered how they could live in a world where young people and children were trafficked and then sold or forced into prostitution and modern slavery? And how the hell was this happening on her doorstep? Something about Rishi's description of what had happened to him and his brother had really got to her. She wasn't going to rest until she found the bastards who had robbed Nitira of her son, and Rishi of his brother.

'Anything on the forensics from our crime scene at Denbigh or our victim's body yet?' she asked to no one in particular.

Garrow looked over. 'Forensics have two DNA samples from the victim's body, but they've run them through the database and got nothing.'

'Thank you, Jim,' Ruth said, frustrated that the forensic evidence so far wasn't giving them any kind of lead. 'What about CCTV, traffic and ANPR? Have we got anything on Friday night that might help us?'

'Good news, boss.' Georgie pointed to the screen. 'This is the CCTV from Vale Street in Denbigh. I've looked back and Chopra drives past these traffic lights once he's left the Simla restaurant at around 11.45pm every night. Obviously, I can't tell if he's on the way to pick anyone up from this.' She gave Ruth a meaningful look. 'But on Friday night, he drives past these cameras at 8.35pm.'

Great!

Ruth's eyes widened. 'Which would fit into our timescale for Carmel's murder?'

'Yes, boss,' Georgie nodded.

'Right, Dan, I want Chopra's BMW seized and brought back here for forensics asap,' Ruth said with a steely determination.

'I'm on it, boss,' French replied.

Ruth frowned. 'Jim, how long before we get Chopra's DNA from our sample?'

Garrow looked over and pulled a face. 'Not until the morning, boss.'

Shit!

Chopra would appear before the magistrates in the morning and face various criminal charges relating to taking Rishi to the Marine Hotel. However, it was likely that Chopra would be released on bail rather than go to prison on remand. She didn't want him disappearing off to India. What she needed was something concrete so she could charge him with Carmel's murder. Then he wouldn't be granted bail and he would no longer be a flight risk.

'As soon as we get Chopra's DNA, I need forensics to test it against the two DNAs they have from the crime scene and the body,' Ruth explained as she looked back at the scene boards. 'If Chopra suspected that Carmel was going to try to contact the police, that gives him plenty of motive. And now we know he left work early on Friday night, that gives him opportunity. He would have had to have taken Carmel in his car.'

French frowned. 'Do we know if Carmel was murdered before or after he was found at Denbigh Asylum?'

'Amis couldn't tell us that,' Ruth said. 'He just said that Carmel had been dead for four to six hours.'

'If Chopra did murder Carmel and then decide to take his body in his BMW to hide at Denbigh Asylum,' French said, 'how did he do that on his own? Carmel was above average size. And trying to move a body like that from a car boot, across the hospital site, and then down into the basement isn't a one-person job, is it?'

'There is another question,' Garrow stated with a quizzical expression. 'Denbigh Asylum is a regular haunt for local teenagers. But there wasn't much of an attempt to hide Carmel's body down there. The killer must have known that it was only a matter of time before our victim was discovered. Why didn't they do more to hide him?'

Ruth nodded. It was a fair point. 'Maybe the killer got disturbed?' she suggested. 'But you're right Jim, it is odd that they left the body lying in the room with no attempt to hide it.'

'You think Chopra had help?' Ruth asked, realising that what French had deduced was probably true.

'Maybe Singh helped him?' Georgie suggested.

'Possibly,' Ruth said. 'But I feel that Pavan Singh keeps his distance and doesn't like to get his hands dirty. But Rishi told us that Kabir Malik sacked him and Carmel from the restaurant for no reason. He implied that this was a regular occurrence. Let's see what we can find on Kabir Malik. It might be that Pavan Singh, Kabir Malik and Rohan Chopra are running this trafficking ring together.

And if they thought Carmel was going to jeopardise it by talking to the police or even the press, then maybe they killed him?' Ruth looked at her watch. It was 7.30pm. 'Right, Chopra is up before the magistrates at lunchtime tomorrow. Let's see what a night in the cells does to him. Dan and Jim, I want you to interview Chopra first thing in the morning. If he was wobbly earlier today, then he might well be willing to talk by tomorrow morning. And see what he's got to say about Kabir Malik.' Ruth looked around IR1. 'Anyone got anything else?' There were shakes of heads. 'Right, no one stays here past 9pm. Go home, get some sleep and be back here first thing.'

'Boss,' Garrow said as he frowned at his computer screen.

'What is it, Jim?' she enquired as she walked over.

'I've just got the results back from traffic for Friday night,' he explained. 'They were running Chopra's plates through their ANPR records to see if they got a hit.'

'And?'

'Nothing on Chopra's BMW yet,' Garrow said. 'But they've got this car coming out of Denbigh on the B4501 on Friday at 6pm.'

'Okay,' Ruth said, still uncertain of the link.

'The B4501 is the road out of Denbigh towards the asylum,' Garrow said. 'And I recognised the registration.' He gave her a meaningful look. 'It's Gareth Steel's car.'

Chapter 32

Georgie came out of a small supermarket on Llancastell High Street with a box of ginger tea, fish fingers, ketchup and a white loaf. She'd read that ginger was good for severe morning sickness, and for some reason she was craving a fish finger sandwich. She was pretty sure that it was too early in her pregnancy to be suffering cravings – wasn't it?

'Georgie!' shouted a voice as she reached her car.

A figure came striding towards her.

It was Ben.

'You're not stalking me, are you, Ben?' Georgie joked.

'Obviously,' Ben replied with a grin. 'You should see what I've got at home. Night vision goggles, balaclava, gaffer tape.'

'I'm glad as an officer of the law that you can make flippant jokes about stalking,' Georgie teased, with her tongue planted firmly in her cheek. Gallows humour was sometimes the only way to survive as a police officer.

Yeah, okay, he is seriously cute, she thought to herself.

Ben pointed to The Crown pub opposite. 'Come on, I'll buy you a drink.'

'No, it's all right. I'm really tired. Maybe another time,' Georgie said. There was part of her that wanted to go home, slump on the sofa with a mug of tea and a fish finger sandwich and snooze in front of the telly. But there was also part of her that felt a frisson of excitement at the thought of spending a bit of social time with DI Stewart.

'Please,' Ben groaned. 'Don't make me drink on my own.'

'So, you drink on your own and you have stalking equipment at home? You're quite a catch,' Georgie quipped. 'Why wouldn't I want to join you for a drink?'

'You see?' Ben laughed.

Georgie pretended to think for a few seconds before shrugging nonchalantly. 'Half an hour, because I'm knackered.'

'Great,' Ben said, gesturing as they crossed the road.

The pub smelled of stale beer and cheap food. It was one of the few pubs at the centre of Llancastell that hadn't been turned all gastro.

Heading for the bar, Ben looked at her. 'What will you have?'

'Sparkling mineral water,' Georgie replied.

'What?' Ben pulled a face. 'Have a proper drink.'

'I'm driving,' Georgie replied.

'Come on.'

'Ben, I'm fine with a mineral water,' she snapped. 'And I don't think you should force me to drink alcohol, do you? Do you want to try to get me drunk or something so I can't drive?'

Ben looked startled by her outburst.

There was an awkward silence.

'No, I ... err ...' Ben was lost for words for a few seconds. Then he mumbled, 'Gosh, I'm really sorry, I ...'

Georgie laughed and nudged his shoulder. 'I'm just fucking with you. But you should see your face.'

'Bloody hell. You sod.' He let out a sigh of relief. 'Fair play, you had me there.'

'But I will have a mineral water, thanks,' Georgie said.

'Yeah, well, I'm not going to mess with you from now on,' Ben said with a wink.

Georgie smirked. 'No, not if you want to keep your balls in the right place.'

He nodded with a grin. 'Right, good to know.'

'That's your MO, is it?'

'What is?'

'Pressure women into drinking alcohol,' Georgie said. 'Then wait until they're over the limit so you can take advantage of them.'

'Oh God. I think you've got me all wrong, Georgie,' Ben protested with a flirty smirk. 'I'm not the *shag monster* that you seem to think I am.'

'Shag monster! Jesus!' Georgie snorted.

'Yeah, I just made it up,' Ben laughed. 'I thought it sounded good.'

'It does,' Georgie agreed. 'I'm going to use it myself.'

'Great.'

'Okay, tell me three things that will prove that you're not a predatory shag monster.'

Ben shrugged. 'Okay, that's easy. I ...' Then he paused for thought.

'But not that easy,' Georgie teased him.

'Hey, give me more than two seconds,' Ben protested. 'Okay. I've got it. I take my mum shopping once a week. I help coach my niece's under-11 football team. And I cry every time I watch *Marley and Me*.'

Georgie raised an eyebrow. 'Yeah, not bad. Although if you didn't cry at *Marley and Me*, that would make you an actual psychopath.'

'True.' Ben then looked at her. 'Oh, and I only ask girls out for a drink that I really like.'

Jesus, he really is too much.

'I see. You are aware that this is 2021 and I'm a woman, not a girl?' Georgie said with a wry smile.

'Sorry.'

Georgie looked at him. 'Is that what you think this is?'

Ben shrugged innocently. 'What?'

'You do know that this is as far away from a date as you can get?'

Ben took a moment and then gave her a sexy grin. 'Yeah, but you've been thinking about it.'

'No, I haven't.' Georgie couldn't help but laugh at his unabashed cockiness. It was sexy.

'I'm pretty sure you have.'

'Are you now?'

'I know I have.'

'If you're expecting a goodnight kiss, then you're way off,' Georgie told him, but she felt her pulse quicken.

'Okay,' Ben said with a smirk. 'I was actually hoping for a bit more than a kiss.'

'You cheeky twat.' Georgie gave him a playful hit and then looked at her watch. 'Thirty minutes and I'm out of here.'

'We'll see,' Ben said.

Chapter 33

Stretching out her toes, Ruth leaned back on the sofa as her partner Sarah massaged her feet.

'God, what are you after?' Ruth joked.

Sarah smiled. 'At least being a copper for the past thirty years hasn't made you cynical.'

'Ha ha,' Ruth laughed. 'Don't stop. This is heaven. And can you pass me my wine?'

'Are you taking the piss?'

'Obviously,' Ruth grinned as she stretched out her hand to take the large glass of white wine that Sarah was passing over to her.

'Don't most coppers take early retirement?' Sarah asked.

'Yeah, they do,' Ruth admitted. 'Minimum retirement age is 55 and lots take that.'

Sarah gave her a knowing look. 'Three years to go then?'

Ruth frowned. 'You think I should retire?'

'Maybe,' Sarah shrugged.

'And do what?' Ruth asked.

'Erm, spend time with me,' Sarah said, pinching her foot hard.

'Ow, that hurt,' Ruth wailed.

'It was meant to,' Sarah joked. 'Is that such a horrible idea? Spending your days with me?'

'No, of course not,' Ruth reassured her. 'I just hadn't thought about retirement yet.'

Sarah gestured upstairs. 'Might be an idea. Especially if we're going to have Daniel permanently.'

'That's a good point,' Ruth agreed, but realised that she really hadn't given retirement any proper thought. 'The weird thing is that when I first moved to North Wales, I was hoping to get a boring desk job and retire as soon as I could.'

'Yeah, I wouldn't describe you as having a 'boring desk job',' Sarah observed dryly.

'No, definitely not,' Ruth said. 'But I guess there has been a series of things that have kept me very much focussed on the present. My relationship with Sian and then losing her. Getting you back and dealing with everything you've been through. And now Nick, Amanda and Megan. I feel like I've been firefighting ever since I got here.'

'True,' Sarah agreed, and then gave her a serious look. 'Do you think they'll ever get their lives back to some kind of normality?'

'God, I hope so,' Ruth sighed, but she could feel the tension growing in her body as she thought of Amanda and Megan sitting in the hotel room with an armed guard outside their door.

Ruth thought for a few seconds.

'The good news is that I don't think Nick will face criminal charges for escaping from Rhoswen,' Ruth said.

'The bad news?'

'If I'm brutally honest, I can't see how Nick, Amanda and Megan can go back to living as they were before if they stay in North Wales,' Ruth said darkly.

'Because Curtis Blake will get his revenge one way or another?' Sarah asked.

'Exactly,' Ruth replied. 'And that means they will have to go into witness protection, change their identities and move away. And even then, they won't ever be able to relax completely.' Ruth gave Sarah a dark look. 'It's so awful that I'm trying not to think about it.'

Chapter 34

It was the following morning. As she had promised, Georgie had left the pub after thirty minutes, gone home and snoozed on the sofa. She and Ben were now in Interview Room 2. She composed herself, then leaned across the table to start the recording machine. A long electronic beep sounded as Georgie opened her files and gave Ben a look. Even though nothing had happened between them the previous evening, there was definitely a growing attraction.

'Interview conducted with Rohan Chopra, 8.45am, Interview Room 2, Llancastell Police Station. Present are Detective Inspector Ben Stewart, the suspect's solicitor Frank Clinton, and myself, Detective Constable Georgina Wild.' She then glanced over. 'Rohan, do you understand that you are still under caution?'

'No comment,' he mumbled.

Georgie looked over at him, but it was hard to say whether a night in the holding cell at Llancastell Police Station had rattled him enough to persuade him to talk. Georgie had seen several suspects break down and confess after a prolonged period in a holding cell. It gave a suspect a preview of what their time in a prison would be like.

'For the purposes of the tape, I'm going to show the suspect item reference 287G.' Ben pulled out a photo. 'Rohan, can you tell me what you can see in this photograph, please?'

'No comment.' Rohan didn't even bother to take a look. His overnight stay hadn't had the desired effect.

'Rohan, can you take a look at the photograph for me please?' Ben snapped.

Rohan sat back deliberately and glared over at Ben.

'For the purposes of the tape, the suspect has refused to look at item reference 287G,' Ben explained. 'The photograph is of Rishi Chowdry. Would it surprise you to know that Rishi told us that he and his brother Carmel didn't steal anything from the Simla restaurant and that sacking young employees was common practice?'

'No comment.'

Georgie fixed Chopra with a stare. 'Rishi also told us that he and his brother were told by you that they would be reported to the police for stealing unless they did the work that they were told to do. Is that correct?'

Chopra looked fed up and huffed. 'No comment.'

'I'm showing the suspect item reference N767.' Ben turned another photo around for him to look at. 'Do you recognise the man in this photograph, Rohan?'

Chopra looked down at his feet. 'No comment.'

'For the purposes of the tape, item reference N767 is a photograph of Kabir Malik, the owner of the Simla restaurant,' Ben explained. 'Can you tell us if Kabir Malik was aware that you were falsely accusing young people of theft in his restaurant in an attempt to force them into prostitution and modern slavery?'

Chopra sniffed and looked at Clinton. 'No comment.'

Georgie flicked through the statement that Rishi Chowdry had given them and then looked over at him. 'Rishi also describes how you assaulted his brother Carmel at the flat they lived in on Graig Terrace. Is there anything you can tell us about that?'

'No comment.'

'We also understand that Carmel Chowdry had threatened to go to the police to tell them about what you were doing,' Georgie said. 'Is that correct?'

'No comment.'

'And when Carmel Chowdry told you he was going to go to the police, not only did you assault him, but you also threatened him.' Georgie moved her finger down Rishi's statement. 'You said if he went to the police, *that would be a very serious problem.* Can you tell us what you meant by that, Rohan?'

Chopra shook his head. 'No comment.'

'Did you mean that you would kill Carmel if he went to the police?' Ben asked.

'No,' Chopra snapped.

They waited for a few seconds. It looked like the pressure of the interview was finally getting to Chopra.

'You see Rohan, it does look very suspicious, doesn't it?' Ben said in a calm, almost friendly tone. 'You attack and threaten Carmel. Then a few days later, he's dead. That really doesn't look good for you, Rohan.'

Chopra shook his head again. 'I didn't kill him.'

Georgie shot a look at Ben – Chopra was unravelling.

'Then who did?' Ben asked loudly.

'I don't know,' Chopra replied quietly. 'If I knew, I'd tell you. But I don't.'

'Rishi claimed you told him that unless he did what he was told he would get into trouble with a man you called 'The Boss',' Ben said. 'Can you tell me who that person is?'

'I don't know. I never met him,' Chopra muttered.

'Was this man, The Boss, responsible for Carmel's murder?' Georgie asked.

Chopra pulled a face as he shook his head emotionally. 'I don't know.'

'Did Kabir Malik have anything to do with Carmel's murder?' Georgie asked.

The question seemed to stop Chopra in his tracks. He didn't say anything, but scratched his nose.

There were a few seconds of tense silence.

'No comment,' he whispered eventually.

Chapter 35

Ruth and French walked into the garage and tyre yard where Gareth Steel worked. There was a radio blasting music from somewhere. The air was thick with fumes from a lorry that sat to one side with its diesel rumbling.

A blond-haired man in his 20s dressed in blue oil-stained overalls approached, wiping the dirt from his hands with a rag. 'Can I help?'

Ruth pulled out her warrant card. 'DI Hunter and DS French, Llancastell CID,' she explained. 'We're looking for Gareth Steel. We understand that he works here.'

The blond man grinned. 'Oh dear, has he been a naughty boy?' he joked.

They ignored him.

'Right,' the blond man said after a beat. 'He's over in the tyre yard.'

'Thanks.' Ruth turned and began to make their way across the garage site.

The sky above was virtually colourless, but in the distance it looked like dark rain clouds were heading their way. The concrete ground was uneven and broken, strewn with weeds and oil stains.

As they got to the far left-hand corner of the site, they saw a large garage with someone crouching down and using a large socket wrench.

Gareth Steel.

'Mr Steel,' Ruth called over as they approached. He looked up from where he was crouching. He then saw French and his face fell.

'What now?' he groaned.

'Can we have a word?' Ruth asked with a forced smile.

He pointed to the tyre he was working on. 'I'm a bit busy at the moment, to be honest.'

'That's all right,' Ruth stated lightly. 'It won't take long.'

French looked at him. 'Or we can do it at the station back in Llancastell?'

'Jesus,' Steel growled as he got up and let out an audible sigh. 'Right, so what is it?'

Ruth could see he had a Union Jack flag tattooed on his hairy forearm. Underneath there was some writing – *There's no black, in the Union Jack.'*

French frowned. 'You told us that you were at home all evening on Friday?'

'Yeah,' Steel snapped angrily. 'Well, I was.'

Ruth gave him her best sarcastic smile. 'But you weren't, were you, Mr Steel? Because we have CCTV of you in your car in the middle of Denbigh on Friday evening. We then spotted you again driving into a car park over by Braxton roundabout.'

Steel glared at them. 'So what?'

'Well, lying to police officers in a murder investigation is a criminal offence,' French explained calmly. 'If you don't tell us why you were driving in Denbigh at that time, we're going to arrest you for obstruction. And then we're taking you back to Llancastell Police Station to question you in connection with Carmel Chowdry's murder.'

'You can't do that!' Steel barked.

'Yes, I think you'll find that we can,' Ruth said. 'And we will.'

After a few seconds, French reached for the cuffs that were hanging from his belt. 'Right, put your hands behind your back.'

Steel shook his head. 'All right, all right. I'll tell you where I was,' he grumbled.

French took out his notebook and pen. 'That's very helpful of you.'

'I was … I was with a woman,' Steel said quietly.

Ruth raised an eyebrow. 'I take it you're married?'

'Yeah, I am,' Steel replied. 'And I don't want my wife to know about it, okay?'

'Can you tell me who you were with on Friday evening?' French said.

Steel hesitated and then muttered reluctantly, 'Abi Williams.'

'And is Abi Williams married?' Ruth asked.

Steel nodded. 'Yeah, her husband works nights.'

'And you were at her home?'

'That's right.'

'We're going to need an address,' French said.

'Why?' Steel protested.

Ruth looked at him. 'I know you're going to find this difficult to believe, but sometimes people lie to us. So, we have to check that what they tell us is the truth.'

Steel rolled his eyes and then nodded.

Chapter 36

Ruth and French arrived at the address that Steel had given them for Abi Williams. The cottage was tidy, but looked a little tired and neglected. The path to the front door was laid with stone, but it was functional rather than decorative. At the windows, heavy curtains were pulled shut. The front garden was devoid of any flowers or plants.

French gave an authoritative knock on the door and took a step back.

A few seconds later, a woman opened the door cautiously and peered at them. She looked like she'd just woken up. Her face was heavily made up, as though she was still in her 20s, but her body and posture suggested she was closer to 50.

'Hello?' she asked. Her voice was deep and husky, and Ruth immediately had her down as a heavy smoker.

They flashed their warrant cards.

'We're looking for Abi Williams,' Ruth explained.

'That's me,' she said, looking perplexed as she rubbed her eyes. 'What's going on?'

'Just a few routine questions. Nothing to worry about,' French reassured her.

'Is it okay if we come in?' Ruth took a step towards the door. She found that this normally made people open the door to allow them inside. Unless they were seasoned criminals who were used to the police knocking on their door.

'Erm, yes.' She ushered them inside while checking that no one in the road was watching.

The hallway was dark and shadowy. The house smelled of burnt toast and cigarette smoke.

'Sorry,' Abi said, pushing her dyed blonde hair back. 'I was asleep. I worked the night shift, you see.'

'We just need to check a couple of things with you in connection to an investigation,' French explained.

Abi frowned and asked, 'Is it to do with that bloke that was found murdered up at the asylum?'

Ruth looked at her. 'I'm afraid we can't discuss the details of our case or our investigation.'

'Terrible though, wasn't it?' Abi shook her head. 'My nephew and niece go up there with their friends. I've told them not to. It's not safe, is it? Anyone could be up there. And the place is falling apart. They could fall through the bloody floor or a ceiling could come down.'

Ruth shot a look at French as if to say, *I don't think she's really getting it*.

'Could you tell us where you were on Friday evening?' French asked as he took out his notebook and pen.

'Friday evening?' Abi's face dropped. 'That was the night of the murder, wasn't it?'

French nodded. 'Yes, that's right.'

'Why do you want to know where I was?' Abi asked, now sounding annoyed. 'I didn't have anything to do with what happened up there.'

Ruth gave her a forced smile. 'If you could tell us

where you were on Friday evening, that would be very helpful.'

Abi frowned. 'I was down The Plough.'

'And that's The Plough Inn on Bridge Street?' French asked to clarify.

'That's right,' Abi said cautiously.

'Can you tell us what time that was?' French said.

'Got there about seven, I suppose,' Abi said. 'Left about ten thirty. I remember because people were saying there was something going on at the hospital because of all the cop cars ... Sorry, police cars.'

Ruth and French shared a look. That didn't fit with Gareth Steel's alibi. Either Steel or Abi were lying about their whereabouts on Friday evening.

'Do you know a man called Gareth Steel?' Ruth asked.

'Gareth? Yeah, of course. We went to school together.' Abi frowned. 'Why? Is he in trouble or something?'

French looked up from his notepad. 'Did you see Gareth on Friday evening?'

'No,' Abi shook her head with a puzzled expression. 'Why? Did he say that he saw me?'

'Gareth told us he came over here on Friday evening and spent time with you,' French explained.

'I don't bloody think so!' Abi said, sounding offended.

Ruth narrowed her eyes. 'Do you know why Gareth might have told us that?'

'No. I've no bloody idea.'

'Can you describe your relationship with Gareth?' French said.

'Relationship? I don't know what you're talking about,' Abi snapped. 'I'm a happily married woman. And I wouldn't go anywhere near Gareth Steel with a bloody barge pole!'

Ruth's instinct was that Abi was telling them the truth.

And that meant for some reason Steel had lied about his whereabouts on Friday evening twice – which was very suspicious.

'And if we go and talk to the staff at The Plough,' French said, 'they will confirm that you were there on Friday evening.'

'Of course they will,' Abi replied with a shrug. 'Because I was.'

Chapter 37

Ben and Georgie were driving over to Denbigh to talk to Kabir Malik. Even though they had chatted about the case to start with, they had then briefly touched on where they grew up and families.

Pulling down the sun visor, Georgie peered at her reflection in the small mirror.

'God, I look tired,' she muttered under her breath.

Ben looked over at her. 'You really don't.'

'That's the wonders of make-up,' Georgie joked.

Ben laughed as he pushed the indicator to turn right and head into Denbigh.

Unless it was her imagination, Georgie was getting that pink-tinged pallor to her cheeks that she'd seen on a couple of friends who'd had babies. That pregnancy glow. Her hormones were going mad too.

Closing the sun visor, she squinted at the light outside. The spring sunshine was giving off a hard glare which glinted in the glass, and the car was incredibly warm. If she wasn't careful, she was going to doze off.

Then a wave of nausea swept over her. Buzzing down

her window, Georgie took a deep breath and then put her face close so that the rushing wind battered against it. It was cool, refreshing, and lessened the feeling of sickness.

'You feeling okay?' Ben asked.

'Yeah,' Georgie replied as she took in a deep breath of fresh air. 'I'll be fine in a minute.'

'Why? Are you feeling sick?'

Georgie gave a slight nod but didn't reply. She just needed some more fresh air to settle her stomach.

Ben frowned at her. 'Well, I know you're not hungover because you drank mineral water. Unless you went back home and demolished two bottles of wine?'

Georgie pulled a face. 'God no. I had a cup of tea and a fish finger sandwich.'

'Nice,' Ben said with a curious smile.

Georgie looked at him. 'What?' she asked.

'Nothing,' Ben said. 'It's just that you're not drinking, you've got a flushed face and you feel sick every morning.'

Georgie raised an eyebrow. 'You think I'm pregnant?'

'As a detective, that would be my guess.' Ben narrowed his eyes. 'But you don't have a boyfriend or husband, so you can't be. Maybe it's a virus or something?'

Georgie buzzed up the window. For some reason, in that moment, she decided to tell Ben. Maybe it was because she was aware there was a growing attraction between them. She didn't want to be put in the position of Ben making a move on her and then having to tell him – which would be incredibly awkward for the both of them.

'No, it's not a virus.' She then looked at him. 'I am actually pregnant.'

'Oh, right.' Ben took a few seconds to process this and then said with an understanding expression, 'Well, it's none of my business.'

There was an awkward silence.

'You don't need to make allowances for me, though,' Georgie said. 'I'm not ill or anything.'

'No, of course not.' Ben nodded awkwardly. 'But just to let you know, if we go anywhere that's dangerous, I am going to bear that in mind.'

They pulled up outside the Simla restaurant.

'Sorry.' Georgie pulled a regretful face. 'I probably shouldn't have told you, but as it came up I ...'

'No, no,' Ben said with slight embarrassment. 'That's fine.'

'I feel I should probably explain, but ...'

'Hey, you don't need to explain.' Ben smiled at her. 'If you're happy, that's great. And, as I said, it's none of my business, is it?'

'Thanks for understanding.' Georgie got out of the car. She couldn't read Ben's reaction. Was he disappointed to find out that she was pregnant? She wasn't egotistical enough to think that. Or was he thrown by such a personal revelation when they didn't really know each other?

Georgie resolved to give it no more thought as she pressed the buzzer that French had described when he had visited Malik with Garrow.

'Hello?' said a female voice on the intercom.

'Hi there,' Georgie replied. 'We're CID officers from Llancastell. We'd like to speak to Mr Malik if he's around?'

There were a few seconds of silence.

Georgie frowned at Ben.

'Hello?' the female voice said. 'I'm not sure he's in.'

Georgie glanced at Ben. It sounded suspicious to her.

'If you can let us in, please,' Georgie stated sternly, 'then we can talk about it.'

'Erm, ... okay,' the voice replied uncertainly.

Then more silence.

'Jesus,' Ben muttered under his breath in frustration.

The buzzer sounded. Georgie pushed open the door, and they went up the stairs to where Malik's offices were located.

A woman in her 20s, looking a little flustered, gave them a nervous smile. 'Hi there.'

Georgie and Ben flashed their warrant cards.

Ben asked sceptically, 'So, Mr Malik isn't in?'

'I've had a look around,' the woman said, 'but I can't seem to find him.'

'Where's his office?' Ben asked bluntly.

'Over there.' She pointed to an open door. 'But I've checked, and he's not in there. Let me just check the kitchen,' she explained nervously as she turned and left.

Georgie pointed. 'Come on,' she said under her breath. 'She's definitely lying.'

They marched over to Malik's tidy office, but it was empty.

'What are you doing?' Ben asked.

'Having a look.' Georgie went around to the other side of his desk.

'You know that we don't have a search warrant?' Ben pointed out. 'Anything we find in here won't be admissible in court.'

'I don't care.' Georgie pulled out a camera and took photographs of the papers and notepad on Malik's desk. 'I'm not taking anything.' Then she reached over to the mug of coffee that was sitting on a dark red coaster. 'It's still warm,' she growled.

'Bastard,' Ben hissed angrily.

Malik had been in his office when they'd arrived and had clearly done a runner.

Chapter 38

Ruth and French walked purposefully into the garage and tyre yard where Gareth Steel worked. He had lied about his whereabouts on Friday night twice, which was incredibly suspicious. Given that he'd been beaten by Carmel and Rishi Chowdry, he had a strong motive to seek revenge. In terms of a police investigation, Steel currently had all three criteria needed to make him a prime suspect – means, motive and opportunity.

The young blond-haired man, whom they had spoken to earlier, was changing a battery in an old van. He spotted them, gave them a puzzled look, and then wandered over.

'You've just missed him,' he informed them.

French frowned. 'Sorry?'

'Gareth,' the blond man said with a shrug. 'I assume you're looking to talk to him again.'

'Yes, we are,' French replied. 'When will he be back?'

He pulled a face and then looked at his watch. 'He's delivering and fitting a tyre up on the coast. Three or four hours. If it goes on any longer, he might just go straight home.'

Ruth looked at him suspiciously. The blond man might have had a cheeky, chirpy expression on his face, but the rest of him showed he was jittery. 'Can you give us the address of where he's gone?'

He looked stumped. 'Sorry, love. Gareth took the order paperwork with him for the customer to sign.'

Love? You twat!

Ruth pursed her lips. 'That's a shame,' she said with more than a hint of sarcasm.

The blond man pulled out his mobile phone. 'I could give him a call, but knowing Gareth, he'll have it turned off.'

Ruth and French exchanged a look – they both thought he was lying to them.

'Yeah, I have a strong feeling that his phone will be turned off,' Ruth said dryly. She then pointed over to the tyre yard. 'Don't mind if we have a look around, do you?'

'Erm, no.' The blond man scowled. 'Wasting your time, though. I can tell Gareth you're looking for him, if you want?'

Ruth gave him a forced smile. 'That's all right, but thank you for your help.'

They turned and walked across the concrete yard towards the bays where two young men were fitting tyres. They looked up.

Ruth pulled out her warrant card. 'Llancastell CID. Gareth Steel around?'

The two men shook their heads in unison. 'No, sorry.'

Wandering inside, Ruth and French came into a small reception area that had an old coffee dispensing machine, a water cooler, and a television mounted on the wall. It was tuned to BBC1 with the sound turned off but the subtitles running. A daytime property show was on.

Ruth cast her eyes around and then spotted an office

on the far side. It was empty. There was a desk, a computer and three chairs. The walls were covered in tyre adverts, a Liverpool FC calendar, and other assorted paperwork.

Out of the corner of her eye, Ruth spotted a foot coming from behind a desk. She looked at French, rolled her eyes, and pointed.

Really?

'Either you've lost a contact lens, Gareth, or you're hiding behind that desk from us,' she remarked sardonically.

There was movement and Steel stood up and looked suitably embarrassed.

'Bit old to be playing hide and seek, aren't you?' French quipped dryly as he took his cuffs from his belt. 'Gareth Steel, I'm arresting you for obstruction. You do not have to say anything. But it may harm your defence if you do not mention when questioned something which you later rely on in court. Anything you do say may be given in evidence.'

Chapter 39

An hour later, Ruth sat at her desk in her office which was adjoined to IR1 and, for a moment, her mind was drawn to Nick. The CPS and Probation Service had still given no indication if Nick would face serious criminal charges for his escape from HMP Rhoswen. It was hard to gauge how much the mitigating circumstances could be brought to bear on any sentencing. She guessed it would be a major factor – but she could be wrong. She couldn't bear to think of him having to spend any more time in prison. He, Amanda, and Megan had been through enough in recent weeks. Surely the CPS would ask for leniency at sentencing and give him a suspended sentence. Of course, there were no guarantees. And she had no idea if Nick would ever return to active service as a police officer.

Trying to put all that out of her mind, she took a long swig of water and sat back to look at her computer screen. Digital forensics had picked up that Carmel Chowdry had a Facebook page. Ruth was now trawling through it to see if there was anything useful on it. The good news was that Carmel had been using the page while he was in the UK.

Clicking on a photograph, Ruth saw Carmel with his arm around a teenage girl. The next photograph showed them kissing and laughing. The caption read – *Me and Derifa*. It had been taken three weeks ago. The girl, Derifa, wasn't Asian, but if Ruth had to guess, she would think she was from an Arabic country. Ruth wondered where Derifa was now and if she could shed any light on what had happened to Carmel? The first thing they had to do was to try and track her down.

Ruth moved to Derifa's Facebook homepage. It featured a photograph of her and Carmel arm in arm. Behind them, there was what looked like a hand car-washing place, but there was no mention of where it was. The photo was taken a month earlier, so she would assume that it was somewhere in Denbighshire. She wondered if digital forensics could track down Derifa's IP address from her Facebook account. That might then give them a home address. However, if she was using a mobile phone to access the Facebook account, that might be a non-starter.

'Boss,' said a voice.

It was French standing by her open door.

'Hi Dan.' Ruth turned her chair to face him.

'We've processed Gareth Steel,' French said. 'He's in a holding cell downstairs.'

Ruth nodded. 'Let's get him fingerprinted and get his DNA. Then we can see if we can match that with what forensics found over at the asylum. And let's pull in his car.'

'Have we got enough for a search warrant yet?' French asked.

'Leave it with me, Dan,' Ruth reassured him. She could see that French thought Gareth Steel was now their prime suspect.

'What's that?' French asked, pointing to a photo on the screen.

'Seems that Carmel Chowdry had a girlfriend while he was here,' Ruth explained. 'Derifa Mousa.'

'Sounds Muslim to me,' French observed. 'Any way of tracking her down?'

'Nothing on her Facebook page,' Ruth said in a frustrated tone. 'Just this photograph of them at a hand car wash. And by the looks of their clothes, they're both working there.'

'And that fits with what we know about the trafficking operation in general.' French peered closely at the photograph. 'That church in the background …'

Ruth looked closely and saw that in the top right-hand corner of the screen there was a white church set back from the road. 'What about it?'

'I know where that is,' French said. 'It's on the Whitchurch Road just before you get to Denbigh.' Then he looked at her. 'Yeah, and there is a car wash at a petrol station just down from there.'

Bingo.

Chapter 40

French and Garrow entered Interview Room 1. The duty solicitor, Tom Duckett, 30s, smart, dark hair and a beard, had arrived and had been briefed on Steel's arrest. Duckett was sitting next to Steel, who was now dressed in a regulation grey tracksuit, as his clothes had been taken for forensics. He had also been swabbed for his DNA. He sat with an angry expression on his face, as though being arrested and interviewed was a total waste of his precious time. French shot him a look as he sat down at the table as if to say, *maybe you should have thought of that before giving us two fake alibis.*

French then leaned across the table to start the recording machine. A long electronic beep sounded as French opened his files and gave Garrow a quick look of acknowledgement.

'Interview conducted with Gareth Steel, 5.20pm, Llancastell Police Station. Present are Detective Constable James Garrow, duty solicitor Tom Duckett, and myself, Detective Sergeant Daniel French.' French then glanced over. 'Gareth, do you understand you are still under caution?'

Steel was looking up at the ceiling, and for a few seconds, seemed to ignore his question. Then he casually lowered his head to look at French. 'Yeah, of course,' he hissed. 'This is a waste of my time.'

French ignored him, reached for a folder, pulled out a photograph and turned it to show Steel. 'For the purposes of the tape, I am showing the suspect item reference 938Y. Gareth, can you look at this photograph and tell me what you can see?'

Steel let out an audible sigh, shifted his chair, pulled out reading glasses from his pocket, and then peered at the photograph. 'Yeah, it's my car. So what?'

'Item Reference 938Y is a photograph of your vehicle at traffic lights coming out of Denbigh on the B4501 on Friday evening.' French looked over at him. 'Is there anything you can tell us about that?'

Steel pulled a face. 'What do you mean?'

French glanced over at Garrow, who opened his notebook. 'When we first spoke to you for our investigation, you told us that you had been home all night on Friday and that you hadn't been out. Is that correct?'

Steel shrugged. 'Yeah. I suppose so.'

Garrow frowned. 'You suppose so. Did you or did you not tell us that you had been home all night on Friday?'

'Yeah, I did,' Steel replied.

Garrow then looked over at him and pointed to the photograph. 'But you lied to us, didn't you, Gareth? Can you tell us why you lied to us?'

'I told you all that this morning,' Steel growled.

'Ah yes,' French nodded and then flicked a page of his notes. 'You told us that you had left your home to visit Abi Williams. Is that correct?'

French hadn't revealed to Steel yet that not only had they spoken to Abi Williams, but he had also rung The Plough Inn to confirm that Abi had been in the pub all night and no one had seen Steel. Withholding this information allowed them to force Steel to tell them 'a provable lie' under caution on tape. It was a valuable tactic when putting a suspect under pressure to tell them the truth.

'Yes.' Steel shook his head in a patronising manner. 'Listen, I've told you all this.'

French fixed Steel with a stare. 'Problem is, Gareth, Abi Williams doesn't know what you're talking about. She does remember you from school, but she has no idea why you told us that you two were having an affair. In fact, I think it would be safe to say she was very angry at the suggestion. Is there anything you can tell us about that?'

'Of course she said that!' Steel scoffed. 'She's a married woman. I'm a married man. She's not going to admit to two coppers that have just turned up on her doorstep that she's shagging someone behind her husband's back, is she?'

French shared a look with Garrow. It looked as if Steel hadn't thought through his lie in any detail. And that meant they now had him over a barrel.

'There's another problem with what you told us, Gareth,' French informed him. 'Abi Williams was drinking in The Plough Inn in Denbigh from late Friday afternoon through to about ten o'clock.'

'So she says!' Steel snorted.

French looked over and then pointed to his notes. 'Actually, we spoke to the landlord of The Plough. A Hugh Sporle. Not only did he confirm Abi was in his pub all Friday, he was also adamant that you weren't. Would you like to comment on this?'

The colour drained from Steel's face. French looked at

him and waited for a few seconds for the tension to build. They had just proved that Steel had lied to them, and they wanted him to squirm.

That was the thing about being a copper. You weren't always dealing with criminal masterminds. In fact, sometimes you were dealing with someone as moronic as Steel, who hadn't thought his alibi through more than one step. It was pitiful.

Steel shifted uncomfortably in his seat. His eyes roamed around the room nervously as he tried to take in what they'd told him and how he was going to respond.

'Gareth?' French said. He waited again before pointing to the photo on the interview table. 'Can you tell us what you were doing driving close to Denbigh on Friday night?'

Gareth stared at the floor and shook his head.

'For the purposes of the tape, the suspect shook his head in response to my question,' French said.

'Listen Gareth,' Garrow said in a softer voice. 'We understand it must have been very upsetting when Carmel and Rishi attacked you outside The Royal Oak.' Garrow pointed to his face. 'You've still got the bruises. So, no one is going to be surprised if you decided to go and find Carmel. Maybe you just wanted to confront him? And maybe things just got out of hand?'

'No,' Steel snapped. 'I didn't have anything to do with what happened to him, okay?'

Garrow nodded and leaned forward. 'Look at it from our point of view. The young man who attacked you only days earlier was stabbed to death on Friday night. You lied to us twice about where you were that night. We know you were in your car on Friday evening, but you won't tell us why. Can you see how that's very suspicious?'

Steel didn't respond, but he fidgeted nervously.

French stared at him for a few seconds. 'We're going to

seize your vehicle, Gareth. And then we're going to search your home. And I'm pretty sure that our forensics team is going to find something, however small, that shows that you stabbed Carmel Chowdry to death on Friday night. So, why don't you do us all a favour and tell us what happened?'

'I didn't kill him,' Steel snapped. 'That's not why I was driving at that time.'

French moved his chair back. 'Okay, tell us what you were doing then.'

'I was meeting a friend,' Steel mumbled feebly.

French sighed in frustration. 'You need to stop lying to us, Gareth.'

'I'm not lying!' Steel thundered. 'I met a friend. A man. His name is John.'

French raised an eyebrow. 'You met a man named John? Come on, Gareth!'

'You just need to tell us what you were doing on Friday night,' Garrow said. 'With your friend John.'

'We go over to this place outside St Asaph,' Steel said. 'A car park by the Offa's Dyke Path. And there are other people there. It's not something I want to admit to.'

French frowned for a few seconds. *What the bloody hell is he talking about?* Then the penny dropped.

'Are you telling me that you and your friend went 'dogging' in a car park near St Asaph on Friday night?' French asked.

Gareth nodded, but didn't say anything.

'Nice try,' French said, but he did wonder if Steel was telling the truth. It might account for his refusal to tell them where he was.

French looked over at Garrow – *well that's the first time I've heard 'dogging' as an alibi. I'll give him that.*

Chapter 41

Ruth and Georgie were heading to where French had said that he'd seen the hand car wash. Ruth, who was driving, saw that Georgie was texting on her phone.

'How's the dishy DI Stewart?' Ruth asked teasingly, gesturing to her phone.

Georgie frowned. 'That's not who I was texting.'

Ruth shrugged. 'Okay. I was just asking.'

There were a few seconds of silence.

'Dishy?' Georgie laughed. 'I haven't heard that word since I was a kid.'

'I'm not keen on the word 'fit',' Ruth admitted. 'But I like the word 'dishy'. It sounds innocent enough, but everyone knows exactly what you mean.'

'Maybe you should start using it again,' Georgie suggested with a wry smile.

Ruth grinned. 'Maybe I will.'

'Anyway, I've scared *Ben* off by telling him I was pregnant,' Georgie explained.

Ruth's eyes widened. 'What did you do that for?'

'I was feeling sick again. He remembered I didn't drink

when we went to the pub. He made some jokey comment about those being signs of pregnancy, so I hit him with it,' Georgie said.

'Wow,' Ruth nodded. 'What did he say to that?'

'He was definitely shocked. He knows I don't have a husband or boyfriend.'

'Did you explain?'

'God no,' Georgie replied defensively. 'Nothing is going to happen between us.'

'Oh right,' Ruth said, but then gave a half-smile.

'What?'

'Nothing. It's just that I know that you like him.'

'I don't!'

'The lady doth protest too much.'

'Are you really quoting Shakespeare at me?'

'Oh.' Ruth pulled a face. 'I didn't know it was Shakespeare.'

Georgie frowned. 'Hamlet, isn't it?'

'Since when were you so well read?' Ruth teased her.

'Hey. I'm not a complete imbecile,' Georgie protested. 'Anyway, we're getting off the point. I think there's some attraction there. But I'm pregnant, so nothing can happen. End of story.'

'Yeah,' Ruth agreed. 'Sounds like the sensible thing to do.'

Georgie looked up and pointed. 'This is it, isn't it?'

Ruth slowed the car as they came around a bend. Up to their right was a church set back from the road. Further along was a petrol station and on the far side of that, a hand car washing service.

Pulling into the petrol station, Ruth could see two Asian men spraying down and washing a car in a parking bay. A smart 4x4 was parked close by with all its doors open. Inside, a figure in a black baseball cap was hoovering the interior.

As the figure turned, Ruth recognised her.

Derifa Mousa.

'That's her,' Ruth gestured as she pulled into a parking space.

They got out of the car. The wind picked up and Ruth pulled up the collar of her coat. Even though she was wearing a nicotine patch, she craved a cigarette.

Pulling out their warrant cards, Ruth and Georgie approached.

'Derifa Mousa?' Ruth called over the noise of the hoover.

Derifa looked startled as she turned to look at them. She didn't say anything.

'Okay if you turn that off?' Georgie suggested politely as she pointed to the hoover.

Derifa nodded but looked terrified. She leaned down to turn off the hoover but, in a flash, sprinted away from them and towards the back of the garage.

'Shit!' Ruth growled as Georgie looked at her.

'Great,' Georgie groaned sarcastically.

'Stay here,' Ruth said sternly to Georgie.

'Why?'

'Because,' Ruth said.

Ruth turned and ran after Derifa, who was now climbing over a fence to the rear of the garage forecourt.

Jesus, I'm getting too old for this.

Reaching the fence, Ruth pulled herself up and over clumsily. She jarred her knee as she landed on the other side.

'Bollocks!' she huffed.

Fields stretched out as far as the eye could see, although

there was a wooded area about two hundred yards to the left.

Derifa was still running flat out.

I'm never going to catch her. She's a bloody teenager! Ruth thought.

With her arms pumping, Ruth broke into a steady run, trying to remember the last time she had actually gone for 'a run'. It was one of the things she had enjoyed when she first moved to North Wales. A daily run in the countryside. But life and her job seemed to have got in the way of all that. It was at times like this she wished she'd carried on.

Derifa darted left, heading for the woods.

Ruth followed, but it felt like Derifa was getting away from her.

To her right, barbed wire and an aluminium fence marked out a field where sheep were grazing. A couple of them looked at Ruth with disinterest as she sprinted past.

Now running flat out again, Ruth nearly lost her footing in a muddy puddle. The thick, dark rainwater immediately seeped into her shoes and socks. It was cold and very uncomfortable. With the back of her hand, Ruth wiped the sweat from her forehead.

Glancing up, she spotted that Derifa had reached the edge of the woods. A moment later, she disappeared behind a line of trees.

Shit!

Sucking in air, Ruth's lungs burnt. Giving up smoking seemed to have done little for her aerobic fitness.

A few seconds later, she reached the edge of the woods. Her eyes scanned around, looking for movement.

Nothing.

Straining her hearing, she couldn't hear anything but the chirp of birdsong and the wind rattling gently in the branches and leaves above.

Where the hell has she gone? Ruth wondered. *And why the hell did she run off like a bat out of hell?*

Ruth's pulse was thundering as she took deep breaths and continued to scan the woods. Derifa must have stopped, otherwise there would be the sound of someone moving. Ruth's heart sank. If Derifa had decided to sit tight and hide in the woods, how were they going to find her? At that moment, she was only helping them with their enquiries so she couldn't justify the manpower or hours to launch a search of the woods.

Then suddenly the distant sound of rustling. A twig cracked. Derifa appeared and headed up the slope of the woods.

'Derifa!' Ruth called. 'Wait there! We just want to talk to you. You're not in trouble.'

In the distance, Derifa turned back to look for a second before running again.

Ruth gave an audible groan as she broke into a sprint again. Her legs felt heavy as she slipped again and lost her footing on a muddy bank.

Bloody hell.

As she ran up the increasingly steep footpath, the wood became progressively darker with the tightly knit rows of Welsh birch, pines and oaks towering overhead.

Ducking and weaving through the branches, Ruth pumped her fists as she jogged. She could see that Derifa was now limping. Ruth was finally gaining on her.

'Derifa!' Ruth panted as loud as she could. 'Just wait there!'

Derifa looked back again and was close enough for Ruth to see her pained expression.

But she wasn't for stopping. She turned again and limped on.

Ruth was only twenty yards behind when Derifa fell to the ground and yelped. She grabbed her ankle.

'Just wait there,' Ruth said as she slowed to a walk.

Derifa looked up at her from the ground. Her face was sweaty, but she looked utterly terrified.

'Please, don't hurt me!' Derifa yelled as she cowered.

Ruth crouched down, trying to get her breath back. 'Hey, I'm not going to hurt you. I'm a police officer. Why are you running?'

'I'm scared,' Derifa cried as she grasped her ankle and winced.

'I just want to talk to you about Carmel,' Ruth told her.

Derifa looked confused. 'Carmel? I don't understand. I thought you were going to make me go back home.'

'Home?' Ruth asked quizzically. 'Where's home?'

'Aleppo,' Derifa said, her chest heaving from the run. 'Syria.'

'Right,' Ruth nodded. 'No. I'm not here to make you go home. I need to talk to you about Carmel Chowdry?'

'Yes.' Derifa nodded. 'But I don't know where he is. He has vanished.'

'I'm really sorry, Derifa.' Ruth gave her a sad look. 'Carmel is dead.'

Chapter 42

Ruth and Georgie were sitting in Interview Room 2 at Llancastell Police Station. Derifa sat opposite them with 'an appropriate adult', a smart-looking woman in her 40s, as she was under the age of eighteen. Derifa had been checked over by the FME – the forensic medical examiner – the doctor who was attached to the station. He confirmed that Derifa was suffering from nothing more than a sprained ankle and verified that she didn't need to go to the University Hospital for an X-ray.

Ruth could see that she was still very upset and shocked by the news of Carmel's death. As she moved a strand of hair from her face, Ruth spotted an intricate tattoo of flowers on the back of her right hand.

'Derifa,' Ruth said very gently. 'As I've explained on the way here, we just want to talk to you about Carmel so that we can find the person who harmed him. But we are going to record this interview in case we need to use anything you tell us in court. Is that okay?'

Derifa blinked and gave a faint nod. She was still clearly shaken up by the news of Carmel's death.

Georgie, who had taken out a pen and notepad, looked over at her with a sympathetic expression. 'You're from Aleppo in Syria? Is that correct?'

Derifa nodded again but didn't reply.

'Could you tell us the circumstances in which you left Aleppo?' Ruth asked quietly.

Derifa frowned and thought for a few seconds. 'My brother Rifat and I had come home from school. And then the military came to my home. They took my brother away and told him he had to fight with them. And they told my parents they were going to come back. I think they were going to ... attack me and my mother. My mother told me I must run away from home. My uncle drove me across the border to Turkey. And then the ... Red Cross?' She looked at them to make sure she was correct and they understood.

Ruth nodded reassuringly. 'The Red Cross. Yes.'

'They bring me to this country. And I then stay with a family. In Ruthin?' Derifa asked.

Ruth and Georgie nodded.

'But the man. The husband. He was a bad man,' Derifa whispered with a dark look on her face. 'So, I ran away. I went to Denbigh.'

This wasn't the first time Ruth had heard a story like this in North Wales. There had been a couple of cases of Ukrainian teenagers who had sought refuge in the UK only to be preyed upon by sexual predators. Even after all the crime she had seen in nearly thirty years on the job, stuff like that made her despair.

Georgie looked up from where she was making notes. 'And you were in a relationship with Carmel, is that right Derifa?'

'Yes,' she nodded sadly.

'Can you tell us the last time you saw him?' Ruth enquired.

'Friday morning,' Derifa said. 'We work at the car wash together.'

'And you all lived in that same flat?' Ruth said, thinking that it was probably the same set up as the flat they'd found in Denbigh. One bedroom, terrible living conditions, no food.

'We used to,' she replied. 'But I have a room of my own in a B&B now.'

'And you were working with Carmel on Friday morning.' Ruth looked at her. 'Then what happened?'

'A man came to see him. He said that The Boss wanted to talk to him,' Derifa explained. 'Carmel went off to speak. I was working inside the car. Then when I turned around, Carmel was gone. I asked, have you seen Carmel? But no one saw what happened to him.'

'And the man that Carmel was talking to?' Ruth asked.

Derifa shrugged. 'I don't know. He was gone too.'

'Do you know the man's name?' Georgie said.

'No.' Derifa shook her head.

Ruth frowned. 'Had you seen him before?'

'Yes,' she replied. 'He came to our flat. Three, maybe four times. But some of the others, they call him 'Roe' maybe?'

Georgie raised an eyebrow. 'Roe?'

'Yes,' Derifa said. 'Sorry.'

Ruth gave her a kind look. 'You don't need to apologise.' Then a thought came to Ruth. She reached over to a folder and pulled out a photograph. She then turned it so that Derifa could have a look.

'Is this the man that came to speak to Carmel on Friday morning?' Ruth asked.

Derifa looked for less than a second before she nodded. She seemed troubled by the sight of the image. 'Yes. That is him.'

Ruth looked at Georgie. 'Roe. Short for Rohan … Rohan Chopra.'

Chapter 43

'Right everyone.' Ruth pointed to the scene boards which had been updated with more information. 'Rohan Chopra. We now have an eye-witness that saw Chopra with Carmel on Friday. Just before they both disappeared.'

Georgie frowned. 'And we know from our interview with Derifa that Chopra told Carmel that The Boss, whoever that is, wanted a word. So, do we think there's someone else involved in Carmel's murder?'

Ben got up, went over to the board, and pointed to several photos. 'I'm assuming Chopra was referring to either Kabir Malik or Pavan Singh. Seems to me that Singh is sourcing these children and teenagers from India with the promise of an education, well-paid employment and a new life. Malik, with the help of Chopra, is using his restaurant to filter them through to other forced labour such as prostitution or the car wash. So, Chopra must have been taking Carmel to see either Malik or Singh.'

'Unless that was just a ploy to get Carmel to go in the car with him,' Garrow suggested with a shrug.

'Possibly,' Ruth said, trying to piece together what they had. 'Kabir Malik must have known what was going on at his restaurant and what Chopra was up to. He either turned a blind eye to it or was involved.'

'Given that he did a runner when we went to speak to him,' Georgie said, 'I would suggest it's the latter.'

The phone rang on a nearby desk, and Garrow picked it up.

'How are we doing at trying to track down his whereabouts?' Ruth asked.

Georgie shook her head. 'Nothing. We sent a uniform patrol to his house, but there was no reply. The car was gone, and it didn't look like anyone was in.'

'What about this video footage that was taken by the teenagers who discovered the body?' Ruth asked. It was starting to drag on and it could be a vital piece of evidence.

'Digital forensics have had to send it away to get it cleaned up properly,' French explained. 'But I will keep pushing them, boss.'

'Thanks, Dan,' Ruth said and then asked, 'Where are we at with Gareth Steel?'

French pulled a face. 'His alibi is that he was 'dogging' on Friday night in the car park by Offa's Dyke Path, just outside St Asaph, with a friend of his called John.'

There were raised eyebrows and snorts of laughter from some of the team.

'Jesus,' sighed Ben. 'I thought I'd heard everything.'

Ruth gave a withering look. 'And will this friend John give us a statement to say that he was with Steel?'

French nodded. 'Steel seems to think he will, but he's already given us two false alibis.'

'Okay,' Ruth said. 'We can't rule Steel out. But we don't have any forensics linking him to our victim or the crime scene. Let's check his alibi anyway … but my instinct is that Carmel's murder is somehow linked to Chopra, Malik and Singh.'

Garrow looked over with some sense of urgency. 'Boss, that was the forensic lab.'

'Tell me it's good news,' Ruth said with a sigh. They needed a significant breakthrough in the investigation and ideally something to link a suspect to Carmel and the murder scene.

'Chopra's DNA is a match to the DNA found under Carmel's fingernails and on his clothes,' Garrow said.

Great!

'What about the crime scene?' Ruth asked hopefully. Having Chopra's DNA under Carmel's nails and on his clothes was a decent breakthrough. However, a decent defence lawyer could claim that had happened in the car and throw doubt on the evidence.

Garrow shook his head. 'No, boss. We've just got this unidentified DNA at the crime scene.'

Ruth immediately wondered if the unidentified DNA belonged to either Malik or Singh. Had one of them helped Chopra to murder Carmel to keep him quiet?

'Okay, we now have enough to rearrest Chopra and question him about Carmel's murder.' Ruth got up from where she was perched on a table. 'I'll get the arrest and search warrants now. And then we're going to Denbigh to pick him up.'

Chapter 44

An hour later, Ruth and Georgie pulled up outside the address they had for Rohan Chopra – a small terraced house in the centre of Denbigh. Ruth clocked his BMW outside. It was significant.

'Looks like he might be in,' Ruth suggested, pointing to the car. She then clicked her Tetra radio. A uniformed patrol was going to the rear of the property in case Chopra did a runner out to the back alleyway. 'Three six to Alpha Charlie nine, over.'

The radio crackled. 'Alpha Charlie nine to three six, receiving, go ahead, over.'

'We're at the target property now,' Ruth explained. 'Stand by, over.'

'Received three six, out,' said the voice.

Ruth looked at Georgie as they got out of the car. 'If Chopra resists arrest, let me and the uniformed officers deal with it. I don't want you to end up in hospital again.'

Georgie rolled her eyes, but nodded. 'Okay,' she said reluctantly.

Overhead, the sun stole very slowly behind a bank of

dark grey clouds and darkness seemed to fall over the road as though someone had dimmed the lighting. The road itself was deserted.

Ruth approached the front door and pulled out both the arrest and search warrants. She gave the door an authoritative knock and took a step backwards.

The wind blew a coke can across the pavement as a church bell rang out for a few seconds.

Ruth knocked again and then looked at Georgie.

Nothing.

'Three six to Alpha Charlie nine, over,' Ruth said into her radio. 'We're getting no response from target property. Stand by in case our suspect attempts to escape from the rear of the target property, over.'

'Alpha Charlie nine, received. Standing by,' the voice replied.

Moving to the right, Georgie went over to the ground-floor window, cupped her hands and looked inside.

'Anything?' Ruth asked.

Georgie shook her head. 'Nothing, boss.' Then Georgie looked over at her as she took out her mobile phone. 'I've got an idea.'

Ruth knew that the property was a couple of miles from the centre of Denbigh. If Chopra had gone anywhere, it was very likely that he'd driven.

Crouching down, Ruth pushed open the letter box and called, 'Rohan Chopra? It's Detective Inspector Ruth Hunter. Can you come to the door please?'

Of course, Chopra could well be hiding inside his house somewhere.

'Boss.' Georgie gestured to her mobile phone. 'We pulled all Chopra's phone records. I've got his mobile phone number here. If I ring it now, you might be able to hear it.'

'That's a good idea,' Ruth nodded as she turned her head so her ear was beside the letterbox.

There were a few seconds of silence followed by a buzz and a mobile phone ringtone coming from inside the house.

Ruth looked at Georgie and nodded. 'Yeah, he's in there.'

Georgie gave her a shrug as if to say *So, what do we do now?*

'Rohan, it's Detective Inspector Hunter here,' Ruth yelled through the letterbox, now convinced that he was sitting inside somewhere and refusing to come to the door. 'We have an arrest and search warrant. If you don't come and answer the door, we'll be forced to break it down to enter.'

Ruth waited to see if she could hear any sound of movement.

Nothing.

Rolling her eyes, Ruth shook her head at Georgie. 'Looks like we're kicking his front door down.'

As Ruth turned her head, she peered inside, scanning the hallway.

On the wall by the entrance to the kitchen, there was a dark smear across the white paintwork.

It was blood.

Standing up, Ruth shot Georgie a dark look. 'We're kicking it down now. There's blood inside.'

Taking a few steps back, Ruth thought that it had been quite a while since she kicked down a door. If the door was just on the latch, it usually opened easily. If it was locked with a Chubb, then it was far more difficult.

Stepping forward, Ruth booted the door with the sole of her foot with everything that she had.

BANG!

The front door flew open, smashing against the hall wall behind with an almighty crash.

"Three six to Alpha Charlie nine, over,' Ruth said into her radio. 'We've made a forced entry into the target property. We believe the suspect might be injured, over.'

'Alpha Charlie nine, received, on our way,' the voice replied.

Ruth and Georgie, who was now at her side, snapped on their blue forensic gloves as it now looked like they were entering a crime scene.

The hallway was neat and recently decorated. A jacket, black overcoat and umbrella hung from the hooks to one side. Ruth got a faint waft of cigarette smoke but it was stale as though this was the home of a smoker.

'Rohan?' Ruth called cautiously.

Chopra could be lying somewhere injured in the house. His attacker could still be inside the property. The blood could also belong to someone else.

Pushing the door to her left, Ruth entered the living room. It had been tipped upside down as if there had been some kind of altercation. There were a few drops of blood on the door frame. It looked like the attack had taken place in the living room. Whoever had been injured had staggered from the living room and down the hallway where they had grabbed at the door frame to the kitchen.

As they moved further down the hallway, spots of blood marked where they had tried to make their escape.

Glancing into the kitchen, Ruth saw that the blood spots didn't continue across the light-coloured tiled floor.

'Boss.' Georgie pointed over to the bottom step. 'Looks like it goes up the stairs.'

'Okay,' Ruth replied.

The two uniformed officers hurried through the door and approached.

The Denbigh Asylum Killings

'Ma'am,' the male officer said, slightly out of breath.

'Can you check the ground floor carefully, constable?' Ruth asked politely. 'And if you've got forensic gloves, can you put them on? And can you look for any signs of forced entry at the back of the house?'

'Yes, ma'am,' the officer nodded as they turned to search the kitchen and utility room.

Ruth and Georgie moved up the carpeted stairs, continuing to follow the trail of blood. Had someone attacked Chopra in his home? Was someone scared that he was going to talk if he was arrested again?

Getting to the top of the stairs, Ruth spotted a large framed cricket photograph hanging on the wall. It was a signed picture of the India cricket team in 2018.

Turning left along the landing, Ruth and Georgie came to a door that led into what looked like the main bedroom. It was neat and tidy, but a little soulless. The bed had grey bedding and there was a row of shoes and trainers lined up precisely under a full-length mirror.

As Ruth did a very quick check under the bed and in the wardrobe, Georgie moved ahead down the landing.

'Boss?' Georgie said with a sense of urgency. She had found something.

Hurrying out of the bedroom, she saw Georgie standing by the doorway to the bathroom.

'He's in here.' She gestured inside.

Ruth poked her head around the door and saw Chopra's blood-soaked corpse lying in the bath. There was a large stab wound to his stomach and his shirt was matted with blood.

He was dead.

Chapter 45

The area outside Rohan Chopra's home was now a hive of activity. The road had been cordoned off with blue and white evidence tape and was being managed by several uniformed police officers dressed in luminous green jackets. Two marked patrol cars were also parked across either end of the road with a big blue sign that read *Road closed due to police incident.*

A group of neighbours stood in a huddle behind the cordon discussing what might have happened. A couple of journalists and photographers had also arrived on the scene to see if there was a major story developing, especially as there had been another murder in Denbigh only a few days earlier.

Ruth and Georgie stood outside as French, Garrow and Ben drew up in an unmarked car.

'Brace yourself,' Ruth said under her breath. 'Brad Pitt's here.'

'Sod off,' Georgie whispered.

It probably wasn't the time to make jokes, but Ruth had learned a long time ago that humour was often the only way to survive in this job.

The SOCO van outside the property was now busy with SOCOs, dressed in their white nitrile suits and masks, coming and going from the house with bags of evidence.

Getting out of the car, French, Garrow and Ben approached.

'Where did you find the deceased, boss?' French asked.

'Upstairs in the bath,' Ruth explained. 'A lot of blood, so I think he'd been stabbed and bled out.'

'Same MO as Carmel Chowdry the other night,' Garrow observed.

Ben raised an eyebrow. 'Anyone see anything?'

'Not sure yet,' Ruth admitted. 'I've got some plod going door to door to talk to the neighbours. Jim and Dan, can you do follow up with the neighbours? Did they see cars they didn't recognise, anyone loitering around? You know the kind of thing.'

'Yes, boss,' Garrow said as they turned and walked away to knock on doors.

Ruth looked at Ben. Not only was he a DI, but he was from a different unit, so it was up to him what he wanted to do. 'Georgie and I are going inside to talk to Professor Amis if you want to join us?'

'I've just had lunch,' Ben joked. 'But why not?'

Georgie joked, 'I bet you look good in a white forensic suit, especially the hat.'

'I'm pretty sure that no one looks good in a forensic suit,' Ben laughed. 'And the hat makes me look like some deranged lunatic behind a deli counter.'

'Mmm, I don't think you need a hat for that,' Georgie quipped.

'Nice. Very good,' Ben retorted sarcastically. 'And what's with the boots?'

Georgie snorted. 'I know. God, they never fit, do they?'

Ruth rolled her eyes. 'Fascinating as all this is, shall we just get suited and booted and go inside?' She resisted the temptation to say, *Please stop flirting right in front of me. It's nauseating.*

The three of them spent the next five minutes over by the SOCO van getting into their suits, masks, and ill-fitting boots.

As they wandered towards Chopra's house, Georgie glanced over at Ruth. 'If we think the MO for this murder is the same, *and* we know there is a strong link between Carmel Chowdry and Rohan Chopra, then it's a fair bet that it's the same killer. And that means we can probably rule out Gareth Steel as a suspect.'

Ruth nodded. It was a good point, and one she hadn't yet thought of. 'Yeah, you're right.'

'Have you put in for your sergeants' exams yet, Georgie?' Ben asked as they entered the house.

She shook her head. 'Not yet.'

'You should,' Ben said encouragingly.

Ruth nodded. Even though she suspected Ben's comment was motivated by feelings other than genuine concern for Georgie's professional development, she had long suspected that Georgie should work towards the rank of detective sergeant.

As they came into the hallway, two SOCOs came down the stairs with evidence collected in small bags that now rested on a white plastic tray.

'Is Professor Amis upstairs?' Ruth asked, gesturing to the stairs.

'Yes, ma'am,' the SOCO responded.

They went upstairs, along the landing, and arrived at the bathroom where Amis was leaning over Chopra's body in the bath. At the other end of the bath, a SOCO was taking photographs with a forensic camera and a high-powered flash.

'And then there were three,' Amis said, making a joke that Ruth didn't understand.

'Bit of a mess, isn't it, Tony?' Ruth stated.

'Oh, I've seen far worse,' Amis stated with an almost bragging tone to his voice. 'But that's a story for another time.'

'We take it our victim was stabbed?' Georgie asked.

'Yes.' Amis nodded and then pointed to Chopra's bloody abdomen. 'Very similar stab wound to the young man I looked at earlier this week.'

'Same killer then?' Ben asked.

Amis furrowed his brow. 'Hard to tell. But given the number of murders they have in Denbighshire in a year, I'd find it hard to believe that it was coincidental.'

'Yeah, it's not Midsomer is it?' Georgie joked, and Ben laughed a little too hard.

These two? God give me strength, Ruth thought to herself. Maybe she was actually just a bit jealous of those first flushes of excitement at the beginning of any relationship.

'Did you find anything else?' Ruth asked.

'Your victim was stabbed in the back in the living room. Staggered into the hall and up the stairs. There was some kind of struggle in here,' Amis stated, pointing to a cracked mirror and deodorant, aftershave and toothpaste scattered across the floor. 'He was pushed into the bath and then stabbed in the abdomen again from the looks of it.'

'Right,' Ben said. 'Any sign of the weapon?'

'No,' Amis replied. 'There is something that I need to flag up downstairs.'

'Go on,' Ruth said, intrigued by what he was going to say.

'The glass panel to the back door was smashed,' Amis explained. 'So, initially forensic officers thought that the killer broke in there.'

'I feel a *but* coming,' Ben said.

'There were fragments of glass on the outside as well as the inside. They'd fallen down the drain, so whoever did it wouldn't have noticed,' Amis said.

Ruth frowned. 'You think the glass in the back door was broken from the inside?'

'It had to have been,' Amis said. 'There's no other explanation for that glass to be on the outside.'

Georgie looked confused. 'I don't get it.'

Ben glanced at her. 'The killer wanted us to think that they broke in via the back door.'

Georgie nodded as the penny dropped. 'Because Chopra let them in through the front door. He knew his killer.'

'And if there were no signs of a break in, the killer knew we'd conclude Chopra let him in,' Ruth said. 'And that would narrow down the list of suspects.'

'And it would take any thought off the table that this was a random act, or a burglary gone wrong,' Ben stated.

'Sounds about right,' Amis agreed. 'We've also got a partial footprint downstairs.'

'Enough to get a foot size?' Ruth asked hopefully.

'Maybe,' Amis said. 'You'll need to get it back to the lab. My guess is a size 6 or 7.'

'Small then?' Georgie remarked.

'A woman?' Ben suggested.

'Or a smallish man,' Ruth said.

'Or a teenager,' Amis chipped in. 'I can tell you more after my preliminary PM later today.'

'Thanks Tony.' Ruth turned to go back down the landing and head for the stairs.

A SOCO came towards her with a sheet of notepaper in an evidence bag. 'Ma'am, I thought you might want to see this sooner rather than later. I found it by the computer in the office,' the SOCO explained.

'Thanks,' Ruth said with a kind smile as she took the bag with her gloved hand. She looked at it as she walked down the stairs and came into the hallway.

'What is it?' Georgie asked.

Ruth held the evidence bag up so Georgie and Ben could read it too:

R I A M A N 4832. THE BOSS?? KM AND PS

BEN FROWNED. 'ANY IDEAS?'

RUTH POINTED. 'I'M GUESSING THAT KM AND PS ARE Kabir Malik and Pavan Singh. As for the letters and numbers, I've no idea.'

'And why does this name *The Boss* seem to keep cropping up? It's like some terrible mafia film,' Georgie said as they went outside and took off their forensic suits.

A few seconds later, French and Garrow arrived.

'Everything all right, chaps?' Ruth asked as she stepped out of the noisy nitrile suit.

French looked at her. 'Next door neighbour, a Mrs Baker, says she saw a man sitting outside Chopra's house last night. I thought you might want to come and talk to her.'

Ruth nodded – it sounded very interesting.

Chapter 46

Twenty minutes later, Ruth sat down on Mrs Baker's sofa, which had been covered with a thin flower-printed bedspread and then tucked neatly down the back. While French and Garrow continued their house to house, Ruth had brought Ben and Georgie to discuss what Mrs Baker had seen the night before. Ruth hoped that having three police officers in her living room wasn't too intimidating for Mrs Baker, who was peering at them through horn-rimmed glasses. Ruth wondered if she should have come on her own, but it was too late now and Mrs Baker didn't seem unduly fazed. She had a pale complexion, grey hair, milky blue eyes and a long nose that descended in a straight line from her brow. She looked a little like an old Victorian school mistress in her white blouse, black cardigan and long skirt.

The living room was cluttered, stuffy and smelled of old-fashioned Pears soap and stewed tea. There was an old highly varnished coffee table and a television set in the corner. A larger table under the window was covered with an assortment of trinkets – little vases, porcelain figurines and dried flowers.

Ruth gave Mrs Baker a kind smile. 'My colleagues tell me that you saw something unusual last night outside Mr Chopra's house, Mrs Baker. Is that right?'

'It's Eileen, please,' she said, and she smoothed out the wrinkles on her skirt.

'Could you tell us what you saw?' Ruth asked in a gentle tone.

'Well, I was putting out the bins. It was garden waste this morning,' she explained. 'And I saw a car parked outside Mr Chopra's house.'

Georgie, who was writing in her notepad, looked over at her. 'Our colleagues said that you saw someone inside the car?'

'Yes. You see, that's the strange thing,' Eileen said. 'The engine of the car was running, but the headlights were turned off. That's why I looked over. Because of the noise. And then I thought 'That's a bit odd.' Why would you sit there with the engine running and the lights off?'

Ruth nodded positively. 'Yes, that is strange. Could you describe the person who was sitting in the car for us?'

'Yes. He was an Indian chap,' Eileen explained and then touched her chin. 'With one of those beards.'

'A goatee?' Ruth suggested.

'Yes, I think that's what they call them,' Eileen said with a nod. 'Handsome fella like that man that was in *Doctor Zhivago*.'

Ben and Georgie looked blankly at Ruth. She assumed they'd never even heard of the film.

'Omar Sharif?' Ruth said with a half-smile. She didn't like to point out that Omar Sharif was in fact Egyptian and didn't really look Indian, but she got the idea.

Georgie leaned forward on the sofa. 'How old do you think this man was?'

'About forty, I'd say,' Eileen replied.

Reaching for her phone, Ruth clicked on an image of Kabir Malik and showed it to her. 'Was this the man that you saw in the car?'

Eileen peered at the photo and then nodded. 'Yes, that's him.'

They all exchanged a look. It was a significant development.

Ben frowned. 'Eileen, can I just check? It was dark when you went outside, is that right?'

'Yes,' she nodded.

'If the car's lights were turned off,' Ben continued, 'I'm just wondering how you saw this man so clearly?'

'Oh,' Eileen pointed to the road outside. 'He was sitting right under that great big streetlight.'

It was a pertinent thing to check, Ruth thought to herself. It was the sort of question a decent defence lawyer would ask Eileen if they were at trial.

'And what time was this do you think?' Georgie asked.

'It was seven,' Eileen stated. 'The news had just finished on the telly. And that's when I take the bins out.'

'Do you know how long the car was parked there?' Ruth enquired.

'Well, I looked outside about ten minutes later to check if he was still there,' Eileen said. 'And he was gone by then. I suppose whoever he was waiting for had come out. Do you think this man has something to do with what's happened to Mr Chopra?'

Ruth narrowed her eyes. 'What gave you the impression that this man was waiting for someone, Eileen?'

'You could tell. He was looking up at the house from the car. You know, like he was impatient or something,' she said. 'He had the engine running. It just looked like he was waiting for someone to come out and he looked like he was in a hurry.'

Ruth exchanged a look with the others. Whoever Malik was waiting for had more than likely killed Chopra.

Chapter 47

Taking a deep breath, Ruth stretched out her back with an audible groan as she sat at her desk. With another murder to investigate, she was feeling the pressure from the top brass within the station to get a quick result.

There was a knock on the door. It was Garrow.

'Hi Jim,' Ruth said, sitting upright in her chair.

'Boss,' he said with a quizzical expression, gesturing to a printout in his hand. 'I've found something that I need to run past you.'

'Go for it.'

'I was just doing a bit of a trawl through Carmel Chowdry's social media stuff,' Garrow explained. 'I came across his Facebook Messenger. On the day before he was murdered, he had a conversation with Derifa Mousa.'

'Okay,' she said curiously.

'It's a pretty heated exchange.' Garrow looked down at the printout. 'So, this is Thursday evening. Derifa writes, *I know you were with her. Don't lie to me, Carmel.* Two minutes later, Carmel replies, *Why are you so jealous all the time?* Then she writes back, *If you have been with her, I'm going to kill you.* Carmel says, *That's not the first time you've said that.* Derifa replies, *Yeah, well, I mean it. I will stab you if you betray me.*' Garrow looked up. 'That's it. That's the last time either of them was on Messenger, boss.'

Ruth took a few seconds to process this. 'My instinct is that this is just young people being melodramatic. But the timing of this and the fact that she threatens to stab him is definitely a concern. What do you think?'

Garrow thought for a moment. 'I think the evidence against Chopra and then Malik is overwhelming. They have a very strong motive. Plus, if we think the same person killed Chopra, that doesn't tie in with Derifa murdering Carmel in a jealous rage, does it?'

'No, it doesn't,' Ruth agreed. 'Let's keep that on the backburner for now. Thanks Jim.'

'Boss,' Garrow replied as he turned and left.

Looking out into IR1, Ruth saw the CID team was in there for an impromptu briefing. The developments in the case were coming thick and fast, so she needed everyone to be up to speed.

She walked out of her office, across the room, and then perched on a table. Ruth sipped water from her bottle before looking up at the scene boards, which were now covered in an array of photos, writing, maps and other information. On the top right, *R I A M A N 4832. The Boss?? KM and PS* was written in blue marker. At the moment, they didn't know its significance.

'Okay, everyone. This is now a double murder investigation,' she stated with a dark expression. 'Time is of the essence. I don't want anyone else being caught up in this before we find our killer.'

French came through the doors into CID holding a bunch of folders and approached. 'Boss, this is the stuff from the planning committee of Denbighshire County Council.'

'Okay,' Ruth said. 'Anything interesting?'

'Plenty,' French replied knowingly. He plonked the folders down heavily on the desk and then grabbed one. 'Denbighshire Council's planning committee had recently given Tealand Properties Ltd, who have owned the hospital buildings and site since 2016, planning permission to convert the hospital into apartments.'

Ruth frowned. 'I'm still not seeing the connection, Dan.'

'The building work was due to start on Saturday morning. Obviously, they've had to put that on hold because it's now a crime scene,' French explained.

'You think that Carmel Chowdry's murder is somehow connected to the building work that was about to start?' Georgie enquired.

'Possibly,' French said. 'The west wing of the hospital was due to be completely demolished on Saturday morning with diggers. It's the only part of the building that's not Grade II listed. The work would have seen that part of the site razed to the ground and the basement filled with concrete.'

Ruth's eyes widened. 'So, if Carmel's body hadn't been discovered by accident, it would now be hidden in concrete.'

French nodded. 'And probably never seen again.'

Garrow looked over. 'Which means that whoever murdered Carmel in that basement and left his body there knew that twelve hours later it was going to be submerged in liquid concrete.'

'Good way of disposing of the body,' Ruth said as she processed what French had said.

'Gets better, boss.' French gave her a knowing look. 'I

did some digging around Tealand Properties Ltd. They seem to be owned by a holding company, Redland Enterprises, that is based in the Channel Islands, which is pretty suspicious in the first place. These days Companies House keeps records of all limited companies, even if they are offshore, to stop money laundering. Not only do Redland Enterprises own Tealand Properties. They also own Adventure Travel.'

Ruth remembered the name, but for a moment couldn't remember why. Then it came to her.

'Kabir Malik?' she said.

'Exactly,' French said with a nod.

Ben frowned. 'That doesn't necessarily mean that Malik knew about the building work at the hospital.'

Georgie sat forward on her seat and narrowed her eyes. 'Bit of a bloody big coincidence though, isn't it? We think that Carmel Chowdry had threatened to go to the police to report what Singh, Malik and Chopra were up to. He's murdered and left in a basement of a building owned by the same parent company as Malik's travel company. Come on.'

Ben shrugged. 'Well, since you put it like that.'

Ruth was already walking towards her office. 'Georgie?'

'Yes, boss?'

'While Dan and I go to Chopra's post mortem,' she said, 'can you and DI Stewart go over to Denbigh, arrest Malik and bring him back here for a formal interview?'

'Yes, boss.'

Chapter 48

Georgie and Ben turned into Smithfield Road at the centre of Denbigh as they headed towards Malik's offices above the Simla restaurant. They stopped at some traffic lights.

'You don't really drive like a man,' Georgie observed as she looked over from the passenger seat.

'Thanks,' Ben snorted, pulling a face.

'That's a compliment,' Georgie laughed. 'What I mean is that you're calm behind the wheel. When I was in uniform, I got put with some right boy racer knobheads.'

'Oh right,' Ben grinned. 'I just don't need to overcompensate for anything by driving like a moron.'

Georgie raised an eyebrow as the lights changed and they pulled away. 'I hope you're not bragging.'

'No,' Ben smiled. 'That would be completely inappropriate, wouldn't it?'

'Yes, it would.' Georgie looked at him quizzically. 'Although there is a saying, if you've got it, flaunt it.'

'Oh my God,' Ben laughed. 'I'm not even sure what we're talking about now.'

'Neither am I,' Georgie chortled. She felt so comfortable in Ben's company and the more time she spent with him, the more she saw that she might have misjudged him at first.

'Here we go,' he said as they parked outside the restaurant.

Unclipping her seatbelt, Georgie opened the door, got out and walked over to the door that led to the upstairs offices. Then she spotted that there was a handwritten note on the door to the restaurant - *Due to tragic circumstances, we will be closed until further notice.* Given that Rohan Chopra ran Simla, it wasn't surprising.

'Here's a question,' Georgie said, looking at Ben, who was fishing out his warrant card.

'Okay.' Ben rolled his eyes. 'Yes, I'll have dinner with you tonight.'

'Not that,' she said. 'If Malik was waiting for someone outside Chopra's house when he was murdered, who was inside?'

'I'm guessing there's someone else they're working with.'

'The Boss?' Georgie said disdainfully.

'Maybe,' Ben said as he reached over to the buzzer and pressed it.

'Hello?' said a woman's voice.

'DI Stewart and DC Wild. We'd like to speak to Kabir Malik, please.'

'I'm afraid he's not here at the moment,' the voice said.

Ben shot a dubious look at Georgie. They knew that Malik had been warned of their presence the last time they visited.

'Where is he?' Ben growled.

'I'm not sure,' the woman replied. 'I think he's out of the country.'

'Okay,' Ben snapped. 'Well, I'd like you to let us in anyway.'

There was no reply.

Out of the corner of her eye, Georgie spotted a sleek black Mercedes C-Class drive past at speed.

She glanced at the driver.

It was Malik.

'He's in that car!' Georgie yelled as she ran to their car.

'Bollocks!' Ben sprinted to the driver's door and jumped in.

'Control from Alpha five-two,' Georgie said into her Tetra radio as Ben hit the accelerator.

'Alpha five-two from Control. Go ahead, over.'

'We're in pursuit of a suspect, Kabir Malik. Black Mercedes C-Class. Heading west along Denbigh High Street, over.'

'Received Alpha five-two, stand by.'

'Bastard,' Ben hissed under his breath as they rapidly built up speed.

Georgie peered through the windscreen. 'Where the bloody hell is he?'

She then glanced over and saw they were already going 60 mph. They hurtled round a bend, and she put her hand out onto the dashboard above the glove compartment to steady herself.

'You okay?' Ben asked, looking over with concern.

She frowned. 'Erm, yes. This isn't my first high-speed pursuit,' she joked sarcastically.

'I know.' Ben pulled a face. 'I know. I was just thinking, what with you …'

'I'm fine,' she snapped and pointed. 'Just catch the bastard!'

'Okay,' Ben nodded.

Georgie heard the squeal of the back tyres as they rounded another bend at speed.

Malik's Mercedes honed into view about two hundred yards ahead.

'There,' Georgie said, pointing.

Ben accelerated, the engine roared, and Georgie felt herself pushed back in her seat.

They went hammering up a hill and then pulled out to overtake a white minibus full of primary school kids who looked out and waved.

Georgie put her hand up tentatively so as not to be rude and then grabbed the radio again.

'Control from Alpha five-two, we have visual on target vehicle,' Georgie said as she looked at the satnav map on the dashboard. 'We're heading south-west on the A543, over.'

'Alpha five-two, received,' a voice said. 'We have a uniform patrol en route, will advise.'

Ben glanced over at her and frowned. 'How did Malik know we were coming?'

'I don't know.' It was a question that made her feel uneasy.

'You think someone tipped him off?' Georgie asked.

'Maybe it was a coincidence, but …'

'Police officers don't believe in coincidences,' Georgie interjected.

'No, we don't.'

A moment later, they screamed through a village.

Georgie held her breath. If a pedestrian, cyclist or car pulled out now, it would be catastrophic.

Malik's Mercedes was now only a hundred yards ahead of them.

And Georgie could see the reg. 'Control from Alpha five-two, I have target vehicle's registration, over.'

'Go ahead, Alpha five-two.'

'Registration Yankee Whiskey Oscar, One Nine Lima, over.'

'Registration received, Alpha five-two.'

Just up ahead, a tractor pulled out of a field in front of them.

Ben had to slow quickly to avoid smashing into the back of it.

'Shit!' Georgie put out her hands as they were thrown forward by the rapid deceleration.

'God, are you okay?' Ben asked.

Georgie rolled her eyes. 'Ask me that again and I'll punch you.'

'Bit harsh,' Ben muttered as he then pulled the car out onto the other side of the road and stamped on the accelerator. The whole car lurched as the engine kicked in.

Peering ahead, Malik had managed to put another two or three hundred yards between them.

'Bollocks, he's getting away,' she grumbled.

'Not if I've got anything to do with it.' Ben moved rapidly through the gears and they hit 80 mph.

Georgie looked over at Ben, who was staring intently at the road ahead.

God, he really is very attractive. Do NOT fall for him.

BANG!

'Fuck,' Ben shouted as he grabbed the steering wheel. 'Blow out.'

The tyre had gone.

Georgie grabbed her seat as the car careered out of control.

She felt like her body was being thrown backwards and forwards as they skidded sideways, then backwards.

Oh God, if we hit anything now, we're going to flip over.

Then a metallic thud.

Ben shot out his arm across her to instinctively protect her from the impact.

Georgie closed her eyes as glass exploded everywhere.

Chapter 49

Ruth was now back in IR1, studying the scene boards as she nursed a mug of coffee in her hand. She and French had been over to the University Hospital in Llancastell to talk to Professor Amis about his preliminary post mortem on Rohan Chopra. He had died from a deep stab wound to his abdomen, although there were three less severe stab wounds to his chest and back. These matched their view that Chopra had been attacked initially in the downstairs living room. He had tried to get away from his attacker by fleeing upstairs, only to be wrestled into the bath where he received the fatal wound.

She looked over at Garrow and French. 'Any word from Georgie or DI Stewart?'

French shook his head. 'No, boss.'

Ruth pointed at the scene boards. 'Okay, I'm going to run through this. Pavan Singh traffics Indian teenagers and young people to the UK on the false promise of an education and well-paid employment. Kabir Malik, Rohan Chopra and unidentified persons then take their passports and use threats and manipulation to force them into modern slavery or prostitution. Carmel Chowdry threatens to report them to the police or to the press, so Chopra and possibly Malik murder him. Chopra is then arrested by us for sexual exploitation of a minor. Singh, Malik and the others in the trafficking ring decide that Chopra is too much of a risk and murder him, too.'

French nodded. 'Seems spot on to me, boss.'

'Jesus, what a mess.' Ruth looked back at the boards. 'And if our eye-witness is correct about Malik waiting outside Chopra's home, then we don't know who killed Chopra.'

'Maybe it's this person called The Boss who keeps cropping up,' French suggested.

'Maybe.' Ruth's eyes settled on *R I A M A N 4832. The Boss?? KM and PS.* Then something occurred to her as she peered at the letters and numbers again.

'Something up?' French asked, clearly noticing her expression.

'Malik owns a travel company, doesn't he?' Ruth went to where the letters and numbers were written.

'That's right.' French looked down at some notes. 'Adventure Travel.'

Ruth pointed to *4832*. 'This could be a flight number. RIA? Isn't there a Royal Indian Airlines?'

'Yes,' French nodded with a quizzical look.

'Royal Indian Airlines, flight 4822, leaving from MAN, which is Manchester airport,' Ruth said, thinking out loud, and then looked at French. 'Can we check it?'

French jumped onto his computer and tapped away at the keyboard. A moment later he looked at her. 'Royal Indian Airlines Flight 4832 flies from Manchester to Mumbai this afternoon at 5pm.'

Bloody hell!

Ruth grabbed her phone and dialled Georgie's number.

Chapter 50

Georgie blinked open her eyes. The car had finally come to a stop and thankfully hadn't flipped over. Her back and shoulder ached from the impact. Both airbags had deployed and there were pebbles of safety glass which had showered all over her.

Glancing over at Ben, she saw that he wasn't moving and his face was turned away from her.

Oh, my God!

Her stomach lurched.

'Ben?' she croaked. 'Are you okay?'

He didn't move for a couple of seconds. Then he turned to look at her. His face had a thick trickle of blood from a gash in his forehead.

'Yeah,' he blew out his cheeks, as he tried to get his head together. 'What about you? Are you okay?'

'Yeah,' she said with a grimace. 'Nothing a good chiropractor can't fix.'

She peered out to see that the bonnet of the car was badly crumpled. The dashboard was tilted at an angle and the windscreen smashed. It was a mess.

Georgie's phone rang, and she saw it was Ruth.

'Boss, we've been in a crash,' she said, answering it.

'Oh God, are you both okay?' Ruth asked, sounding concerned.

'I think so.'

'Are you sure?'

'Yes. Honestly. We're both fine,' she reassured Ruth.

'What about the car?'

'Write off, I'm afraid.'

'Right,' Ruth said. 'Just as long as you're both okay.'

Georgie looked over at Ben. 'Just a few cuts and bruises but nothing serious.'

'Good,' Ruth sighed. 'What happened with Malik?'

'He did a runner,' Georgie explained. 'We were chasing him when we crashed.'

'Right. We think he's flying to Mumbai from Manchester this afternoon,' Ruth explained. 'We need to get you guys picked up and checked over.'

'There should be a uniform patrol here any second now, boss.'

'Right, okay,' Ruth said. 'And we might need to ban you from leaving the station at this rate.'

Georgie smiled. 'I'll see you when we get back, boss,' she said as she ended the call.

Ben had a strange frown on his face. He looked over at her. 'There's a strong smell of petrol in here. We need to get out.'

Now he'd mentioned it, Georgie noticed the fumes were getting stronger and stronger.

Reaching down to where her seatbelt was clipped in, she went to release it.

It was stuck.

'I can't get this out,' she said, panicking.

Ben jumped out of the car, ran around to her side of

the car and pulled open the passenger door, which was damaged and dented.

Georgie looked down as she frantically pushed the red button to release the seatbelt.

Nothing.

It must have got jammed by the impact of the crash.

If the petrol ignited, she was going to be burned alive.

She looked at Ben as her pulse quickened. 'I'm serious, Ben, I can't release it. It's jammed.' She was beginning to feel terrified.

'Hold tight.' Ben leaned across her and yanked at the seatbelt where it was stuck.

The petrol fumes were getting thicker and more potent. The fuel tank must have cracked in the crash.

'For fuck's sake!' Ben growled as he pulled desperately at the belt. 'I can't seem to get it out.'

Looking down, Georgie saw where the electrical wires had been ripped from the dashboard and were now hanging precariously in mid-air. One spark from them, and they were both going to go up in flames.

Georgie looked directly at Ben. 'Get away from the car, Ben.'

'Don't be ridiculous!' he snapped. 'I'm not leaving you in here.'

'There's no point us both dying,' Georgie said as her heart thundered in her chest.

'I'm not going anywhere,' Ben said emphatically as he gave the belt another almighty yank. 'Bloody hell!'

Nothing.

It was stuck.

There were a few seconds of silence.

Georgie braced herself. She sensed the car was going to explode any second.

Placing his foot against the handbrake to give himself

leverage, Ben wrapped the slack of the seatbelt around his hands.

He jerked it with everything he had.

The belt lock flew out and Ben went flying backwards, nearly losing his balance.

Moving quickly, he grabbed Georgie by the arm and dragged her out of the car.

They sprinted away from the car and down the grassy verge of the long country road where they had crashed.

As they got about 30 yards away, there was an almighty BANG!

The car erupted into a ball of flames.

The force of it knocked Georgie, and she fell against Ben, who put his arms around her.

'Jesus,' she whispered as she looked at the black outline of the car, now consumed by a ferocious fire where she had been sitting only seconds earlier.

Keeping her arms around Ben, she looked up at him. He then pulled her a little closer as they looked directly at each other.

'That was close,' he whispered.

'Yeah,' she whispered, her eyes locked onto his. 'That was really close.'

Ben smiled, his eyes twinkling. 'Why are we whispering?' he asked.

'I've no idea,' Georgie whispered with a little laugh.

Their eyes locked again.

Ben leaned in slowly and kissed her firmly on the mouth.

She didn't resist.

Chapter 51

Ruth and French had been searching Manchester airport for over twenty minutes, but there was no sign of Malik anywhere. She was still waiting for security to contact her to confirm whether Malik had checked in for the flight.

Taking the escalators to the first floor shopping precinct, Ruth scanned the busy concourse. It was early April, which meant it was the school Easter holidays, so the airport was incredibly busy. They then showed their warrant cards to gain access to the business and first class lounges, but Malik was nowhere to be found.

As they returned to the main shopping area, Ruth glanced at her watch and then looked at French. 'Forty minutes before take-off.'

'Head for the gate?' French suggested.

'Yeah,' Ruth agreed as they turned and headed down towards Gate 5 where the flight to Mumbai was departing from.

They arrived and saw that the flight hadn't boarded

yet. Ruth scanned the waiting passengers but couldn't see Malik.

She took out her warrant card and headed for two members of the flight's cabin crew who were standing by ready to check boarding cards and passports.

'Hi there. DI Hunter and DS French, North Wales Police,' she explained. 'We're looking for a passenger who we think is on this flight. Do you have a passenger list?'

The female flight attendant, 30s and brunette, shook her head. 'I'm sorry, we don't.' She then pointed to a computer terminal and a scanner. 'It's all done automatically. But I don't have an actual passenger list I can look at or give you.'

'Okay,' Ruth said with a frustrated expression. 'Thank you.'

French looked at her. 'If Malik is on this flight, then he's going to have to walk past us to board.'

Ruth nodded as her eyes scanned the waiting passengers, as well as those now arriving at the gate.

'DI Hunter?' asked a voice.

Ruth turned to see a short man with ginger hair approaching. He was wearing a lanyard and carrying documents.

'I'm Nigel Trelford, Head of Security for the airport,' he said. 'We spoke earlier.'

'Yes, that's right,' Ruth said.

'You're looking for a passenger, Kabir Malik, is that right?' Nigel asked.

'Yes,' Ruth replied. 'We have reason to believe that he's on this flight today.'

Nigel pulled a face. 'I'm afraid Mr Malik is actually on a different flight to India. BA 343 to Delhi.'

Ruth exchanged a look at French. At least they knew

Malik was definitely flying to India, so they could now arrest him.

'Thanks. Which gate is that flying from?' French asked.

Nigel looked out of the huge windows and pointed to a plane that was speeding along a runway in the distance. 'I'm afraid that's the flight to Delhi.'

Chapter 52

Sitting on the bed in his cell, Nick had borrowed Danny's phone again to check on Amanda and Megan. They were fine, but obviously it was frustrating that they were stuck in limbo in a hotel room. Nick was due to travel to Mold Court tomorrow afternoon for a meeting with his lawyer, the CPS and Probation Services. It would be in this meeting that he would learn whether the CPS would press charges over his escape from HMP Rhoswen. If they were going to press charges, then Nick might get bail, as it was a lesser charge than previously. However, he would still have to go to trial and might well get a custodial sentence.

On top of all this, Nick still had the issue of Blake to deal with. Now that he had hatched a plan for the following morning, he could feel his anxiety growing. If he botched it, then he could end up dead or facing more criminal charges. But he knew that he wasn't going to allow Blake to ruin the rest of his and his family's life. He refused to go into a witness protection scheme and go into hiding. And that left only one option.

Looking down at the phone, Nick dialled Ruth's number. She was keeping in touch with Merseyside Police, who were effectively responsible for Amanda and Megan's ongoing safety.

'Hello?' Ruth said.

'Ruth, it's Nick,' he said quietly. Danny was lying on his bed, reading a tabloid newspaper.

'Hey, how are you?' Ruth asked. She sounded tired and preoccupied, but that went with the job.

'You know. Still living the dream,' he replied caustically.

'I'm going to see if I can come over to Mold tomorrow,' she explained.

'It's fine. I know you're up to your eyes with this investigation,' Nick said, although he secretly would have liked to have seen her tomorrow.

'I really don't think they're going to press charges, Nick,' Ruth said optimistically. 'Although you committed a crime, no one got hurt when you escaped. And not only did you clear your name, you uncovered a stack of evidence against Blake and the Croxteth Boyz.'

'Yeah, I know all that,' Nick admitted. 'I just don't want to get my hopes up only to have them dashed.'

There were a few seconds of silence.

'What about Blake?' she asked.

'I'm dealing with it,' Nick said under his breath.

'Sounds ominous.'

'I can't talk to you about it on the phone,' Nick explained. 'Best that we don't even acknowledge it.'

'I understand,' Ruth said.

'How is the investigation going?' Nick asked. He missed the CID team at Llancastell and the day-to-day excitement of being a police officer.

'I'm pretty sure we've got a prime suspect,' Ruth

replied. 'I've just got to go to Delhi to question him unless we get enough evidence to charge him with murder and then get him extradited.'

'Delhi? Well, it's better than driving up to Rhyl,' Nick joked.

'True,' Ruth laughed. 'To be honest, I'm not looking forward to Delhi. Or having to deal with the bureaucracy of the Indian Police Force.'

'Now you've said it …' Nick laughed, '… I'm glad I'm in here. I'll let you go. And please don't feel you need to come tomorrow.'

'Hey, I've got to come,' Ruth quipped. 'I miss seeing your hairy face every day. I assume you've grown that thing back?'

'That thing?' Nick chortled. It was so good to have a bit of flippancy and humour. He brushed his hand over his jawline. 'Yeah, it's nearly back you'll be pleased to know. Night, and get some sleep.'

'Yeah, night Nick.'

Chapter 53

Ruth had slept for seven hours last night, which was unheard of. However, it had left her feeling a little foggy headed as she came out of her office to take the 9am briefing.

'Okay, listen up,' she said as she took her customary position perched on a table beside the scene boards. 'As most of you know, Kabir Malik flew to Delhi yesterday. And because we don't have enough evidence to charge him with murder, I might have to fly out to Delhi in the next couple of days to formally question him. The Indian government won't get involved in any kind of discussion about extradition until we can charge him. Which means we need to work flat out to get that evidence now.' She pointed to his photo. 'We have an eye-witness who saw Malik sitting outside Chopra's house at the time of his murder. There are the allegations that the Simla restaurant was part of a trafficking ring out of India. And we have his involvement with Tealand Properties who were due to start renovating Denbigh Asylum. Unfortunately, none of that puts him physically at any of the murder scenes. What about forensics?'

Garrow looked over. 'Until we have Malik's DNA or fingerprints, forensics say it's going to be difficult to link him to our victims or our crime scenes.'

Ruth furrowed her brow. 'I just don't think we have enough for an arrest or a search warrant.'

'We've got two DNAs from the Denbigh Asylum crime scene,' Ben said, sitting forward in his chair. 'And if we think Malik was waiting outside Chopra's home, then there's someone else involved. And that person might have been responsible for both murders.'

'Good point,' Ruth agreed, but it felt like the investigation was now at a standstill. 'I want us to run Malik's plates through traffic and ANPR. Let's see if we can get a hit for the times of either of our murders. What about Malik's phone records?'

Georgie glanced over. 'Still waiting, boss.'

'Just a quick update on Gareth Steel,' French said with a wry expression. 'I've done my best to research 'dogging'. I couldn't find any mention of a meeting at the car park at Offa's Dyke Path. There are a couple of regular places in North Wales, but Offa's Dyke Path car park isn't one of them.' French then raised an eyebrow. 'If anyone wants details, talk to me afterwards.'

There were a few murmurs and laughter from the team.

Ruth frowned. 'What about this 'John' who was going to back up Steel's alibi for the night of Carmel's murder?'

French shook his head. 'I've left several messages on the phone number that Steel gave me but I've heard nothing back.'

'And Steel has lied about his alibi twice before,' Garrow pointed out.

'Okay,' Ruth said. 'Let's see if we can track him down. I'd like to be able to eliminate him fully.'

'Boss.' Garrow signalled that he had something else. 'Email from forensics. They had that video footage that those teenagers shot on the night of Carmel's murder cleaned up. They're not sure if it's going to be of any use.'

Ruth pulled a frustrated face. 'Have they sent it over, anyway?'

'Yes, boss.' Garrow gestured to the large monitor that was mounted to the wall in IR1. 'Do you want me to play it on there?'

Ruth shrugged. 'Might as well. It's probably cost us a fortune to get it digitally enhanced.'

Clicking on his keyboard, Garrow linked his computer to the screen and then went over to turn on the monitor. He then went back to press play.

The screen was filled with the footage that the teenagers had shot when they arrived at Denbigh Asylum.

The camera wobbled as they ducked under the yellow tape and the teenagers went down the stone steps. It was dark and very difficult to make out anything.

'Hello?' a voice called. 'Any psychos or paedos down here?'

The camera then jolted suddenly as a rat darted across the floor.
'Shit!'
'It's just a rat,' said a voice.
'I hate rats.'
There was some more mumbling which the microphone didn't pick up.
The camera moved around the first room to the left before coming

up and focussing on the corridor ahead.

There was the faintest outline of a figure in the corridor. The person ran towards them.

'Shit!'

'Come on then,' shouted a voice.

The figure ran past the camera. It was dark, and they were wearing dark clothing and a hoodie pulled up over their head.

The camera wobbled.

'Who the hell was that?' asked a voice.

The footage stopped.

Ruth was pretty sure that there wasn't anything in the video that was of any use. 'Anyone see anything?'

'It's just too dark,' Garrow said.

Ruth pointed to the screen. 'Can you just play it again and then freeze it as the person goes past them?'

Garrow obliged, freezing the image of the blurred dark figure up on the screen.

'Bloody hell,' French groaned. 'I can't see anything.'

Ruth moved closer to the screen and squinted. The person's hood completely obscured their face. It was so frustrating.

Then something caught Ruth's eye.

It was the person's hand which was up by their chest as they ran.

'Can you zoom in a bit on that?' Ruth said, going up to the screen.

Garrow tapped at his computer, and the image magnified.

Ruth peered again.

There was something on the back of the person's hand.

An intricate tattoo of a flower.

Ruth looked at the team. 'That's Derifa Mousa.'

Chapter 54

Nick sat on his bed, leaned down and tied the laces of his navy-coloured Nike trainers. He was wearing shorts, a t-shirt and a tracksuit top. If his plan was to work later, he needed to look as if he was playing 5-a-side on the prison astroturf later that morning. He had identified the time slot after the AA meeting finished over in the chaplaincy.

For a moment, he was taken back to his first night in a cell in Rhoswen. Like most prisoners, he had hardly slept a wink. He had no idea who his cell mate was except that he was big, hairy and Albanian. Nick knew that if he closed his eyes then he would fall asleep. And if he was asleep, he was vulnerable. He didn't want to be woken by his cell mate attacking or sexually assaulting him. He needed to be on his guard. Luckily, Yakiv turned out to be a decent bloke and he needn't have worried.

A figure appeared in the doorway, breaking his train of thought. It was Danny, returning from the shower. Nick could see how heroin had ravaged Danny's body. His ribs were clearly visible across his torso, as were the scars of track marks up the inside of each arm.

'Bloody hell, man,' Danny laughed. 'I thought you weren't interested in footie? Thought you was all about rugby.'

'I bumped into some old mates from North Wales,' Nick lied. 'They asked me to make up the numbers this morning.'

'Good for you, pal.' Danny went over to his bed and got dressed. 'Make sure you stretch. First time I played, I pinged me bloody hamstring.'

'Will do.' Nick went over to the printed 5-a-side timetable that Danny kept beside his bed. 'I assume C Blake here is Curtis Blake?' Nick had never hinted to his cell mate that he had had any dealings with Blake or even knew who he was.

'Yeah, that's right.' Danny gave him a quizzical look. 'You're not playing with that Scouse lot, are you? They're bloody animals.'

'No,' Nick reassured him and shook his head. 'I just know the name from the news, that's all. Big time drug dealer, isn't he?'

'Something like that. I try to stay clear of blokes like that … Hey, you've got that hearing or meeting thingy later, haven't you?' Danny asked.

Nick hadn't gone into any details other than he was meeting the CPS to see if they were going to press charges and take him to trial.

'Yeah,' Nick nodded. 'They're taking me over to Mold at 4pm. Got to wear my civvies in case I don't come back here.'

'So, I could be getting a new bloody cell mate tonight, eh?' Danny then grinned at him. 'Thank God for that.'

'Oh cheers,' Nick laughed. 'Yeah, well, I don't want to get ahead of myself.'

'Well, I bloody hope they let you out, mate,' Danny said with a kind smile. 'You're a nice fella.'

'Thanks Danny,' Nick said.

Danny gestured to the cell next door. 'They've took Daz over to the CSU this morning.'

CSU stood for the Care and Separation Unit. It was effectively solitary confinement for prisoners. The cells were damage proof. No TVs, and everything was bolted to the walls and floors. In the unit, there was no canteen, one phone call a day and only 30 minutes of exercise.

'What for?' Nick asked.

'Punching a female screw because she wanted to check his mouth for pills,' Danny explained.

'How long?'

'Two weeks, I think. Poor bastard,' Danny replied as he headed for the cell door now he was fully dressed. 'I'll see you down on the pitches this morning, eh?'

'Looking forward to it,' Nick said.

In fact, he prayed that everything that morning went like clockwork because if it went wrong, it was going to be catastrophic.

Chapter 55

Ben and Georgie walked down the corridor in the rundown B&B in the middle of Denbigh where Derifa Mousa was staying. The young woman on reception had confirmed that as far as she knew, Derifa was still in her room. Ruth and French had gone to the rear of the building as they could see there was an alleyway and they didn't want Derifa doing a runner. She'd already done that at the car wash.

The red patterned carpet was threadbare and the paint on the wall chipped. There were a couple of cheap-looking water colour prints of Snowdonia in wooden frames hanging in a row. Cigarette smoke lingered in the air as they got to Room 9.

Ben knocked on the door and took a step back.

As Georgie pulled out her warrant card, she was still trying to piece together the investigation. Derifa had been filmed running from the room where Carmel's body had been found. Did that mean she was guilty of his murder? They were convinced that whoever killed Carmel had also murdered Rohan Chopra. How did she fit into that scenario?

The door opened by about two inches and Derifa peered out nervously.

'Derifa,' Georgie said calmly, showing her warrant card. 'We need to ask you some questions. Can you let us in, please?'

'Can you hang on a second?' Derifa asked, and then she pushed the door closed.

From inside the room, there was the sound of movement – banging, drawers closing etc.

Georgie shot Ben a look. *What the hell is she doing in there?* Then silence.

'Bloody hell,' Ben growled as he banged aggressively on the door again. 'Derifa, you need to open this door.'

Nothing.

'Maybe she's done a runner?' Georgie suggested.

Ben frowned. 'We're on the first floor.'

'I've seen plenty of people jump out of first-floor windows in my time,' Georgie stated.

'True,' Ben agreed as he nudged his shoulder against the door to see how much force it would need to be opened. From the looks of it, not very much.

Ben took a couple of steps back from the door and looked at Georgie. 'We haven't got time to stand here all day.'

'You going to pay for it?' Georgie joked as she gestured to the door.

Ben slammed his shoulder into the door, and it burst open, smashing against the wall behind.

Georgie immediately spotted Derifa sitting on the windowsill of a large open window and attempting to climb out.

'Oi, stay there!' Georgie thundered.

As Georgie rushed over, Derifa turned and lowered herself from the windowsill with her hands.

Looking out, Georgie realised why Derifa had been reluctant to jump in the first place. The back of the B&B dropped down into a sunken garden below that was at the same level as the basement. Effectively, it was a two-storey drop to the gravel below and well over 25ft.

Derifa was now hanging on to the windowsill with her fingertips.

Georgie looked down at her as she went to grab her and pull her back up.

'Derifa, don't jump. You'll break both your legs, or your neck,' Georgie warned her.

'I don't care,' Derifa wept.

Reaching down, Georgie grabbed the back of Derifa's coat.

'Get off me!' Derifa said, struggling.

With every ounce of strength that she had, Georgie pulled Derifa back into the room where she fell onto the carpet.

What the hell is Ben doing?

'Jesus,' Georgie gasped as she pulled Derifa's hands behind her back and cuffed them. She then turned round to see that Ben was looking through Derifa's stuff.

'You okay?' Ben asked.

'Just about,' she huffed. 'Could have done with a hand, though.'

Ben pulled a face. 'God, sorry.' He then held up a trainer and looked over. 'Size 6 trainer here. Dark stains on the soles. Could be blood.'

He spotted something else, crouched down on the floor, and frowned as he looked under the bed.

'There's something taped under here,' Ben said as he

reached under and then pulled out what looked like a headscarf.

'What is it?' Georgie asked.

'That's not mine,' Derifa yelled.

Opening the scarf up, Ben showed it to Georgie.

There was an eight-inch knife with what looked like bloodstains on the blade.

Georgie's eyes widened.

'Derifa Mousa, I'm arresting you on suspicion of murder,' Georgie said. 'You do not have to say anything. But it may harm your defence if you do not mention when questioned something which you later rely on in court. Anything you do say may be given in evidence. Do you understand what I've just said to you, Derifa?'

Derifa looked shocked but nodded slowly.

Chapter 56

As Nick leaned forward on his seat, he checked his watch. There was only five minutes left of the AA meeting. The next thirty minutes were going to define the rest of his life. He felt sick in the pit of his stomach and his heart was pounding.

Phil looked out at the group. 'Is there anyone else who would like to share today? Remember, better to get it off your chest here in safety than take it back to your cell.'

Nick took a breath to steady himself. He could do with the meeting ending five minutes early. Glancing around at the other prisoners, he looked for any sign that one of them was going to share. They were either staring into space or readying themselves to leave.

'Right,' Phil said with a kind smile as he sat forward in his chair. 'Thanks everyone. It's been a great meeting.'

'Thanks Phil,' said a prisoner, who went over and shook his hand.

Nick had the list of all the prisoners who were due to attend that day at his feet. It was the job of one of them to do a roll call and then hand the list over to Mike, the SMS manager, when he arrived.

'Have you got a pen, Phil?' Nick asked, knowing full well that Phil never had a pen and always sent the prisoner doing the register off to the chaplaincy office to borrow one.

Phil did his usual routine of patting his pockets. 'Sorry. You okay to get one from the office for me?'

'No problem,' Nick said, getting up from his seat.

Taking a nervous swallow, Nick headed for the office as he had done before. A woman in her 40s gave him a suspicious look, as she had done earlier in the week.

'Okay if I borrow a pen for Phil?' Nick asked cheerily. He had already spotted a lanyard and security pass lying on the desk closest to the door.

The woman rolled her eyes. 'As long as I get it back this time.'

'Of course, I promise,' Nick replied with a grin.

Swiping the lanyard as he went past, Nick shoved it into his trouser pocket as he came into the room and handed the pen to Phil.

'Up to no good?' joked a voice.

It was Mike, one of the prison's SMS officers, who was dressed in his sports gear with a whistle hanging around his neck.

'Just stealing another pen for Phil,' Nick joked.

Phil called out the names of the prisoners as he took a roll call.

'I need a favour, Mike,' Nick said under his breath.

Mike raised an eyebrow. 'That sounds ominous.'

'I'm going to be late for my 5-a-side.' Nick pointed to his watch. 'Okay if I come with you to the pitches from down there?' he asked, pointing out to the corridor where the door down to the astroturf was situated.

'Don't see why not.' Mike gestured to the printout he was holding. 'As you're down on my list.'

'Yeah, I am,' Nick replied. He had signed up for football the day before.

Phil went round, shaking everyone's hand.

'Right you lot,' Mike said. 'I need you out here in the corridor tout de suite.'

Some of the prisoners frowned – they had no idea what he was talking about.

'Didn't know you were bilingual, Mike,' Nick quipped.

'One of my many talents,' Mike laughed as he locked the door behind them all. He then glanced at Nick. 'Give me five minutes for a jimmy and you can come down with me.'

'Thanks, Mike.' Nick looked down the corridor and saw Tony Connell and Jayden Roberts coming out of the NA meeting and lining up further down.

Nick gave Connell a nod. Connell and Jayden gave Nick a slight nod back.

Right, we're on. Time to get my life back.

Chapter 57

Derifa was now dressed in a regulation grey tracksuit as her clothes had been taken for forensics. She had also been swabbed for traces of DNA. Georgie leaned across the table to start the recording machine. A long electronic beep sounded as Ruth opened one of her files.

'Interview conducted with Derifa Mousa, Llancastell Police Station. Present are Detective Constable Georgina Wild, duty solicitor Patrick Blanham and myself, Detective Inspector Ruth Hunter,' Ruth stated, and then glanced over. 'Derifa, do you understand that you are still under arrest and that we are going to be questioning you in connection with the murders of Carmel Chowdry and Rohan Chopra?'

'Yes,' Derifa replied, sounding angry but terrified. She was fidgeting and jigging her foot.

Ruth waited for a few seconds as she pulled one of the files in front of her. Then she looked over. 'Derifa, can you tell us where you were last Friday between 5pm and 9pm?'

Derifa took a moment to respond. Then she said, 'I was in my room at the B&B.'

'And you're sure of that, are you?' Ruth asked her calmly.

Derifa frowned and then glanced at Blanham. 'Yes. I was tired after work. I don't understand.'

Georgie reached into a folder and pulled out a photograph. 'For the purposes of the tape, I'm showing the suspect item reference 832B.' Georgie turned the photo so that Derifa could see it. 'Could you take a look at this photo, please, and tell me what you can see?'

Derifa, who looked utterly baffled, peered at the photo – a still from the video shot by the teenagers. 'I do not understand. I can't see anything.'

Georgie pointed to the far right of the image. 'If you look carefully, you can see a person's hand, can't you?'

Derifa squinted and then pulled a face.

'You don't agree?'

Derifa huffed. 'Yes, I can see a hand.'

'Do you notice anything about the hand?'

Derifa groaned but didn't look at the image again. 'No. I do not understand why you are asking me this?'

'You see, on the back of this hand, there is a tattoo,' Ruth said, and then pointed, 'which is identical to the tattoo on the back of your hand, isn't it?'

'I don't know,' Derifa replied, but her voice trembled.

'Why did you lie to us, Derifa?' Ruth fixed her with a stare. 'We know that you were at Denbigh Asylum on Friday evening.'

'I wasn't,' she replied in a whisper.

'You were,' Ruth snapped. 'You need to tell us what you were doing there.'

'I don't know.'

'You don't know why you were there?' Ruth asked.

Derifa blinked. She was rattled.

Ruth locked eyes with her. 'Because your boyfriend

Carmel Chowdry was found murdered in that building. So, you're going to need to tell us what you were doing or we're going to charge you with his murder.'

There was silence for a few seconds as Derifa tried to compose herself.

'Derifa?' Ruth said.

'I followed him,' she cried as she started to unravel. 'That's all. I didn't hurt him.'

'Why did you follow him?' Georgie asked.

'I thought he was meeting someone there,' Derifa mumbled as she wiped a tear from her face.

'Someone?' Ruth said with a frown. 'You're going to have to be more specific.'

Derifa shrugged.

'Did you think that Carmel was going to meet another girl there?' Georgie asked forcefully.

Derifa nodded.

'For the purposes of the tape, the suspect has nodded to confirm that she did believe that Carmel Chowdry was going to meet another girl at Denbigh Asylum,' Georgie stated.

Ruth sat back and waited for the tension to mount. Then she looked over at Derifa with a quizzical expression. 'So, you followed Carmel to the hospital. Did you see him meet another girl?'

'No,' she whispered.

'But you decided to attack Carmel anyway, is that right?' Ruth asked.

'No.'

'But we have you on video leaving the room where Carmel was murdered,' Ruth said. 'And we have the knife that we believe killed him hidden in your bedroom. How can you explain that?'

'It's not my knife,' Derifa replied as she started to cry again. 'I promise you.'

George frowned. 'Then why was it hidden under your bed?'

Derifa sniffed and wiped her face. 'I don't know.'

'Okay,' Ruth said. 'You followed Carmel, but he didn't meet a girl?'

'No, he met a man,' Derifa said.

'He met a man?' Ruth asked, wondering if there was any truth in what she was saying. They had the video and the murder weapon, after all.

'Can you describe this man?' Georgie asked.

'Not really. He was a long way away,' Derifa explained. 'And he was wearing a dark coat and a hat.'

Ruth looked at Georgie – it felt like Derifa was making this up as she went along.

'What kind of hat?' Georgie asked, unable to disguise the doubt in her voice.

'I don't know,' Derifa said. Her voice was unsteady. 'Like a cap. But quite big.'

Ruth frowned. She didn't know what she was talking about.

'Like in that TV programme,' Derifa said. 'Like in the Peaky Blinders.'

Ruth raised an eyebrow. 'This man was wearing a Peaky Blinders-style cap?'

'Yes,' Derifa said.

'Then what happened?' Ruth asked.

'I tried to follow to see where they went,' Derifa explained as she wiped tears from her face. 'Then I saw the man leave. I went down to the basement and saw Carmel lying there. Then I heard voices, so I ran.'

Ruth narrowed her eyes. 'What about the knife, Derifa?'

Suddenly, it was all too much. Derifa broke down and sobbed, putting her head in her hands.

Blanham looked over with a serious expression. 'I think my client could do with a break, don't you?'

Ruth nodded as she leaned over to the recording equipment, pressed pause and said, 'Interview suspended at 2.47pm.' She then looked at Blanham as she got up from the table. 'Let's reconvene here in an hour.'

Chapter 58

Nick watched carefully as Mike opened the door that led to the staircase down to the pitches. There was a security pad on both sides of the door. Nick also watched carefully to check there was no other way of opening it from the other side.

As they walked down the steps, Mike gave a little cheerful whistle.

'You seem to enjoy your job,' Nick remarked, trying to pretend that his whole body wasn't tight with fear. Looking up, he scanned the ceilings for CCTV cameras. There weren't any, which wasn't surprising as this was technically a staircase only used by prison staff.

'I used to work in industry. Boring work but well paid,' Mike said. 'So I retrained. It's badly paid but I get to give something back and help people.'

Nick gave him a wry smile. 'Even the lunatics in here?'

'You know that two-thirds of the blokes in here committed their crime while under the influence of drugs or alcohol,' Mike said as they got to the bottom of the steps. 'If we don't tackle the addiction in here, they're going to go back into society and do exactly the same thing again. And they end up back in here. I've seen it too many times.'

'Fair point,' Nick agreed, even though his mind was elsewhere.

They came out into a small alleyway at the side of the chaplaincy building and then turned right.

There were three full size astroturf pitches in front of them with various prisoners and officers hanging around waiting for the games to start at the allotted time slots.

'Enjoy your game,' Mike said as he headed off to where he was refereeing.

'Thanks.' Nick immediately turned his attention to finding Blake.

Blake knew that Nick was on the VP wing. Therefore, it was virtually impossible for Blake and his crew to get to Nick inside the prison. Except Nick was going to give them the golden opportunity they'd been looking for.

On the far side, there was an area sectioned off where prisoners from the VP wing could play football in safety. Obviously, they couldn't play with the general prison population. However, Nick had counted on Mike not checking whether he was a vulnerable prisoner. There was no need. After all, why would a vulnerable prisoner want to take the risk of being out with the other prisoners? It would be suicide. In any other circumstance, someone on the VP wing would flag up their status rather than hide it.

And that was how Nick intended to entrap Blake.

Scouring the waiting prisoners, it wasn't long before Nick spotted a group of shaven-headed thugs in luminous green bibs doing keep-ups and passing the ball back and forth. In the middle was Blake who was shouting and laughing.

Nick walked across the pitch so that he was now less

than 50 yards away. Clearly, Nick couldn't appear as if he'd seen Blake and his crew.

Then, out of the corner of his eye, he saw a sudden movement.

Glancing up, he saw Blake and three of his thugs marching quickly towards him.

They'd spotted him and they weren't going to let him get away.

Nick locked eyes with Blake, and gave a suitably terrified look before turning and sprinting back the way he'd come.

After about ten seconds, he glanced back. As planned, Blake and the others were now running after him full pelt. If they got hold of him now, they'd pull him out of the view of the CCTV cameras and screws and beat him to death.

But that was what Nick was counting on.

Come on you fuckers! See if you can catch me.

Chapter 59

Perching herself down on a desk, Ruth frowned as she tried to piece together what Derifa had told them and how that fitted their double murder investigation. Most of the team were at their desks, making phone calls or working on their computers.

Georgie approached and handed her a coffee. 'You look confused, boss?'

'Thanks,' Ruth said, taking the coffee. 'I am confused,' she admitted. 'Derifa Mousa does have motive to murder Rohan Chopra as well as Carmel. Different motives, I grant you. But Chopra was an aggressive bastard to Derifa and everyone she knew.'

'But why is Kabir Malik sitting outside Chopra's house at the time of his murder?' Georgie asked. 'Why has he trusted Derifa to go inside to murder Chopra? She's a teenage girl, and he's a grown man.'

'True,' Ruth agreed. 'Why not do it yourself?'

'What if we have two different killers?' Georgie suggested.

Ruth frowned. 'MO is the same. So my instinct is that it's too much of a coincidence to be a different person. We have Derifa on camera. She had the murder weapon. And we have the texts she sent threatening Carmel Chowdry.' Ruth looked at Georgie. 'Derifa killed him. But why did she go with Kabir Malik to Chopra's home and attack him? That's still not clear.'

'Was there something going on between her and Malik?' Georgie said.

'Maybe,' Ruth said. 'If Malik wanted Chopra dead because he was scared that he was going to give evidence against the trafficking ring, maybe Derifa agreed to do it.'

French, who was holding a phone, looked over and gestured. 'Boss, the forensic lab wants you to go and look at something.'

'Thanks Dan.' Ruth gestured to Georgie. 'Come on. Let's see what they've found.'

Ruth and Georgie headed for the main doors to IR1 and then out into the corridor towards the back staircase.

'I kissed Ben,' Georgie admitted as they walked down the stairs.

'What?' Ruth exclaimed under her breath. 'When did that happen?' She wasn't sure that was a good thing and was afraid that Georgie was very vulnerable at the moment. Maybe she'd made a mistake by making jokes about Georgie's growing attraction to Ben.

'When he pulled me out of the car,' Georgie explained as they walked out of the side entrance and headed for the forensic building across the road. 'The car exploded. He put his arms around me to keep me safe. And then we kissed.'

'Yeah, I think if Ben had pulled me out of a car and saved my life I might have kissed him. And I'm gay,' Ruth joked and then gave Georgie a look. 'Just tread carefully, okay?'

'I know,' Georgie nodded. 'There is something between us but I know I've got to protect myself at the moment.'

They entered the forensic building and headed for the lab to their left. It was brightly illuminated with several rows of forensic equipment – microscopes, fume hoods, chromatographs and spectrometers – as well as vials and test tubes of brightly coloured liquids.

A lab technician in a full forensic suit, mask, and gloves approached them at the doorway. 'Can I help?' she asked.

'DI Hunter and DC Wild,' Ruth explained. 'We had a call in CID that you'd found something?'

'Yes,' the lab technician nodded as she handed them forensic gloves and masks to put on. 'I'll take you over.'

Ruth and Georgie followed her over to the chief lab technician, Hilary Salmon, whom Ruth had met a few times since arriving at Llancastell nick.

'DI Hunter,' Hilary said from behind her mask. She was holding a test tube and looking at a computer screen with a graph on it.

'What have you got for us?' Ruth asked.

'We've got the DNA and fingerprints from your suspect, Derifa Mousa,' Hilary explained as she pointed to the screen. 'As you can see, we've managed to match them to DNA found on clothing that we took from Carmel Chowdry.'

Ruth looked at Georgie. It was a breakthrough.

Hilary then held up an evidence bag with a small green vape inside. 'We also have Derifa Mousa's thumbprint and DNA on this vape,' she explained.

Ruth frowned. 'Where did you find the vape?'

'SOCOs found it on the living room floor at your

second crime scene,' Hilary explained. 'Rohan Chopra's home. So, we can place your suspect at both crime scenes.'

Ruth looked at Georgie. It was a significant breakthrough.

Chapter 60

With another glance back, Nick saw that Blake was sprinting after him with the others about twenty yards behind. So far, so good.

As Nick ducked inside, he sucked in air as he ran full pelt up the stairs that he had just come down with Mike from the chaplaincy.

Taking two steps at a time, he pumped his arms with everything he had.

Come on, keep going.

The muscles in his thighs burned. At the top of the stairs, he could now see the security door that led into the corridor of the chaplaincy.

As he bounded up the last few steps he grabbed the security pass he'd stolen from the main office. His hand was shaking from nerves and the stress of running. Slamming the lanyard against the door's security pad, he waited for the red light to flash and the door to click as it unlocked.

Nothing.

Are you fucking joking me?

He could hear the footsteps of Blake and the others pounding up the staircase after him.

'Please work, please,' Nick muttered as he tried the pass again.

Nothing.

Jesus.

In about ten seconds, he was going to be battered to death down the staircase.

Looking at the pass, he stammered, 'Come on, come on …'

The footsteps and shouts were getting closer and closer.

Shit. This is not good.

Rubbing the plastic lanyard on his top, Nick carefully placed it in front of the security pad.

Nothing.

Then a second later, *CLICK.*

The red light flashed.

Thank God!

Pushing the door open, Nick turned and made sure that it was left open by about a foot.

He then pushed himself flat against the wall on the other side and held his breath.

The sound of trainers on the steps and heavy breathing got louder.

Here we go!

Blake came through the open security door into the corridor and looked around.

Nick stepped out and punched him in the jaw as hard as he could.

He then hit the security door with his shoulder, slamming it shut. It locked itself with a clunk.

Blake's thugs would now be stuck on the other side, with no way of getting it open. Which left Blake on his own and vulnerable.

Blake staggered and shook his head.

Sprinting down the corridor, Nick darted left into the Muslim prayer room and slammed the door shut behind him.

The room was huge and cavernous. There were ornate Muslim prayer scrolls hanging from the walls. Several prayer mats were laid out in a row.

Over to the right, fifty or so grey plastic chairs were piled high.

Looking up, Nick checked again that there were no security cameras. He knew that prisons weren't allowed CCTV inside places of worship as it contravened prisoners' human rights.

He was right.

Then he stared at the door, waiting for Blake to follow.

The door burst open.

Blake came in with his face full of thunder.

Got you!

'What the fuck are you doing in here?' he growled as he clenched his fists.

Nick's pulse was racing and his stomach was unbearably tight with nerves.

'I like it in here,' Nick said with a shrug. 'It's peaceful.'

'You do know I'm going to kill you,' Blake said as he approached.

'Yeah, I don't think you are,' Nick said, trying to hold his nerve.

'And just so you know,' Blake hissed. 'When I've kicked and choked the life out of you, I'm going to make sure that your wife and daughter end up in the ground next to you.'

Out of the corner of his eye, Nick spotted movement from behind the mountain of chairs.

Connell and Roberts stepped out from behind the chairs, blocking off Blake's escape route to the door.

'Hello Curtis,' Connell said, as Roberts went to close the door to the corridor and check that no one was around.

Nick could see that Connell had a thick piece of rope wound around his hands.

Blake's eyes roamed nervously around the room, and he readied himself to fight them. 'You think I can't take on the lot of you, eh?'

Jayden smirked. 'I think it's unlikely, you twat.'

In a flash, Connell and Roberts were on Blake and overpowered him.

Pulling him to the ground, Connell wrapped the rope around Blake's throat and began to pull.

Roberts sat on Blake's legs and had his arms pulled behind his back.

Blake struggled furiously, but he was beginning to choke. He looked up at Nick. The anger had gone, and he now looked scared.

Sucking for breath, Blake continued to kick and thrash around. But he was weakening. He looked at Nick again with a pleading expression.

Nick took no pleasure from watching them slowly strangle the life out of him. But there was just a huge sense of relief. He thought of his old girlfriend, Laura Foley, who had died from heroin supplied by Blake. The hundreds of others who had suffered and perished from the drugs he'd supplied or the violence that he'd inflicted on anyone that got in his way.

Connell looked up at Nick with an expressionless face. 'We're going to string him up from that window,' he explained, pointing. 'Make it look like suicide.'

'Okay,' Nick said quietly as he gestured to the door. He couldn't watch anymore. 'I'm gonna go now.'

As he came out into the corridor, Nick's head was in a

spin. Curtis Blake would be dead in a matter of seconds. He couldn't help but be overwhelmed by the significance of that.

Just keep it together, Nick.

Walking down the corridor, he turned left and headed for the main office as he retrieved the pen from his pocket.

'Just bringing this back,' Nick said cheerfully as he waved the pen at the woman he'd seen earlier.

'Okay, thanks,' she said without looking up.

He dropped the lanyard and security pass back on the desk he'd taken it from and headed towards a prison officer who was chatting to the prison chaplain, a man in his 60s, very overweight with a shock of white hair. Nick had had several conversations with the chaplain before and after some of the AA meetings in Rhoswen.

Nick looked at the prison officer. 'I was helping out at the AA meeting,' he explained as he gestured to the empty corridor. 'But it looks like the guys have gone without me. Sorry.'

The chaplain gave the prison officer a nod, as if to confirm that Nick wasn't lying.

'Okay, I'll take you back over if you come with me,' the prison officer said.

'Thanks. That's great.'

Chapter 61

Ruth and Georgie were now marching through the ground floor of Llancastell nick. Ruth had made a very quick call to her contact at the CPS, who confirmed that given the huge weight of evidence, Derifa Mousa could be charged with the murders of Carmel Chowdry and Rohan Chopra. They would need more evidence before the trial, but it was enough for CID to meet the CPS threshold to charge.

'Do you think that anything Derifa went through in Syria might account for her actions?' Georgie wondered as they walked towards the custody suite.

'You mean something like PTSD?' Ruth asked.

'Possibly,' Georgie replied with a shrug.

'We can request that a full psychological examination takes place before she goes to trial,' Ruth said, thinking that was probably a sensible thing to do.

'She just seems so young,' Georgie said with a frown. 'And the murders were so cold blooded and violent.'

'I agree.' Ruth gave a thoughtful nod. 'It does suggest

that there might be some kind of underlying mental health condition. Or maybe she was forced into doing it?'

Ruth showed her warrant card to the custody sergeant who was in charge of the holding cells at the station.

'We've got a suspect,' Ruth said. 'A Derifa Mousa?'

The sergeant ran his finger over the computer screen. 'Cell six. Follow me, ma'am.'

They followed the burly sergeant to the corridor where all the holding cells were.

It was Ruth's legal duty to verbally charge Derifa with two counts of murder, now that things had escalated. They would need to continue to interview her. Derifa would then be taken in front of a magistrate in the morning and remanded in custody until the date of her trial. With something like murder, that could take up to six months.

'Here we go,' the sergeant said as he unlocked the cell door.

As he opened the grey metallic door, to her horror Ruth saw Derifa lying on the floor in a huge pool of her own blood.

'Oh my God!' Ruth cried as she went over to her.

Both of Derifa's wrists had been slashed and her whole body was drenched in blood.

'Get the FME and call for an ambulance,' Georgie shouted as the sergeant hurried away.

Ruth felt for a pulse.

Nothing.

Derifa's body was ice cold and her skin purple and blue around her mouth.

'Jesus,' Ruth said as she put her ear to Derifa's mouth.
Nothing.

She looked over at Georgie. 'We're too late.'

Chapter 62

It had been an hour since Ruth had discovered Derifa in the holding cell. Despite the work of the FME and the paramedics, she had lost too much blood. Technically, she had died from exsanguination, which was an extreme version of haemorrhage and fatal blood loss. It had left Ruth feeling sad and frustrated. She wanted to know how Derifa had managed to smuggle a small razor blade into the cell in the first place. There would be a full internal inquiry to establish how that had been allowed to happen.

Ruth sat at her computer, lost in her thoughts, as she typed up her report on the incident down in the holding cell and relevant information about Derifa regarding the investigation.

There was a knock at the open door. It was Georgie.

'Boss, I've written up my incident report and emailed it over to you,' she said quietly.

'You okay?' Ruth said, gesturing for Georgie to come and sit down.

'Yeah. It just feels sad,' Georgie admitted as she pulled over a chair. 'I'm not condoning what Derifa did. But she was so young. And she'd fled her country to find a safer life here. She was vulnerable, which allowed this group of men to bully and manipulate her.'

Ruth nodded thoughtfully. 'She's not the first and, unfortunately, she won't be the last. And I understand the harm caused by violent crime and drugs. But there seems something incredibly evil about the trade in vulnerable human beings.'

Ben arrived at the door and looked in. 'Not interrupting anything, am I?'

'No,' Ruth said. 'We're just picking over what happened down in the holding cell earlier.'

'Horrible,' Ben said with a dark expression. He then gestured to a folder that he was carrying. 'I've been speaking to officers from the MSHU unit over in Harlech. They've ID'd Kabir Malik as running forced labour on a fruit picking farm. They've found twelve Indian nationals packed into two small caravans.'

'Any of the workers willing to ID Malik?' Georgie asked.

'Only one,' Ben explained. 'The rest are too scared.'

Ruth leaned forward. 'I guess the bigger the case we can build against Malik, the more likely it is that we can get him extradited from India.'

Garrow appeared at the door with a grave expression on his face. 'Boss, you need to turn on the television. Something has happened at HMP Rhoswen.'

Grabbing the remote control, Ruth clicked on the small television on the other side of the room which was always tuned to the BBC News channel.

The news anchor looked at the camera. 'It is believed that Curtis Blake was found hanging in a room in the chaplaincy building within the prison grounds at around 12.30pm. A prison spokesman said that he had taken his own life and that they were not looking for anyone else in connection with the incident.'

A photo of Blake appeared on the television screen.

'Curtis Blake was 43 and had been one of Liverpool's most notorious and feared criminals in recent decades.'

Ruth took a breath as she looked at the others. She felt a mixture of shock and also relief.

Chapter 63

Nick sat out in the corridor of the Crown Court in Mold waiting for his solicitor to arrive before they met with the CPS and Probation Service. He was now dressed in his 'civvies' in case the charges were dropped against him and there was no need for him to return to prison. Despite that, a prison officer sat reading a newspaper on a chair opposite, in case Nick needed taking back to HMP Rhoswen.

With no access to any media, Nick was still in the dark as to how Blake's death was being reported in the outside world. However, when he was getting changed – navy trousers, caramel-coloured brogues, black jumper and white shirt – the news that Blake had been found dead had started to spread through the prison like wildfire. The reports from other prisoners had been mixed and muddled. Blake had been stabbed and killed in the showers. Blake had thrown himself from a third-storey window in an attempt to escape, and died. And, Blake had hanged himself.

Nick noticed a figure heading his way.

It was Ruth.

Christ, she's a sight for sore eyes.

'Hey,' Nick said, getting up.

Ruth took out her warrant card and showed it to the prison officer. 'DI Hunter, Llancastell CID. Okay if I have a word?' she asked, gesturing to Nick.

'Be my guest,' the officer replied with complete disinterest.

She sat down.

'How are you doing?' Ruth said quietly as she looked at him.

Nick took a few seconds to try to find an answer. 'It seems like one of my problems has gone away.' Then he gestured to the door marked *Crown Prosecution Service, North Wales*. 'Now I've got to hope that this goes the way it should.'

'I'm sure it will,' Ruth reassured him. 'I've checked. There is a precedent for this legally.'

'Is there?' Nick asked, now curious.

'1982,' Ruth said. 'Terry Daley escaped from Ford Open Prison. He'd been convicted of bank robbery and given eight years. He proved while he was on the run that he was working in a pub at the time of the robbery, so couldn't have done it. For some reason, the defence had botched this as an alibi at trial. Daley gave himself up. The judge took into account the fact that no one had been hurt in the escape and that Daley had served prison for a crime he hadn't committed. He was granted a conditional pardon and served no more time.'

Nick nodded. It was encouraging to hear that there had been another case where the prisoner had not been charged with the escape and was not taken to trial. 'That's good to know.'

Ruth gave him a knowing look and whispered, 'As for

how you managed to solve your first problem, I don't want to know. But you may well have put Amanda and Megan out of immediate danger.'

'I hope so,' Nick whispered back. 'Obviously I haven't heard any reports since I left to come here.'

Ruth glanced over at the prison officer. He was still ensconced in his paper.

'Suicide,' Ruth said under her breath. 'And they're not looking for anyone in connection to the death.'

Nick felt a wave of relief sweep through his whole body. He closed his eyes for a moment and let out a sigh. 'Thank God for that.'

A man in his 40s, in a smart suit and with a briefcase, walked along the corridor towards them.

'This is my brief now,' Nick explained.

Ruth touched his arm and looked at him. 'Good luck.'

Chapter 64

It was late afternoon as Georgie got to her car in the car park at Llancastell nick. The spring sunshine was bright and warm.

Wow, it's virtually sunglasses weather, she thought, remembering that there was a pair of 70s boho-style shades in her glove compartment.

'Hi,' said a friendly voice from behind her.

It was Ben.

'Hey,' she said with a smile. She noticed that it was getting harder and harder for her not to smile when she was in his presence.

'You off home?' he asked casually.

'Yes. I'm shattered,' she sighed. 'And after the incident in custody …'

'Yeah, of course,' Ben said with an understanding expression. He then gestured to the car. 'Mind if I jump in for a second?'

'Erm … Something wrong with your car?' she asked. 'I can give you a lift.'

'No, no, nothing like that.' Ben looked awkward. 'I just

thought …' Then he pointed to the car. 'Actually, is it okay if we have this conversation in there?'

Why is he acting so weird? Georgie wondered.

'Okay.' Georgie opened the driver's door and got in.

Ben got in and settled himself.

'What's wrong?' Georgie asked. She was feeling a little anxious at his behaviour.

He didn't say anything for a few seconds. Then he turned and looked directly at her. 'I'm not very good at this sort of thing …'

Georgie gave him a quizzical look. 'Okay. But you are starting to freak me out, Ben.'

'Sorry.' He pulled an apologetic face. 'It's just that we haven't talked about what happened earlier today. After the accident and everything.'

Georgie locked eyes with him and smirked. 'Are you talking about the fact that you kissed me?'

Ben opened his mouth as if offended. Then he laughed. 'I'm pretty sure that you kissed me back.'

'Did I?' she asked playfully.

'Yes, you did thank you,' Ben said.

'So what?' Georgie said, trying to keep it light-hearted even though her pulse was racing.

'Erm … well,' Ben stammered. 'I just haven't been able to stop thinking about you since we kissed.'

Georgie tried to play it cool, but she couldn't help but break into a beaming smile. 'Can't you now? Well, you're in luck.'

'Am I?'

'Yes, because I haven't managed to think about much else since then, either,' Georgie admitted.

'Haven't you?' Ben sounded incredibly relieved.

'Want to try it again?' Georgie asked as she leaned slightly in towards him.

'Yes, definitely,' Ben nodded as he moved closer and kissed her. Soft at first and then harder. He put his hand gently to the side of her face.

As they moved apart, Georgie grinned. 'Not bad.'

'Thanks,' Ben said, his eyes twinkling.

Georgie's expression changed. She knew they had to have some kind of grown-up conversation.

'Of course, if this is going to go anywhere,' she said. 'We need to … talk.'

'Yeah, of course,' Ben said as he reached over and moved a strand of hair from her face. 'But I'm serious. And I'm going into this with my eyes wide open.'

'Really?' she asked with a serious tone, and then looked directly at him. 'Because I'm pregnant with another man's child. And that is a huge, huge thing to take on for anyone.'

'I want to be with you,' Ben said earnestly. 'So, I'm prepared to take that on.'

'I'm not sure I believe you,' Georgie whispered as she suddenly felt overcome with emotion.

Ben frowned. 'Why not?' he asked gently.

She looked at him and blinked. She was on the verge of tears. 'I'm too scared to really believe you. In my head, I was going to do this all on my own.'

'I understand that you're scared. Why wouldn't you be?' he said, and then leaned towards her. 'But I'm not going to hurt you. I promise.'

They kissed again passionately as the emotion of the conversation overwhelmed them.

Chapter 65

Nick moved his chair away from the table and took a breath. He had been sitting in the hearing with Claudia Steen from the Crown Prosecution Service, Helen Atkins from the North Wales Probation Service, and his solicitor, James Partington. For the past ten minutes, they had gone through various details and legal technicalities.

Nick had been studying Steen and Atkins for signs of how this hearing was going to go, but they weren't giving anything away. His pulse was still racing and his stomach was tight with nerves. Nothing they had said so far gave him any indication of what they had decided. He had given James Partington a couple of furtive glances, but he seemed none the wiser either.

'Listen, Nick,' Atkins said. 'I don't want to prolong this any longer than we have to. It wouldn't be fair to you. And we will be able to give you a longer explanation of our joint decision afterwards.'

Shit!

Nick's heart sank. The words and her tone of voice

convinced him that it was going to be bad news. He braced himself.

'I can tell you that neither the Crown Prosecution Service or the Probation Service believe there is anything to be gained from keeping you in prison any longer,' Atkins explained and then gave him a kind smile.

For a few seconds, Nick tried to process what she meant.

What did she say?

'And spending valuable tax payers' money on charging you with escaping from prison and possibly having to go to trial is impossible for us to justify,' Atkins explained. 'There will be no criminal charges against you going forward.'

Nick blinked for a second as he let out a gasp. He dared not believe it.

'Really?' he asked, still scared that they were going to say something else as a caveat. 'I'm free to go?'

'Yes, you are.' Steen gave him a sympathetic look. 'You were a highly respected police officer, Nick. You were imprisoned for a crime that you didn't commit. And you escaped to clear your name. No one wants to punish you for that.'

Chapter 66

'Oh my God, Nick! That's incredible news,' Ruth cried down the phone as she walked along the hallway in her home. The hearing in Mold had dragged on, so she hadn't had time to wait and see him. She felt completely overwhelmed by relief and joy.

'I know,' Nick said, sounding choked. 'It just doesn't feel real.'

There were a few seconds as Ruth processed what Nick had told her.

'Where are you now?' she asked.

'I'm being taken home.'

'What about Amanda and Megan?'

'I managed to speak to DCI Parker at Merseyside Police.'

'Yeah, I know him,' Ruth said.

'He told me that the Regional Organised Crime Unit believe that now Blake is dead, the threat to Amanda and Megan is minimal,' Nick said. 'It was personal. And with Blake dead, there's likely to be a lot of infighting in Croxteth about who takes control of the drug trade in that area.

They have intel that local gangs are already planning to move in from Norris Green. No one is going to be interested in some feud that Blake had with me. As far as they're concerned, it's ancient history now he's gone.'

'Thank God,' Ruth sighed. 'I can't believe you're all going to be together tonight.'

'I know. Neither can I,' Nick said quietly. 'I was too scared to let myself think it was ever going to really happen. I feel like I'm dreaming.'

'I'm so, so pleased.' Ruth felt her eyes well up with tears. 'You all deserve to be happy after what you've all been through.'

'Thanks,' Nick said. 'I couldn't have done it without your help, Ruth.'

'No problem. I don't feel like I did anything,' Ruth whispered as she wiped a tear from her face. 'I'm going to let you go, as I'm a bit weepy here.'

'I'll give you a call tomorrow,' Nick said.

'Yeah. Just enjoy being together,' Ruth said, 'Lots of love to you all. Night.'

She ended the call and came into the small dining room where Sarah, Daniel and Doreen were sitting, passing around fish and chips that she'd picked up from the chippy on the way home.

'You okay?' Sarah asked as she came over to her.

'They've let Nick go,' Ruth said with a sniff.

'Oh my God, that's brilliant,' Sarah said, giving her a hug.

Chapter 67

Sitting down on the sofa, Nick put his hands on the soft material, almost as if to check it was real and that he wasn't really dreaming. He looked around the living room. It felt like it had been months, even years, since he was last there. He loved the smell of being home. Leaning his head back against a soft cushion, he blew out his cheeks and smiled to himself.

He kicked off his shoes and put his feet down on the carpet. *God, that feels sooo good.*

The house was incredibly quiet. All he could hear was the wind blowing outside and the slight creak of the timber. Peace. He closed his eyes. *I will never take this for granted ever again. I promise.*

Checking his watch, he saw that Amanda and Megan were due back any second. He could feel the growing tension and excitement at his anticipation of seeing them.

He took a few deep breaths to try to compose himself. The past few weeks had been a living nightmare. And now it was over.

Then the sound of the door opening.

Jumping to his feet, Nick rushed to the living room door and glanced down the hallway.

'Daddy!' Megan yelled as she sprinted along the hall towards him.

'Hey,' Nick said as he scooped her up into his arms. 'It's so good to see you,' he said, kissing her cheek and nuzzling into her hair. He loved the smell of her hair. 'Are you glad to be home?'

'Yes, of course, silly,' Megan said.

Turning, he saw Amanda closing the door behind her. Their suitcases were to one side.

Their eyes met, and he felt an indescribable rush of emotion as Amanda walked towards them.

Putting his arm out, Nick pulled Amanda close to him. 'I didn't think this was ever going to be possible,' he whispered.

'Neither did I,' she whispered back, sounding choked.

Chapter 68

Georgie was flicking through Ben's collection of records on vinyl in his living room while he was making them dinner in the kitchen.

'Put on anything you want,' he called out.

'I'm struggling to find anything I like,' Georgie teased. 'Too many boys with guitars.'

Then she spotted *Fleetwood Mac's Greatest Hits* and pulled it out of the sleeve and went over to the record player. 'I take it all back,' she called out.

The song *Dreams* started to play.

Georgie smiled to herself as she wandered over to the bookshelf, which was stacked with novels. It had been such a long time since she had done the whole *getting to know you* thing with someone. It felt exciting.

Under her breath, she started to sing along with the song. 'Thunder only happens when it's raining …'

Running her finger along the books, she saw a series of classics. A boxset of the complete works of F Scott Fitzgerald. George Orwell, Graham Greene and Hemingway. American crime novels by James Ellroy, George Pelecanos and Michael Connelly. Then a very thick biography – *The Life of Mother Theresa of Calcutta*, which surprised her.

There were a few framed photographs resting on the shelves. One of the photos showed Ben graduating in his gown and cap.

'Oh God, don't look at that,' Ben groaned as he came into the room. 'I was so hungover in that photo, and my hair is shocking.'

'Yeah, it is,' she joked.

'Thanks.'

'Where did you go to Uni?' she asked.

'Warwick,' Ben said as he came over to look at the photo. 'Did bugger all apart from play rugby, cricket and drink beer. Got a respectable 2.2 in Social Sciences.'

'Swot,' Georgie teased him.

Ben kissed her and then frowned. 'I'm trying to work out if there are any cheeses that you can't eat when you're pregnant?'

'Brie, camembert, ricotta, mozzarella, blue cheese,' Georgie said, thinking aloud.

'Cheddar?' Ben asked with a grin.

'Yeah, cheddar is fine,' Georgie laughed.

'Good,' Ben said chirpily as he kissed her again and disappeared back to the kitchen.

Peering at another photo, Georgie spotted that it was taken more recently. It was a group of blokes sitting outside a pub on what appeared to be a very cold day. Ben was sporting a very fashionable black flat cap. It really suited him, she thought. For a moment, she remembered Derifa Mousa referring to the hats as *a Peaky Blinders cap*.

Pushing that thought from her head, Georgie resolved not to think about work and have a lovely evening. After all she'd been through in the last two months, she deserved a bit of happiness, didn't she?

Wandering from the living room to the kitchen, she noticed Ben was on the phone, talking in a very quiet voice. He hung up, saw her and smiled.

'Sorry, work stuff,' he said, gesturing to the phone.

'Do you need any help?' she asked, pointing to the food he was preparing.

'Don't worry,' he said with a smile. 'It's all in hand.'

'I was looking at your books,' Georgie said. 'Very impressive. *The Life of Mother Theresa* eh?'

Reaching under his t-shirt, Ben brought out a crucifix, grinned, and gave it a jokey kiss. 'I'm a good Catholic boy.'

Georgie rolled her eyes. 'I'm pretty sure you're not.'

Ben chopped up some red onions. 'That's the thing. Everyone thinks that all Indians are Hindu. But there are twenty million Catholics in India. And somewhere like Goa is completely Catholic.'

Georgie peered at the crucifix that hung down over Ben's t-shirt. 'So that necklace is a crucifix? And Protestants won't wear them, so they only wear a cross. Is that right?'

'Yeah,' Ben nodded and then smiled. 'Don't worry, I'm not madly religious. I go to mass at Christmas with my mum and that's about it.'

'Okay,' Georgie said, feeling relieved. 'Phew.'

'Sorry to bring it up,' Ben said as he chopped away. 'But the first victim, Carmel Chowdry, was an Indian Catholic, and he wore a crucifix.'

Georgie froze as an icy chill swept through her.

What?

Her pulse quickened, and her mouth went dry.

Carmel Chowdry wasn't wearing a crucifix when he was killed because he'd given it to his brother Rishi the day that he was murdered.

Oh, my God. How does Ben know that Carmel Chowdry wore a crucifix?

Georgie took a deep breath to steady herself. There must be some kind of explanation.

What the hell is going on?

'You okay?' Ben asked.

She looked at him with a frown. 'Carmel Chowdry wasn't wearing a crucifix when he was murdered,' she said very quietly.

'Wasn't he?' Ben said nonchalantly as he put the chopped onion rings into the frying pan and they hissed loudly.

'No,' Georgie said, aware that she was feeling shaky. 'He gave his crucifix to his brother on the day of his murder. Rishi was scared and Carmel gave it to him, saying that having it would protect him.'

Ben didn't look up but stirred the onions and garlic in the pan. 'Oh right. My mistake.'

'In fact, the only way you would know Carmel Chowdry wore a crucifix is if you had met him before the day he was murdered. But you hadn't had you?'

'Not as far as I'm aware,' Ben said casually, before looking over at her. 'I don't see what the big deal is.'

'Did you meet Carmel before he was killed, Ben?' she asked, her whole body now rigid with fear.

'No,' Ben laughed. 'How could I?'

Georgie narrowed her eyes. 'Yes. How could you?' Her head was whirring with thoughts. She remembered the cap she'd seen Ben wearing in the photograph in the living room. Derifa had seen a man wearing that type of cap meeting Carmel at the Denbigh Asylum the night he was murdered. And Kabir Malik had been one step ahead of them at every point. He knew every time they were coming to his offices. He even got a different flight. Someone had been tipping him off.

'Georgie?' Ben said innocently. 'What's wrong?'

Taking a deep breath, she stared at Ben. She couldn't believe what she was about to say. 'It's you, isn't it?' she whispered.

There were a few seconds of silence.

'What are you talking about?' Ben snorted as he carried on stirring the food. But she could see that underneath, he was rattled by what she had said. His eyes flitted about nervously.

'Ben?'

'What?' he snapped angrily.

'Look at me,' she demanded.

Putting down the wooden spoon, Ben turned.

Something was very wrong. She could sense it.

'Oh my God, you're the man that everyone called 'The Boss,'' she gasped. 'You're working with Singh and Malik, aren't you?'

'Jesus, Georgie!' Ben exclaimed as he turned to look at her. 'What the hell are you talking about?'

'Tell me the truth, Ben,' Georgie snapped.

He didn't answer.

'They're paying you off, aren't they? And when you thought Carmel Chowdry was going to ruin everything, you somehow lured him to Denbigh Asylum and killed him. And when Kabir Malik was waiting outside Rohan Chopra's house, it was you who was inside murdering him. You planted a vape that you knew Derifa Mousa had been using. And you took the knife to the B&B and while I was cuffing her, you pretended to find it hidden under her bed.'

Ben's face had completely changed. The twinkle and boyish grin had gone. It was like looking at a completely different person. The sight of him terrified her to her very core. He was holding an eight-inch kitchen knife.

'I think we need to go into the living room for a little chat,' he said in a dark, alarming tone.

Georgie was frozen to the spot. She shook her head. 'No, I'm not going anywhere with you. I'm leaving.'

Ben took a step forward, brandishing the knife. 'I can't let you leave here, Georgie, can I?'

'Try and stop me!' she growled, taking a step towards the kitchen door.

Ben moved quickly to block her and held up the knife. 'Don't do anything stupid, Georgie. I don't want to have to hurt you.'

Enjoy this book?
Get the next book in the series
'The Wrexham Killings'
pre-order on Amazon
Publication date August 2023

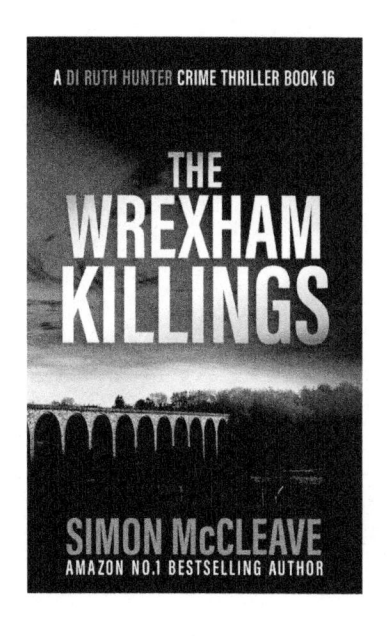

Click here to pre-order your book -
    My Book (UK)
    My Book (US)

The Wrexham Killings
A Ruth Hunter Crime Thriller #Book 16

Your FREE book is waiting for you now

Get your FREE copy of the prequel to
the DI Ruth Hunter Series NOW
http://www.simonmccleave.com/vip-email-club
and join my VIP Email Club

DC RUTH HUNTER SERIES

London, 1997. A series of baffling murders. A web of political corruption. DC Ruth Hunter thinks she has the brutal killer in her sights, but there's one problem. He's a Serbian War criminal who died five years earlier and lies buried in Bosnia.

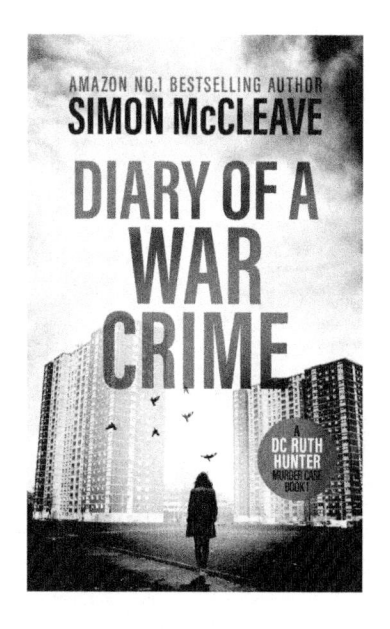

My Book
My Book

AUTHOR'S NOTE

Although this book is very much a work of fiction, it is located in Snowdonia, a spectacular area of North Wales. It is steeped in history and folklore that spans over two thousand years. It is worth mentioning that Llancastell is a fictional town on the eastern edges of Snowdonia. I have made liberal use of artistic licence, names and places have been changed to enhance the pace and substance of the story.

Acknowledgments

I will always be indebted to the people who have made this novel possible.

My mum, Pam, and my stronger half, Nicola, whose initial reaction, ideas and notes on my work I trust implicitly. And Dad, for his overwhelming enthusiasm. Carole Kendal for her meticulous proofreading. Keira Bowie, for her ongoing calm help, especially with the stuff that I tell her makes '…my head melt!' My excellent publicists, Emma Draude and Emma Dowson at EDPR. My designer Stuart Bache for yet another incredible cover design. My superb agent, Millie Hoskins at United Agents, and Dave Gaughran and Nick Erick for invaluable support and advice.

Printed in Great Britain
by Amazon